Spun

Books by

PEGGY TROTTER

Year of Jubilee
Reviving Jules

~Unchained Souls Series~
The Secret Things
The Secret Storm

~Society of Outcasts~
The Misfit Bride
The Lowborn Lady
The Spellbound Schoolmarm

~Up from the Miry Clay~
Tattered Blossoms Rise
Wild Daisies Bloom
Flawed Roses Flourish (Releasing 2025)

Spun

Spun

PEGGY TROTTER

RANSOMED-EVER-AFTER BOOKS

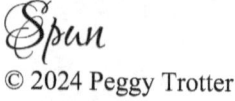

Spun
© 2024 Peggy Trotter

Visit the author's website at: www.peggytrotter.com

Published by Ransomed-Ever-After Books

This novel is a work of fiction. Names, characters, businesses, places, events, and incidents are either the products of the author's imagination or used in a fictitious manner. Any resemblance to actual persons, living or dead, or actual events is purely coincidental.

First Edition, 2024
ISBN-979-8-9897864-2-8
Library of Congress Control Number: 2024920323
Printed in Columbia South Carolina, United States of America

All Scriptures used with this work are from the King James Version (KJV).

Cover Illustration © 2024 by Zanne Davis/Photo by Neuro_Cat: https://pixabay.com/users/neuro_cat-38483528/

Edited by Nancy Clark

Dear Reader~

Please be aware that this novel takes place in the 1870s. Because of that reason, some of the word choices reflect that time period.

The Lord is the light and my salvation; whom shall I fear? The Lord is the strength of my life; of whom shall I be afraid?

When the wicked, even mine enemies and my foes, came upon me to eat up my flesh, they stumbled and fell.

Though an host should encamp against me, my heart shall not fear: though war should rise against me, in this will I be confident.

Psalm 27:1-3 KJV

Chapter One

Near Bellevue, NE—1876

The revolver's cold barrel pressed deeper into her temple. Maggie Robbins tried not to flinch, but failed. Her gaze flicked to the five other men lounging against the cabin's walls. The dim light of the lantern above her head, coupled with the shadows of the men's hat brims, transformed the invading humans into eyeless specters poised for violence.

Even dead, Axel Robbins had placed her and her son in yet another dangerous situation. She rued the day she'd met him. Hatred for her former husband reared up, threatening to extinguish both the fear and rage that now pulsed through her. Not for the first time, she wished for a man's strength to throw off the iron arms that held her captive and clear the room of the vermin. Her throat convulsed. She'd shoot every one. Straight in the heart.

"Don't think I believe that lie." Jeether Moats cleaned his teeth with his hunting knife as he stood before her. "Playing the innocent? You knew what you were doing when you married Ax Robbins. You'd have to be a plain simpleton not to have heard of Pick 'n Ax."

Serenity lay deceptively across the bandit's furry face. But viciousness glittered hard in his eyes. She dropped her gaze and stretched her aching shoulders. The thug holding her arms behind her tightened his grip.

"Now, let's try this again. Where's. The. Gold?" Moats stepped closer. The odious smell of his unwashed body intermixed with the filthy buffalo skin draped on his shoulders wafted to her nostrils. She swallowed the urge to gag and clenched her teeth to stifle the razor-sharp retort that begged release. This was no time for her impulsive nature to jump to the forefront. No matter how many times she'd yearned to muscle over in power, it hadn't happened yet. Better to shut her mouth and bide her time. When the hooligan didn't move, she inched her gaze to his.

His black eyes grew hooded. "Hmmm. Perhaps if one of my men fetched that lily-white youngster from the barn, I'd get a few answers."

"No!"

Moats let out a sharp laugh as he drew the long knife across her jaw. "Listen, little lady. I heard you was cheeky. Ax and I had a right long talk before I shot him and his pa cold dead in Dodge City."

The icy knife edge scraped down her face, and terror lit through her like a grass fire. She squeezed her eyes closed. Maybe this was it.

Her misery would come to an end. Yet, she must stay alive for Corbin. He needed her. "There is no gold."

His blade paused, and her eyelids fluttered open. Moats whirled from her and paced, back and forth, slapping the hunting knife in his palm. She couldn't take her eyes from him. Short of spouting a repeater from her nose and gunning down the invaders in a brutal gun bath, she hadn't a hope of getting away.

Suddenly, the horrid man halted, squared up, legs wide. "Just shoot her, Gibbons."

"Please," Maggie's voice broke on a sob. "I swear I don't know anything."

Moats strolled to her, shaking his head. His gaze dropped and leered at her entire form. "But you is one fine woman. Don't you think so, boys?"

The ghostly spectators nodded and snorted. Repulsiveness and cold-stone dread shot through her like a hot needle. Tears burned the back of her eyes. That would be a horror worse than death. "I'm telling the truth."

Moats's beard parted, displaying rotting teeth in a semblance of a smile. "Then you best be finding it, little gal. I know it's here. Pickett ran his mouth about their big take after stealing my plan. Now, that ain't right, is it?"

"Robbery's against the law."

A mirthless laugh belched from the sickening man. "You hearing this, boys? Mrs. Axel Robbins is giving us a sermon."

Laughter erupted around the room. He reached out a hand and brushed the back of his finger down her face, his deplorable breath

almost scorching her. Sweat broke out across Maggie's skin and she clenched her eyes shut.

"You got one week to find that gold. Don't try to run, pretty lady. 'Cause we'll be around. Got it?"

Her eyes ached, but she forced her lids open and stared at the far wall to keep them at bay. "I'll find it."

"Just what I want to hear." He nodded and sheathed his blade. "Let's go."

The man behind her released her arms, and she sagged against the wall. One by one, the men filed out of the cabin door. She cringed at the slam, stumbled forward to set the bar with fumbling fingers, and hurried on shaking legs to slip out the back. Tears streamed down her face.

She gained the small barn, not much bigger than an outhouse, and jerked the door open. "Corbin?"

The darkened interior, filled with various tools, appeared empty in the gray light of sunset. She bit her lip and stepped inside. Her voice called out in a hoarse whisper, "Corbin?"

Two boards separated at the bottom on the right wall, and she gave a gasp.

"Mama?"

She brushed the moisture from her face, rushed over, and bent to peek inside the small lean-to. Her eight-year-old son held up a candle, his dark eyes searching her face.

"Why are you hiding? You've not holed up in here since your father's last visit."

His grave gaze entreated hers. "I heard voices."

Protectiveness swelled inside her. "Just…visitors."

A sob rose at the lie, and she studied his earnest, frightened face. He pulled back inside the small area and gestured to the far corner. "Look. Miss Honeycomb had her kittens."

"Let me see." Maggie struggled through the small opening and the boards slid together behind her like a hidden door.

She settled on the pile of pine boards that served as a bench and leaned against the stacked wood. The tumble-down mountain of discarded boards camouflaged the secret space on the outside of the shed. Straw lay thick and her son's treasured mementos lined the horizontal support beams—a white rock, a Canada goose feather, an empty cicada shell, and a leather string of Indian beads. These talismans offered comfort in his secret hideaway, a place that had become a second home to him.

Maggie shoved away the uncomfortable thought and shifted her gaze. The proud mama cat purred, perfectly at home on Corbin's small baby quilt. Maggie reached to rub her soft fur. Five tiny kittens nuzzled the cat's belly for milk, their little paws kneading.

"What beautiful babies. I guess they knew how safe your secret spot is, huh?" She managed to pull a smile for him, but his features remained serious.

"Are they friends of Axel Robbins, Mama?"

The smile slid from her face. She cut her glance to the cats nestled in the colorful blanket. Corbin's reference to his father by Axel's given name hardly caused her pause. Corbin had never called him Papa, for he had never been one, outside his obvious assistance in impregnating her, that is. Thankfully, he'd been mostly gone. But

11

she knew the times Ax and his father Pickett had appeared, it hadn't been a blessed time of family bonding.

Shame burned through her for allowing so much pain to taint her son. He didn't need to know more of the sordid tale. Certainly not that his father's killers now held them at their mercy. The silence grew too heavy. "No."

"Are they staying?"

She turned to him, pulled the candle from his hand, blew the flame out and set it on a rickety shelf. Her son huddled against her in the near dark, and she wrapped her arms around him. "Yes."

"You won't marry one of them, will you?"

Sorrow seized her throat, her hands clenched into fists. The poor thing already knew too much. No, she wouldn't be stupid twice. "No. They want gold."

Corbin tucked his head under her chin. A fierce love gripped her, and Maggie tightened her jaw. "Come on. Let's get inside. We've got butter to churn and supper to fix."

Hank Sutter lounged on the rough-cut bench of the cabin's porch when Maggie swung through the door early the next morning. Seeing her was just the thing to get his blood moving. Sure as honey dripped from the comb he was near on freezing.

He shoved the hat to the back of his head and stood. She stutter-stepped, her violet-blue eyes flaring. Hank flicked his gaze from her to the dark-haired boy at her skirt and then back to her shocked face.

"Hank?"

He stiffened and nodded.

Her glare narrowed. "You're part of *them*, aren't you?"

After sucking in a deep breath, he answered. "I'm here to keep an eye on you."

"Well, take your eye and stomp on it." Maggie gripped the boy by the arm, spun, and strode to the end of the porch.

Hank ambled after her rigid form. She hadn't changed much. The woman possessed a disposition of a mountain lion—and just as jumpy. It was no surprise she had no welcome for him. Maggie yanked a cow to the front of the barn and tied her to a post. The boy fetched two stools and a pail.

"Need any help?" He watched the two of them position themselves on either side of the red and white animal.

"Not from you." Maggie lowered herself to the three-legged perch.

He inhaled and squinted westward, knowing once he left the tree line there lay Nebraska's flatland. His gaze shifted to the hills surrounding them where huge red oaks soared and then to the slope below him to the Big Muddy, the Missouri River.

The torturous channel peeking through the leaves moved like molasses. A white steam boat, a sternwheeler headed toward Omaha, chugged north around the bend, the water deceptively placid. Maggie's parents had picked a fine place to homestead. The north side of the big Muddy's bulge to the east made a fine location for a farm. It was the perfect site, one he'd dared to yearn for a lifetime ago.

Hank focused his attention on Maggie and her son. Streams of milk squirted into their bucket. The cow raised her rear leg on

Maggie's side, more than likely ill over the woman's anger-driven squeezes, and despite himself, a smile tugged at the corner of Hank's mouth. He toed a rock at his feet, knowing he should say something, but as usual, not sure what. The same problem didn't nag at Maggie.

"We're milking a cow, not mining for gold," she snapped. "Can't you just leave us be?"

"Thought maybe the grasshoppers had cleaned you out." Feeble diversion. She'd rip him for that.

"Like you cared." She stood and shot him optic daggers.

The boy untied the cow and led her away without a sound.

"Take her to the far pasture," Maggie commanded the boy and then snipped at Hank. "Everyone knows the hoppers came through in '74. Any toddler could tell you that's nigh on two years ago."

"Just making conversation."

She planted an unyielding fist on her hip. Hank knew the lands to the east still battled the nefarious insects. "But you were never very good at dialogue, were you, Hank Sutter?"

He paused. "Reckon not. But then, you weren't much on waiting."

Her nostrils flared, and her eyes widened with sparks of fury. She strutted to him and stabbed him in the chest with her forefinger. "Don't you dare start with *that*, unless you can explain how one waits without knowing they're actually waiting."

Hank let his gaze rove her. Her face portrayed an angry version of the youthful image embedded in his memory, with the addition of a barrelful of sorrow and a few creases around her eyes—those violet-blue eyes—and golden hair of wheat. How many times had he

14

strolled through a ripe wheat field stroking the stalks and thinking of her, hungering for her?

Now, hardness settled on that finely-featured face, drawn in the early morning light, and her full lips puckered into a scowl. "Well?"

He'd give twenty bucks if she'd just touch him again. Scratch that. He'd happily slap down double that amount. Instead he shrugged, looked away, and followed the progress of the boy down the slope.

"I didn't think so." She tramped to the house and slammed the door, leaving tiny puddles of milk in her trail.

Hank grunted. Well, that encounter had gone 'bout like he figured. Time hadn't mellowed her. If anything, her temperament had become quite embittered. He let out a sigh of regret. Wishing the years back wouldn't change where she was and what she'd suffered. Nor would it magically alter anything for him.

He sauntered to his bench on the porch and continued his watch, preferring to stand. Being married to Ax Robbins would jade the patience of Job. Maggie…Robbins. It was hard to cotton to. Always in his mind she was Maggie Sutter, Mrs. Hank Sutter. Always. Even when he knew it was beyond all possibility. He never deserved her. With a low growl, he slumped to the bench, lowered the brim of his hat and leaned against the log wall.

The door to his right burst open and the physical representation of his doleful thoughts stepped out, hands on her hips. He didn't move. Maybe if she thought he was asleep, she'd head back in the cabin.

"I don't want you on my porch."

But she was having none of his avoidance. And the view of her torso and tapping foot indicated her vexation hadn't slackened. He toyed with the idea of keeping his hat lowered. "Got my orders."

"Your orders. Men. So obsessed with their own profit, their own...desires that none of them would stoop to help anyone less fortunate."

Hank raised his arm and thumbed the hat brim back to get a glimpse of her pink face. She near on threw sparks from her eyes, and he was somewhat surprised she could still breathe with her arms knotted at her bosom. Now, that wasn't a rabbit he needed to chase. At least the blush flaming across her cheeks made it worth the tongue lashing. "I suppose so."

"That's right, you dingus."

Their gazes locked and held until she twisted away. He studied her profile. Maggie had been influenced by the best, or in this case, the worst. "Dingus. Hmmm. If I remember right, that's Jesse James's favorite word. Ax must have had some pretty powerful friends."

Her tongue wet her lips, Maggie's classic sign of discomfort. The drab black dress made her too-full lips pop in full blush. Probably best not to focus on her mouth either, one of her many features that haunted his dreams. Then her face froze hard, her blink more like a grimace as she cinched her arms tighter across her chest. "It's not your business."

"No. S'pose not."

She stood a moment. He could decipher her tapping foot. That was never a good signal. Then her arms unlatched from her middle and settled on her hips. "Is that all you can say?'

For a moment, he thought to stride to her, snatch her up, and bend her over his arm in a kiss that would steal the fury from her. But Moats didn't need to know more than he already did. And kissing Maggie now would only delay the inevitable storm.

"I reckon." He stared at the river's tree line. Her breathing grew audible. Here it came…

"The great orator." Her hand flung into the air. "Did it ever occur to you that people needed you, Hank? That I might—" She cleared her throat and then spun to pace a few steps. Then, in a pivot that made the drab black dress skirt twirl tight against her legs, she stomped close. "But no. One day here. The next day gone. Mr. Silence just disappeared."

Hank shuffled his feet. He hoped she didn't recognize that as his sign of regret. "You knew why I left."

Maggie stood a few minutes, just huffing out her boiling anger, squeezing the hands hanging at her side into fists. If she were a man, he'd earn a black eye right about now. But instead, she seemed to shrink. Her hands shook as she lifted them to rub her upper arms, as if below her black cape, she shivered. With the softest, daintiest grunt, she faded back toward the door and for the first time her voice grew soft. "Knowing why wasn't a lot of help to me."

He stood and reached out, his heart sinking when she shrank from him. "I'm sorry, Maggie."

She blinked and flicked a glance at the boy approaching the cabin. Her chin lifted. "You're a stranger, sir. The Hank Sutter I knew is still not here."

The child slipped up beside her, and Maggie laid a protective hand on his shoulder. Without another glance, she ushered the boy into the cabin.

<u>Chapter Two</u>

Maggie eased the final drawer into the dresser and shot a glance at her sleeping son sprawled across the quilt-covered bed, peacefully snoozing. The child had learned to sleep through anything for sheer escapism alone.

She collapsed into the stiff ladder back chair at the table and wiped her forehead. There'd been no false back in the highboy and no extra space at the bottom of the trunk. For two nights she'd tapped each plank at her feet, satisfied no gold rested beneath the floorboards. How she wished she could spin some from straw like the fairy tale she'd often read to Corbin. Then, perhaps her troubles would be over.

The only thing she had to show for her efforts was her mother's watch fob she'd found below the last drawer of the highboy. The

candle she held had set off the gleam of the golden chain. Gold, but not *the* gold.

Her fingers pressed the small brass button at the top. The fob flipped open. Doubtful it even worked anymore, not that she cared. Maggie didn't need the candlelight to remember the embossed rose, for she remembered it well, hanging around her mother's neck.

Missing for ages, Maggie had assumed Ax had pawned the piece, like everything else she hadn't hidden. She'd safeguarded the matching ring by sewing it into the hem of her best dress. By some blessed miracle the furniture had somehow survived Ax's greed.

She tapped her finger beside the pendant. For the thousandth time Hank's somber face crossed her mind. Had anyone ever bamboozled her so? Well, she'd finally told him what she thought of him. That conversation had formulated and festered in her head for the last eleven years. She exhaled and slumped in the chair. Yet, instead of vindication, emptiness filled her.

He'd matured since his sixteenth year. Tall and wide-shouldered even as a youth, Hank's body now brimmed with thick muscle, making him an intimidating presence. His easy, relaxed manner and soft brown eyes ignited an ache of regret in her chest.

At fourteen, she'd been completely smitten with him, and the time-forged bond made them inseparable, at least then. Now, she wanted to take his head off with a shovel handle. With a groan, she dropped her head into her hands. How could Hank be part of this gang?

Besides, Hank was the least of her worries. Though the Moats's Gang that surrounded her was not as notorious as her husband's Pick

'n Ax, Jeether Moats would not be a man to toy with. Axel and Pickett had received their eternal rewards. Meanwhile, she would forever be paying for her rash decision to marry the criminal. And if Hank hadn't left, she'd—

Nope. Not tonight. She'd spent enough lonely nights reminiscing the could-have-beens. What she needed was gold, and lots of it. Little did Moats know that Ax merely stopped by—she refused to say his home—to fulfill his husbandly rights, and none too gentle at that, not to discuss his tactics and strategies on managing his heists and ill-gotten gains.

She picked up the small hammer on the table and then rose. The huge fireplace stood before her, meticulously constructed by her own grandfather with stones from abandoned Fort Atkinson. A sigh worked its way up her throat. She supposed if her own kin were resilient enough to ferry all that material down the Big Muddy, she could rap each one in search of a secret hidey hole.

Her eyes trailed the stonework up the side of the cabin wall in the flickering candlelight. She clenched her hands and cursed her misfortune of marrying Ax Robbins for the thousandth time. Corbin rolled over on the bed, and she stilled. The only good thing from her marriage slumbered in oblivion. Her face relaxed as her gaze swept her son's sleeping form. Her eyes drifted back to the fireplace where a small oval daguerreotype rested on the mantel.

It drew her like a starving man to a church potluck. She cupped it in her hand and pored over it. The photo could've been her, so alike the image. Her mother's grave face stole none of the woman's

beauty. She stood so tall and lithe, untouched by the sickness that would fill her body years later.

Tears threatened, and Maggie rubbed the metal likeness. She planted the picture back on the mantel *No*. She wouldn't waste another moment on the what-if's. It solved nothing, helped no one. She'd made a haunting choice, and now, she must face the consequences.

Her hands sought the first stone. What if there were no gold to be found? She gritted her teeth and tapped with the small hammer. It wouldn't help to focus on such a possibility now. Every effort must be made to find it, if it existed. Muted footsteps outside the cabin wall stilled her hands.

Yes, the sooner she found it, the sooner they'd be gone.

Hank pressed his chest to the cold, wet earth and contemplated the wide expanse of muddy water. At least the moon cooperated, and the sky's darkness resembled a black wool blanket. The ferry, some fifty feet south, had filled to near capacity with passengers. Old Abe Carver's mumbles echoed over the water. Then the man let out a laugh. It must be a profitable night.

Clenching his jaw against the chill, Hank slid into the Missouri River, warding off the shakes and the gasp that rose up his throat. He swam underwater till his hands touched the wet wood. Then, he surfaced. He gripped the boats bottom supports and hand over hand reached the angled bow. The wood now jutted above his head, masking him from the occupants aboard.

His fingers located his favorite notch in the wood, and he burrowed his hand deep in the crevice. The sweeps on either side of the flatboat took their first stroke as the cable behind and above him grew taut. Hank exhaled slowly to disperse the sound of his breath. His whole body hugged the rotting logs beneath the boat as it plodded across the wide river.

Thoughts of the new train bridge crossed his mind while he fought heat loss. Riding in an icy train car seemed quite appealing at the moment. The judders took hold of him like it always did, neck deep in the thick cold liquid. "Too thick to drink and too thin to plow." The familiar phrase danced through his thoughts when the silty water flowed unbidden down his gullet. *Yep, think of something else, not of how cold you are. And—not about Maggie.*

He clamped his mouth closed to keep his teeth from chattering and prayed the river had grown narrower since his last ford. Maggie's angry face lit his memory. She had a right, he supposed, to hate him. He'd left without much of an explanation. Talking to women had never been a strongpoint of his. As kids they'd tromped the wooded hills near the river, she chattering away, and he enjoying every minute of it in silence.

Yet, leaving had been his only choice. If he'd—the shadow of the tree line caught him by surprise, and he let go of his handhold. His body relaxed, allowing the current to suck him away from the boat. He rolled and dove under, letting the water pull him farther down the bank.

Many right-veered strokes later, his hands struck mud. He emerged in a crawl, leery of the ferry boat upstream, but the muffled

voices stayed even-keeled as he slipped into the woods. He paused, shivering near a cottonwood, and turned to gaze across the river. How many times in the last eleven years had he stood on this bank, the Iowa side of the Big Muddy, and stared across, thinking and praying for Maggie? He'd lost count.

He tore his eyes from the black outline of the Nebraska treetops and rubbed his hands up and down his upper arms. A long walk awaited him in soaked clothes. Though the early October weather had been unseasonably warm, the night temperature dipped near freezing. He hoped Ni'-da-wi would have his horse ready.

He jerked as the Indian woman appeared at his side. Mutely she passed the lead rope to him.

"How'd you know I'd be here?" His voice came out in foggy puffs.

"No moon."

He nodded. "Thanks."

She disappeared into the brush, just as she'd materialized. He backed the horse into the cover of the trees, and made fast work of removing his wet clothes before yanking on dry ones. His numb fingers fumbled with the other saddle bag to ease the green wool blanket from its hiding place.

With a grunt, he mounted the horse, grateful Ni'-da-wi had saved him a long walk. Still, several hours of riding stretched ahead. He needed to finish the mission and be back before daylight, which was no small task. With one last glance across the river, he nudged the horse eastward.

Rupert Stilts's face grew red. "What do you mean, there's a complication?"

Hank cleared his throat and stepped nearer to the fireplace. He couldn't get warm. His dip in the Missouri had chilled him to the bone. "The woman. I know her."

Stilts snorted. "And what, pray tell, is the problem? That's the perfect ploy. Beguile her. Ascertain what she knows."

Hank shifted as a ripple of distaste for the man sliced down his spine. "She doesn't know anything."

The compact man, whose slicked-back hair and fancy suit clashed with the primitive cabin, threw his chin up in a derisive laugh. When his head lowered, his black eyes narrowed.

"Now, attend my words, Sutter. I won't have you renege on this. You've a reputation to revive. It may be your very last opportunity. I'm counting on you to complete this quest."

The small man stepped closer and the sour scent of Macassar hair oil gone rancid drifted up to Hank. Stilts's eyes glittered with the reflection of the fire. "But more importantly, Mr. Pinkerton is counting on you. Jack missed the mark. You," he prodded Hank with his bony finger, "will not. Understood?"

Weariness enveloped Hank. He'd made so many mistakes in his twenty-seven years, he couldn't afford another. Becoming a U.S. Marshal required Stilts's assistance. There was no other option. His contact continued to glare, and Hank nodded.

"Now, get back to Bellevue, and finalize the assignment."

Although Hank yearned for a few hours' rest in front of the inviting fireplace, he shouldered his blanket and strode to the exit.

He opened the door and paused. "There'll come a time, Stilts, when I'll be glad to sever our relationship."

The small man smiled, but not with humor. "Be cognizant of this. There is no relationship between you and me, or you and her. 'Tis but business."

They glowered at one another for several tense moments. Then Hank stepped out into the night air, leaving the door agape.

Maggie lay down just as the sun lit the eastern sky. Tears stung her eyes, and her teeth cut into her bottom lip, sending a rushing sound through her throbbing head. She took a quivering breath. No gold. No gold anywhere. She covered her face with her hands to keep the sobs from slipping out. Jeether Moats would be back. She hadn't much time. There had to be a way to get something to placate him.

Behind her Corbin stirred and she froze. He settled his body again, and she exhaled and relaxed. How much could she tell her young son, yet still protect him? He possessed a wisdom beyond his eight years, but did he need to know their lives were at risk? Danger had stalked her from the moment she'd courted Ax Robbins.

A scraping noise came from the porch. Hank? Better him than one of the other leering thugs. She examined the fireplace that took up the far wall. Why couldn't there have been a smidgen of treasure among its stones?

Corbin stirred again, and she swung her legs to the floor. No sense sleeping now. Soon he'd be up and ready for chores. She refused to leave him alone a single moment, so just as well start

breakfast. Exhaustion made it hard to lift the iron skillet. Simple eggs and cornbread this morning would have to do. She'd not chance a visit to the smokehouse. It'd probably already been raided by her unwanted visitors anyway.

After setting the cornbread over the fire, she stepped to the door and unbarred it. Hank sat, arms crossed, head bowed in sleep. The bench seat appeared too narrow, and his long legs bent awkwardly beneath him. The creak of the door made his head jerk up and his shoulders swell as he inhaled a waking breath.

She stepped on the porch and pulled the door shut behind her. "Been out here all night?"

"Pretty much."

A sliver of compassion rose at his thick, weary voice, yet she resisted the emotion and snugged her arms across her chest. "I've got cornbread on. You want to come in?"

His head rotated, and his bloodshot eyes latched on to hers. "Inside?"

Maggie licked her lips and transferred her gaze to the sun rays peeking over the treetops. "If you want."

A long silence ensued. "Not a good idea."

With a shrug she replied, "We *are* old friends."

Hank shifted his long legs to stretch out before him and crossed them at the ankles. "Moats might take offense."

"Moats," she spat, her hands parked on her hips.

"Hush…" His quick surveillance around the yard sent a shiver down her back.

He was right. Her impulsiveness had again taken charge. She sniffed as if unconcerned yet lowered her voice. "Why do you mention that vermin's name?"

"He has first dibs on you."

Blood plummeted from her face, and she stumbled. "W…what?"

She felt a steadying hand upon her elbow. His lips pressed against her ear. "If you don't come up with the gold, he'll exact it in flesh."

His face swam before her. "Hank…"

"Go, Maggie." He pushed the door open and shoved her inside.

She slumped against the closed door, her heart pounding. Her fingers clutched the fabric at her throat to ward off the thoughts of Moats's hands on her skin. Boots shuffled once more on the porch, and thoughts of Hank's mother drifted through her mind. Pity knotted her stomach, while a warm ache for her childhood friend bloomed through her chest.

Mrs. Sutter had found a way to support herself at the expense of her reputation, and her son's respect, with men like Jeether Moats. A low moan emitted from her throat, and she supported her head against a rough plank. *Would* Moats exact his, 'gold' in such a way? She shuddered. No. She'd die first.

Corbin stirred and sat up. He greeted her with a scratchy throat. "Morning."

She took a couple of short gasps before she could respond. "Breakfast is almost ready."

"We gonna milk this morning, Mama?"

Maggie rushed to the chair at the table and eased herself down. "Of course. I've got to get the eggs done."

He slid to the puncheon floor and padded to the table, his gaze on her. "Before we milk?"

She swallowed. "Yes, I'm especially hungry this morning."

He stared at her, and she avoided his gaze. She grabbed the eggs and cracked them into a heavy crock bowl. Then she dipped her fingers in to fetch the shell fragments her unsteady hands had dropped. Corbin continued to study her as she picked up the large spoon to whip in a slab of butter. The child could sense something. Finally, he turned and approached the door.

"Where are you going?"

"The necessary."

Her trembling hands set the bowl down on the scarred table. "Wait till after breakfast or use the honeypot."

His brows drew together. "Mama?

"Do what I say," her voice lashed in command. Silence draped the cabin. She lifted her eyes to his dark solemn ones. "I'm sorry. We have to be careful not to go anywhere alone."

He blinked. "Like when Axel Robbins was here?"

A tear slipped to her cheek, and she pressed her fingers to her skin to conceal it. Her voice came in a harsh whisper. "Yes, just like when your father was here."

<u>Chapter Three</u>

Maggie rose, walked to the fireplace, and poured the eggs into the hot skillet on the hearth. She regretted her strident tone. "You still have your books."

Corbin drew close to the bookshelf she'd constructed with crates and discarded lumber. His face pale and somber, he ran his finger across the five titles that rested there. It had been all she could save from Ax's rage. "Will they take them away?"

She clenched her jaw. *No,* they would not take Corbin's books or anything else. Her mind traveled to the butcher knife she'd hidden in the eaves. Tonight, she'd bring it down. "Sit and read a spell while I cook the eggs."

"Yes'm."

When they emerged from the cabin an hour later, the sun shone bright. Hank no longer sat on the rickety bench, and a shot of dread

stole over her. Her anger for him didn't taint the security she felt when he was about. Emotions jumbled, she set out with Corbin at her side, determined to finish the chores and be back to the cabin as soon as possible.

To her surprise, Hank strode from the shed swinging two pails of frothing milk. Sugar, the red and white cow with her big brown eyes so innocent and trusting, followed the stranger who'd milked her.

"Thought I'd save you some work."

Something strange fluttered in Maggie's middle as she came to a full stop. She unclenched her hands to take the buckets from him.

"I'll drop them off at the door."

She tightened her hands into fists when he stepped past her. Corbin's stare was like a hot brand.

Through compressed lips, Maggie commanded her son. "Take the cow to pasture. Don't go too far. Hear me?"

He nodded and turned to do her bidding. Hank dropped the pails on her porch.

On either side of her, those two silent males completed their tasks while she seethed in between. Why did life never make sense? She took in the disheveled garden behind the house and shivered in the chill air. If only Hank hadn't left those many years ago…She snapped that thought in half and strode after the larger of the mutes. He'd already sauntered back to his post on the bench.

Blinking away her wrath, she moseyed to the porch and perched upon the edge. She ground her teeth before muttering, "Thank you for doing the milking."

Hank pulled a blade from his pocket and set to work skinning a stick. She studied him a moment. His clothes seemed especially rumpled this morning and fatigue lined his face.

"Not get much sleep?" she ventured. Opening Hank was like prying at a freshwater mussel.

He shrugged. This would soon annoy her. She gazed out toward the river and then flicked a glance at Corbin's distant figure. "Why are you doing this, Hank?"

The whittling stopped, and she turned to meet his eyes.

"I got my reasons."

"Not good ones, I dare say."

His eyes dropped back to his task. "Good enough, I reckon."

Her lips tightened. "Been to your mom's grave yet?"

Again his hands ceased. "No."

Her eyes flicked to him. She knew him painfully well. Talk of his mother would break his silence, she was sure. "She talked of you right to the end. Hoped you'd come home."

Hank's jawline firmed. "Drop it, Maggie."

His knife went back to business.

"She practically starved to death."

"Maggie. Enough."

Her face froze. "Why should I? Just because it's an unpleasant thought, an unpleasant memory for you? Think about what you're doing, Hank. You've joined a gang of train robbers with the intent of stealing and raping. Isn't that a bit unpleasant?"

He stood and thrust the knife into the sheath at his waist. "Find the gold, and we're history."

"Really? You believe that? You think Jeether Moats is going to thank me profusely for the gold and then meander off into the sunset waving a fond goodbye to Corbin and me? How do you sleep at night?"

He jumped from the porch and faced her. She jumped to her feet, thrust her chin up, and glared at him. Among the tired planes of his face, his dark eyes searched hers. "Trust me, Maggie. You're safe."

Seething and hating the tears that threatened, she shoved against his chest. "You're a bigger fool than I thought, not to mention a coward. A yellow-bellied scallywag who abandons people the moment life gets difficult. I never knew you'd stoop so low. Well, when Jeether Moats comes for me, I hope you're there to watch."

With a sob, she leaped to the porch, grabbed the pails, entered, and slammed the door.

Burn the man! She plunked the pails on the scarred table top and stormed back to jam the bar into place. He, of all people, spouting concerns for her safety while joined with seven thugs ready to abuse her to get their filthy hands on Ax's heist. The mythical heist. Well, no one was getting in here, especially Hank.

Corbin! How could she have left her son outside, dangling over the clutches of those horrible men? Eyeing the front door, and knowing Hank waited just beyond the strong oak, she scurried to the back, shoving down the rising hysteria. She slid through the back door.

Rounding the cabin, her heart fell. No child in sight. Gripping her bodice she ran around the corner. Surely Hank would—

There, Corbin stood at the edge of the porch, swiping a jagged trail down a skinned stick's length, with Hank's huge knife. The involuntary wheeze she exhaled drew both Corbin's and Hank's attention. The big man straightened from leaning over, guiding Corbin's small hands.

"What in Heaven's name are you doing?" Her demand came out like a pup's whimper.

Corbin's usual still face reflected a touch of a smile. "Whittling."

For a few intense moments, she just focused on breathing and not killing Hank. When Corbin dropped his eyes back to his task, she leaped forward. "Young man, you get in the house right now."

This froze his movements, the somberness on his face thick as the Missouri River mud.

"Yes, ma'am."

He handed the knife and stick back to Hank. Maggie yanked up the front of her skirt and bounded aboard the porch without the aid of the steps and stomped up to Hank. He too, had retreated behind a frozen mask.

"How dare you let him wield a knife!"

Hank shrugged. "He was interested."

"Interested? In a gang member's carving?" She lifted her hand and poked his chest. "You have no right to even speak to my child, let alone hand him a knife. Is that clear?"

All her righteous rage took a hiccup when Hank enclosed her prodding fingers in his huge palm. His warm, comforting hand cradled hers gently. Her throat bobbed at his touch, and she couldn't help but drop her gaze to his rough fingers. His voice, soft as the fuzz at the base of a feather, lifted her gaze.

"He's soon to be a man, Maggie. I was here to keep him safe."

For a moment, lost in his dark eyes, she wanted to lean against him and plead with him to shoulder this mess. A ravenous longing rose up. She wanted to beg him to stand beside her, father her fatherless child, and…stay with her. How freeing it would be to let go, to—

"Mama?"

Like a load of snow sliding off a roof onto her head, Corbin's voice rescued her from her own delusions. She jerked her hand away and tugged the cape around her shoulders. She gritted her teeth. "Leave us be."

She pivoted, grabbed Corbin by the thick wool coat, and stalked to the door. One yank to the leather thong reminded her that she'd barred the front entryway. She lifted her chin and spun, refusing to even glance in Hank's direction, and dragged Corbin with her toward the corner of the cabin. Without a word, she nudged her son through the back door and secured it.

Apparently her life goal was to humiliate herself in front the man she despised the most.

Maggie held the candle out as she wedged her body further beneath the cabin. A spider web tickled her neck, and she recoiled to scrape it away. Horrid place. Just horrid. The crawlspace smelled dank and appeared much larger than the fifteen foot square room above.

From the far corner, two yellow orbs glowed in the weak candle light. A skunk's black and white body froze in the wavering flame. Maggie gulped, clamped her lips closed, and scuttled backward to the opening as fast as she could. She slid out with a shudder and inhaled the night air. Safe to say the gold had not been hidden there.

The crickets chirruped in the woods behind the cabin, and the air smelled woodsy and wet. Low male voices drifted to her ears, and she blew out the candle flame. The dark dampness did little to cheer her so she scrambled up and hurried to the back door, all the while studying the tree line for signs of the owners of the muted conversation. The smell of smoke would not be a clear indicator of their whereabouts, for puffs wafted from her own chimney.

She slipped into the cabin and pressed the bar into place with the stealth of Jesse James himself. The darkness made it hard to make out Corbin's body stretched across the bed. Bless his heart, he had no idea what resided below his slumber. She could only hope the polecats wouldn't care to fill their chosen den with their own foul smell.

And the vermin were welcome to their sanctuary. She wasn't about to evict her unwanted tenants. Her weary body settled into the ladder back chair. Skunks or no skunks, nearly every hiding spot she knew of had turned up empty.

The temperature of the room caused her to shiver. She'd banked the fire and kept it low to avoid throwing light for her search tonight. Now she rose. She needed to rake the ashes for live coals and add a couple logs. With a sigh, she sank to the raised hearth and stirred the fire to life. The room brightened in an orange glow.

Something had to give. Tomorrow, Moats would demand the gold.

She turned her head at the movement behind her. A man sat on the trunk near the front door. With a leap, she gasped, clutched her breast, and glanced to her motionless son. "Who are you?"

He flicked a speck of dust from his sleeve. "A concerned ally."

She blinked, still trying to get her breathing under control. "How'd you get in here?"

"With no trouble at all."

She narrowed her eyes at his unusual sharp enunciation. Her gaze ran over his form as the fire illuminated the cabin. He appeared a dandy in his forties or fifties, with a curled handlebar mustache and petite goatee, hair well-oiled. The black cane he carried gleamed in the dim light and a long dark coat draped over the shoulders of his well-fitted grey suit. His right ankle rested at ease on his left knee as if he passed a pleasant day in a park.

"Get out. You have no right to be here, sir. You've not been invited in."

The left side of his mouth curled, and he tapped his cane on his shiny black boot. "I believe you will be quite interested in what I have to say."

"You're one of them, aren't you?" Her heart hammered in her chest.

"Pshaw. My dear woman, I'm here to offer my assistance."

She flicked a glance once more to her son's sleeping form.

"Have no worries of your young knight. He's quite safe for now."

She stilled and elevated her chin. Her hand crept behind her to search the back edge of the table. Just inside the crack near the window lay the dagger she'd fetched from the rafters.

The stranger leaned back. "I'm sure you're seeking this."

His hand reached beside him, and the glint of the knife blade mocked her. The breath strangled in her throat.

"Now, let's cease all this nonsense and get down to business."

"I have no business with you."

His lips twitched and one brow rose. "Come now. You're a bit wet behind the ears, but surely not a dullard. The deal I have in mind is quite honorable."

Maggie found it hard to swallow. Could she possibly snatch up Corbin and flee the cabin before this ogre barred her path? She gave a slight shake of her head, trying to clear it, denying her own question at the same time. "Who are you?"

He blinked lazily. "You may call me Dr. Rumble Stills."

"Doctor?"

A low laugh echoed from his chest. "Of a sort, yes."

"There's no reason for me to trust you. You broke into my home."

He leaned forward and reached out with his cane as if he were drawing on the floor. His gaze flicked up. "You need gold. I have gold."

Her gasp stopped his cane's motion. "You can't think I'd take a dime from you."

Dr. Stills dropped his foot and stood. She licked her lips and edged closer toward the bed. His moving form approached the

38

fireplace. He picked up the tintype of her mother and leaned his body toward the hearth to direct the light onto the image.

"Put that down and leave at once."

"Or what?" he sneered. "You'll alert the miscreants outside?"

His eyes dropped to the picture he held and studied it closely. "What's your poison, Mrs. Robbins? Frying pan or fire?"

Her heart raced, and she gripped the collar of her blouse. Goosebumps broke out on her flesh. If only Hank could hear, perhaps he could…help? "I beg you, sir, please return my mother's picture to the mantel and kindly depart."

"He'll come, you know." He replaced the photo and brought his hands to the top of his cane, his legs squared behind it. The fire behind him darkened the outline of his rigid form. Still, his gaze drilled into hers. "Oh, yes. He will most certainly come. And he'll demand the gold."

A shudder raced through her. "How…how did you know that?"

He took two strides, pulling a black satin bag from the inner pocket of his long suit coat. At the table he spilled the contents, and several twenty dollar gold pieces clinked into a pile.

Her mouth opened as she scanned the treasure. She pulled her eyes from the gleam of the coins and cut her gaze back to his. "You can't get something for nothing, Dr. Stills."

"True. So very true." He stepped back to the fireplace and pointed to the daguerreotype with his cane. "You may claim that pile in exchange for this."

She shook her head. "You can't have my mother's photo."

He nodded and clicked the cane to the floor. "Understood. Tell me, my dear, who do you think he'll profane first? You or your son?"

Maggie wrapped her arms around her middle. "You're a rat."

"It's a simple deal, Mrs. Robbins. Are we in agreeance or not?"

One more step and the back of her legs hit the solid edge of the bed. Her hand reached back to feel her son's chest rise in sleep. When he gave a contented sigh, she knew she had to protect the future with the past. She ground her teeth.

"Fine. The photo for the gold."

A rare smile lit his features. "Indeed, not a dullard. Very well, my good woman. I trust our exchange will leave you in good stead."

He snatched the tintype from the mantel and concealed it beneath his coat. With a nod of his head, he swung the cane out, strolled to the back door, and unbarred it. "A good evening to you, milady. Perhaps we can do business again soon."

With that, he swung through the door, and Maggie lunged forward to secure it.

Chapter Four

Hank kept his face as expressionless as possible. Where had Maggie gotten that gold? Had Ax stowed it with her knowledge? A sense of disappointed dread soured his stomach. Maggie's face paled as Moats stepped closer to her, and Hank clenched his fists.

"What is this? You expect me to believe this is the sum total?" Moats tipped his head back and gave a shout of laughter. "You take me for a fool. Leonard, find that boy."

Maggie took a step back, her eyes surely searching for the boy. But Moats yanked her forward. "Oh, no. You ain't going nowhere. Taking care of the kid must be hampering you from getting the job done, so we'll tend your boy for a while, till the rest of the gold comes to light."

He let her go, and Hank exhaled a lungful of air.

"Please, not Corbin. He's just a child. I'll find the rest, I promise."

Moats continued his stride toward his black horse. He pointed at Hank. "You, watch her."

Tears washed down Maggie's face. "Please, don't do this."

But Moats yanked the reins, reared the horse, and was off. Maggie stood, squeezing her hands and breathing in quiet sobs. Hank stepped toward her, wishing he could offer some comfort. She turned angry eyes on him.

"Don't you dare come near me." She pivoted and raced toward the cabin. The door slammed shut followed by thumps of the bar being wedged into place.

Hank hung his head. As if he needed more reasons for Maggie to hate him. He scanned the perimeter, wondering if Leonard had located the boy yet. With a sigh, he made his way to the porch and took up his vigil on the bench.

Dad-blamed Stilts. Why couldn't the man understand dealing with a woman posed a much trickier assignment? It wasn't cut and dried. Women came with too much emotion, tears, and guilt, especially Maggie. His fist connected with his other palm. He'd rather deal face to face with Jesse James than take on his childhood crush. No, he was the fool. Maggie wasn't just a crush.

He dug out a rawhide pouch of pemmican, yanked a piece off, and tossed it into his mouth. This assignment was taking a toll. He'd barely eaten in weeks. His jaw gnawed the wad of meat and finally, he swallowed. Tough batch of jerky, much like the situation he found himself in. It couldn't be helped. Hank couldn't back out now.

Leonard appeared from the side of the house and jogged to the snatch of trees down the slope to the right. Hank pressed his molars together. Maybe the kid had snuck off. Or maybe Maggie had stowed him inside. Either way, he'd soon be flushed out.

Indian Joe, the gang's tracker, came striding by. Yep, something was up. The half-breed knew how to spot a drop of blood in red clay. Pity filled his gut. Moats wouldn't coddle the boy, that was sure. Hank took a deep breath.

He pulled out his whittling knife and eased the block of wood from his pocket. Perhaps Maggie's son carried enough of Ax's genes to be devious, although he doubted it with the boy's solemn face and calm demeanor. He scrutinized the arched neck he shaped in his hands. Perhaps Maggie's boy liked horses.

His thumb probed a rough patch on the wood. He lacked practice since he'd chosen a life affixed to a saddle. Working with Moats often turned sedentary, not something he preferred. Sitting around provided too much time to think. Even now, his mind drifted off into comparing Maggie's eyes to the Nebraska sky and her hair to ripe wheat.

A heavy step brought his thoughts to an abrupt end. Moats strode toward him followed by Leonard. "Get the hatchet and take that door down."

Hank rose. "Sure, boss. But I expect she'd open the door."

Moats squinted at him. "Then get it open, one way or another."

"Yes, sir." Hank turned and rapped on the oak.

Silence met his ears.

"Sutter…" Moats's guttural syllables grated across Hank's nerves.

Hank knocked again. "Mrs. Robbins? You best be opening up, or we'll be chopping it down."

A few seconds ticked by before scraping sounds of the bar being lifted lit his ears. The door swung open. Her defiant tear-streaked face wrenched his stomach. She tilted her chin and stiffened her lips. Moats stepped forward.

"Bring the boy out."

Her face went rigid. "He's not here."

Moats turned his head and spurted a healthy stream of tobacco juice on the right doorpost. Spatters freckled Maggie's cheek and, her gaze turned icy. She raised an arm to swipe it away. "You're quite a gentleman, Mr. Moats."

He snorted and stroked his puffy beard. "I think it's about time for Mrs. Robbins and me to get better acquainted."

Hank stepped forward. "You want me to search the cabin?"

Moats went silent, his gaze full on Maggie, and Hank's gut tossed.

"Fine," he grunted and shoved her aside.

Hank and Leonard entered behind him and combed the small space for the boy. Moats stood in the center of the room, arms crossed, while Leonard threw the quilts to the floor and yanked the sheets from the mattress. Maggie's lips quivered, so Hank pulled his gaze away to open the large trunk by the door.

Ripping sounds came from behind him as Leonard slit the ticking and tossed the softened shucks about the room. A strangled moan emitted from Maggie's throat.

"Leonard, that's enough." Hank muttered.

"Shut it, Sutter." Leonard emptied the sack and stepped into the mess covering the floor. The man yanked on the lone strap of his grungy overalls and grinned, but his stare was stony. "I guess he's not in there."

"You best be cleaning this up, Mrs. Robbins," Moats growled. "Never know when I'll need a good bed."

Leonard guffawed. Hank stood stiffly by the door until the all of them had exited the cabin. He threw an apologetic glance behind him, but Maggie had covered her face with her hands. With a clenched jaw and a backbone full of regret, Hank pulled the door closed.

Maggie clenched her arms about her and stared at the corn shucks scattered around the room. It had long grown dark, and fear and loneliness bound her like a vine-covered shack. She hadn't risked taking food to the shed, sure her son lurked in his secret spot. How long would it be before they discovered him?

An owl hooted nearby, and her head popped up. From experience, Maggie knew that was no ordinary hoot owl. Could it be White Moon? Tonight? Of all nights, the girl had impeccable timing. But then, she always did.

Maggie nearly knocked the chair to the floor in her haste to reach the window. She peeked out, but the darkness betrayed no

movement. She could only trust her own senses at this point. Quickly, she unbarred the back door, leery as never before of the stranger who'd invaded her house a few short nights ago.

Maggie paced as she waited. She froze as the door eased open. The small frame that slipped through bespoke Corbin's faithful friend. The small Indian girl stood in the shadows.

Maggie rushed forward, pressed the door closed, and clasped the child's hands. "What are you doing here?"

Humor laced the childish tones. "Father hunting."

The girl's usual reply brought no smile to Maggie's face tonight. Her father often left the reservation to the north without permission and hunted the old grounds near Bellevue.

"I see many bad men."

"Yes." Maggie bit her lip, tears filling her eyes. "They're looking for Corbin."

The girl grew silent.

"Listen, White Moon. I need your help. Remember how you took him to your village last summer when—?"

Maggie stopped. No need to bring up Ax's last terrifying appearance at the cabin. At the girl's shadowed nod, Maggie continued. "I need you to take him there now." She clenched the girl's fingers. "Can you do it?"

"Injun Joe no see. We go."

"What about Mr. Gore?" What would the agent of the Bureau of Indian Affairs do if he caught Corbin within the boundaries of the reservation? And would Corbin be any more safe in the confines of

the Omaha village? Not that Maggie had much choice. She had to send her son away.

"Corbin, good Indian. No get caught. He is The One Who is Quiet, Zonde."

A sliver of relief snaked through her. Yet getting through the perimeter set up around the cabin would be quite a feat. "Go carefully, White Moon."

"No worry. God guides me. I am Mi'-wa-thon—White Moon."

Maggie compressed her lips. The girl's confidence shook her. God? The same God that allowed her mother to die? Who allowed Axel Robbins to enter her life? Who sent Hank away? Acid belched up her throat as White Moon slipped through the door. God had done nothing—*nothing* to help Maggie. So, she would take matters into her own hands. She would protect her own with every breath of her life.

Corbin would be spirited away, protected by a strong contingent of warriors. And she? She would be alone—alone to face the villains surrounding the cabin.

Silent sobs took hold of her body as Maggie slid the bar into place.

Maggie gripped the knife and stared at the back door of the cabin. The trunk she sat upon had long grown hard, but she dared not move. A week had passed since White Moon had spirited Corbin from the men's clutches. An ache snaked through her stomach which broke out in goose bumps across her skin. How she longed for him.

Tears threatened, but she raised her chin. No. She would not be distracted from the task at hand. Since the dandy knew the looming deadline, he would show tonight, and she would be ready. The door eased open and she stiffened. But the form that entered loomed much larger than the stranger's.

Moats?

"It's me, Maggie," Hank's whispered voice met her ears.

She slumped in relief then hated herself for her weakness. "What do you think you are doing?"

The moonlight shimmering through the window behind him revealed the shake of his head. "Not sure."

She huffed. "Get out."

His form eased into the chair, backlit by the ethereal glow. His hushed voice caressed her nerves. "I was there when Mother died."

"What are you talking about?"

"You said I wasn't. That she asked for me."

"You're lying."

He laid his arm on the table. "I'm not. Old Polly and I buried her before the preacher showed up."

She rubbed her temple. "I never saw you."

A silence stretched. "Sometimes things aren't what they seem, Maggie."

Her name ran off his tongue like honey, and she licked her lips in the dark, thankful he couldn't see. "I'm glad for her. She was really sick."

His head nodded in shadow. "Yep."

"Is that what you're sneaking around for? To tell me about your mother's last visit?"

He shifted in the chair. "I'll tell you if you explain why you're sitting here holding a knife…with the door unbarred."

Maggie clenched her jaw and ran her fingers up the cold blade of the knife. "A lady has her secrets."

He stood and Maggie wanted to rush forward, throw her arms around him, and beg him to stay. Instead, she pressed her back to the log wall behind her.

"You've grown hard, Maggie. I should've been straight forward with my intentions. Above all, I wish I'd been here for you."

A sob percolated up her throat, and tears bled from her eyes. She wanted to snap at him, hurt him for abandoning her, but her throat seemed tied with twine.

"I failed you, Maggie. I'm sorry."

In her misery, he slipped through the door and disappeared. She flung the knife to the floor, lurched forward, and slammed the bar into place before sinking to the floor to weep in silent regret.

"I need supplies."

Hank stood on the outer perimeter as Maggie confronted Moats. The blamed woman had marched into their camp first thing in the morning. He had to give it to her. She had nerves of steel. Moats sat on a stump, spooning beans into his mouth. The other members of the gang either lurked about or were about their assignments. Hank leaned to stir the pot of breakfast beans over the fire.

"Supplies? No, no. Seems to me you failed to supply the rest of the heist."

Maggie's chin lifted. "We renegotiated. You extended my deadline."

Bean sauce dripped down Moats's beard. "I can be a plain idiot, cain't I? First the boy disappears and now no gold. Then you expect to head to town for supplies? I ain't no idjit. I don't need you in town babbling about the Moats's gang surrounding your cabin. You go nowhere. Gold first."

Her lips grew tighter, and Hank lowered his head but kept her in his view. Why did the woman have to be so audacious? He jerked his head a tad. Just one of the many things he loved about her.

"You won't get any gold if I starve to death." Defiance blared in Maggie's tone.

Moats laughed and threw a stick in the fire. "I could use a man like you."

The other men, in various positions about the fire guffawed, but Hank clenched his fist. The woman was too beautiful and fiery to flare up in front of a bunch of lustful degenerates. Anger boiled in his gut. Hank kept his gaze on the gang's leader.

"Fine. You go. Get yer business done. No talking or my man will shoot you where you stand. Got it?"

At her nod he continued. "You've got two hours."

Moats turned and scanned the crowd. "Sutter. Get a couple of horses ready and take this fine lady into town."

Hank expelled a sigh of relief. *Thank God.* He hurried to carry out the command before Moats could change his mind about

selecting him. He couldn't protect Maggie from the scum he worked with if he wasn't there. He turned his head a mite. Maggie scurried after him but slowed once she'd left the camp behind.

He quickly saddled two horses and approached her. "Sorry. No sidesaddles."

Maggie snorted. "As if I'd know how to cling to one side of a horse. Surely you know me better than that."

The woman drew close. Nerves jangled through his body. "Need a leg up?"

Her hand pressed against his arm, and he fixed his gaze on hers. "Thank you for visiting last night."

It was about now he'd bring the roof down on top of his head. Never did the right thing flow from his mouth. If she only knew how badly he'd wanted to stay, how badly he wanted to confide in her. But he clamped his lips and soaked in her gentleness, the softness in her eyes, the beauty of her face. A muscle twitched in his forearm.

He reached up to stroke the spikey beard that had developed on his face in the last few days. He wasn't fit to accompany her. What he wouldn't give to be clean shaven and decked out in his best pants and shirt.

Maggie's brows elevated and humor tugged at her lips. "I only have two hours, Hank. Perhaps you could help me board the horse?"

He blinked. "Yes, Ma'am."

His hands spanned her waist and lifted her clear of the horse's back. Her face registered surprise, as he eased her down, and she gave a short laugh.

"Buy a calf and receive a herd."

He cleared his throat. Perhaps he'd gotten carried away. "Sorry. Shoulda just let you step up."

Her lips twitched. "Your bungling charmed all the girls, Hank Sutter."

He mounted and turned a puckered face to her. Maggie? Flirting? Surely not. "My blunders have put me in plenty of hot water. Usually, with you."

They set the horses in motion, and she turned a sunny face in his direction. "It's not your missteps that set me off, Hank. It's your silence. And your absence."

Hank affixed his gaze between his horse's ears. Was she goading him? One wrong word and she'd shred him. Yet silence peeved her, too. His crude tongue never quite framed the right phrase. "Maggie, I don't know—"

She held up a hand to silence him. "No, let's not overthink and regurgitate unpleasant events. I have two hours of escape. Let's pretend."

His brow furrowed. "Pretend?"

A dreamy expression crossed Maggie's features as she leaned back and drew in a long breath. "Yes. Let's fantasize you never left. Let's ride into town like we used to when we were kids. Remember?"

Chapter Five

D id he remember? Glory, did a parched man thirst for water? That memory occupied his thoughts most days. Those times hadn't been exactly carefree, but they carried an innocence he only dreamed of now.

"You're not going to ruin it by saying nothing, are you?"

He turned his head and surveyed Maggie in a blue shirt waist and white pinafore. Like a fairy princess, her dark cloak fell around her shoulders and across the horse's rump. If he squinted, she resembled the young girl of eleven years ago.

"Hank?"

"Sounds perfect."

She smiled. An actual smile that threw him into silence.

"Come to think of it, you were always the strong, silent type." She laughed. "It's probably why we got along so well."

"Possibly."

"Though Retha Guthrie tried her hardest to worm her way between us."

He slid his hands down the reins and settled into the soothing pace. "She could turn a head."

Maggie sniffed. "Hank Sutter, you're horrid."

He studied her stiff features. "Never kissed her, did I?"

She harrumphed. "How would I know?"

Hank grinned. "You know."

Her lips twitched into a smile. "We did though."

Hank grunted. Not a good memory to resurrect. That scene had worn its wear in his head over the years. It was the moment he knew he had to leave.

"Hank? You're doing it again."

His gaze returned to her.

"Do you remember?" Maggie gave a cheeky grin, a blush blooming in her cheeks.

She so transfixed him, he could barely look away. Remember? She'd be shocked to know how many times a day it replayed in his memory—that kiss and what would follow. No, he couldn't tell her that. It might disgust her to know.

"The silence, Hank."

He sat up in the saddle. "I reckon I might recall the event."

They turned left on the path near the river, and she kicked her horse to cut him off. She swerved the dark horse in front of him. He yanked his mount to an abrupt halt.

Her eyes blazed in fury. "That's it? You reckon you recall? Must have been quite an earth-shattering memory with you oozing such excitement."

"Maggie, I..."

She pulled her horse around and nudged the animal into a gallop. Hank groaned and then urged his horse to catch up. Maggie had always been a superb rider when she'd had the opportunity to hone her skills. But he'd given her the mare, and his bigger mount soon came abreast. In the rush of the wind he snaked a hand out to grab the reins and ease both horses to a stop.

The horses heaved and danced about as Hank slid to the ground. In one motion he captured her waist and pulled her from the horse. He yanked the horses and Maggie to the cover of the trees.

She twisted her arm in an attempt to break his grip. "Let me go, you fiend."

Once they reached the security of the trees lining the river, he sent a quick scan to make sure none of Moats's lackeys had followed. Then he released the horses' reins and pulled her farther into the cover.

He whipped her around to grip her upper arms. "What do you want from me, Maggie? I never seem to say the correct thing, and I never shut up at the right time."

She continued to wrestle, shoving and pinching him with all her might. He yanked her against him, and her eyes flared open. But at least she calmed.

"You want to know all about it? Fine. I never kissed Retha or any other woman since you and I snuck to the spring house to hide

your mother's secret box. And about that day? I think about it all the time. How you felt in my arms. What your mouth tasted like. It's like a fire burning in my gut. Why do you think I left, Maggie?

She blinked, her mouth agape. "I…I don't know."

"I had to have something to earn you. I was nothing, Maggie. I didn't deserve a woman like you. I had to make something of myself. Only when I got back, you were already taken."

He released her and turned to pace the river's edge.

Maggie chewed her lip and clenched her skirt in her hand. The only other time she'd seen such passion in Hank had been that day in the spring house. In the cool darkness, their breathing had merged, their bodies melded into one. She'd never experienced anything of that magnitude since.

Shivers shook her in the chill morning air. She stepped forward and laid a hand on his shoulder. "I'm sorry. I didn't know."

He turned, his face set in the usual expressionless mask. "How would you? You didn't wait."

She gritted her teeth. "How could I, Hank? My mother was dying. I had nowhere and no one."

The muscle in Hank's left cheek twitched. "You had Ax."

She spat on the ground. "Oh, yes. He was my beau, all right. Until I married him and discovered what a monster he really was."

Hank's eyes narrowed. "Rumor had it you didn't know."

She shook her head and cut her gaze to the grass. "I was an idiot. A trusting idiot."

He moved closer and caressed her arm. "You were grieving."

She closed her eyes and hung her head. "I couldn't have done much worse picking up your mother's occupation."

He seized her arms, and she gasped in pain. "Don't say that."

A tear worked its way from the corner of her eye. "What does it matter? Your men will soon have their way with me. At least your mother earned cash."

His arms crushed her to him, and he whispered into her hair. "I won't let them hurt you."

Her breathing came in spasms. "You won't be able to stop them, Hank."

He drew back and captured her gaze. "I will."

She shook her head, tears trailing. "Why would you care?"

The look in his eyes deepened, and his hand brushed away the moisture on her face. "Because—I love you, Maggie."

She gasped. "What? You couldn't. Not after everything. I'm Axel Robbins's widow."

His hand wrapped around her jaw and threaded into her hair. "I always have. Why would it change?"

Air refused to flow to her lungs. It felt so good to be held by him. "But you—I—"

The desire on his face stilled her tongue. "Sometimes silence is good, Maggie."

His mouth lowered and her breath rushed from her. His lips ran leisurely over hers and, she pressed against him, tugging at his shirt. He groaned and his arms wrapped around her body like a tailored dress.

A sigh slipped from her, and he whispered her name. The stamp of the horse made his head jerk, but his hooded gaze never left her face. A warmth cascaded through her body, and an intense craving to remain in his arms saturated her every nerve. Oh, heavens, dear heavens. She still—loved *him*. After all this time, after all the agony, all the scandal, she still loved him.

His hand caressed the small of her back as he searched her eyes. Hank Sutter loved her. Hank Sutter her childhood beau. Hank Sutter the love of her life. Hank Sutter…bank robbing, thieving…thug. She jerked away from him and swallowed.

"Maggie?

She shook her head and stepped back. His arms fell to his sides. "You're just like Ax. All full of affection and sweet promises. What will you do once you've bagged your quarry, Hank? Force me to cook, clean, and service you while you gallivant all over the country robbing banks? Sorry, Hank. I unknowingly signed up for that once. I won't be stupid enough to do it again."

The rest of the way to town was as quiet as a double funeral, but Maggie wasn't about to break the silence. Let him stew in the pot of his own making. If he thought she believed he was still in love with her, he had another thing coming. Although the sincerity in his voice and the brokenness on his face dug at her soul, she shoved it away.

How many times had Ax pretended to adore her during their whirlwind courtship? As soon as the judge had pronounced them hitched, his demeanor had soured. Her wedding night had been

nothing but a quick, rough violation, and it was then she'd known—known she'd made the worst mistake of her life.

And as far as Hank only kissing her and no other woman? Pshaw. He was a grown man in every right. She flicked a glance to those broad shoulders, the lithe hips gyrating to the rhythm of his horse's gait. Then she made the mistake of letting her eyes travel up to collide with his. She jerked her head to the road in front of her.

Sure, Hank was fine. He put Ax to shame in both looks and form. But that wouldn't sway her none. Not even their past connection made a difference. He could lie all he wanted about how the only lips he ever touched was hers, and she'd sooner believe Jeether Moats's farewell speech once he received the gold.

Fact was, Hank Sutter was a man, albeit a fine one...a brawny, strapping specimen with dark, bottomless eyes that nearly undid her. But that was beside the point. He was part of the group called men. And the lot of them had dark urges that made them say and do things to acquire such desires. She would have no part of it.

Smoke puffed from the Fortstown Outpost's chimney stacks, now visible through the trees. Ugh, how she wished they could have had time to ride to Bellevue, where she was less known. The usual mixture of Otoe or Omaha Indians and fur trappers were scattered about, loading horses, wasting time, chewing tobacco and all looking like someone she wanted to avoid. Maggie tugged her cape's wool hood over her head.

Hank led them to the nearest hitching post and looped his reins around before reaching to assist her down. As much as she wanted to zap him from her sight, it'd be best—and safest—to be seen as

Hank's woman. So as much as she burned to clamber down from the horse alone, she waited for his attention.

She followed him into the old log structure, keeping the hood down over her eyes, and focusing on the heels of Hank's boots. Her cheeks burned at her own lack of independence, but she consoled herself with the thought that she was only using him for her own gain. Ugh, that unsavory thought made her twist her shoulders in discomfort.

He paused just inside the door and instead of heels, she peered at his toes. She lifted the hood and connected with his steady gaze.

"Remember. Just shopping."

Suddenly using him for her own gain didn't sting as much. "I got it, Hank."

She spun from him and approached the counter. The buckskin-layered man, leering a grin with several missing teeth, almost made her wish she hadn't been so hasty. But she squared her shoulders and fished the list from her pinafore pocket.

"Howdy, perty lady. What can I do you for?"

His guffaw made several ticks flick across her face. She thrust the paper at him. "I need some supplies."

"Shore, shore and then—"

The man's grin wavered about the same time Maggie felt Hank's arm brush her back. The man's lips twitched a time or two, and then he nodded and disappeared. Maggie pressed her eyes closed for a moment. As much as she despised Hank, she couldn't wish him away at this very moment. She needed him…for…protection only.

As she waited, she browsed the small area, avoiding the sudden influx of shoppers whose gazes seemed to latch onto her more than the feeble offerings for sale. But Hank's comforting presence was never far away. And if she knew him, he kept busy shooting down the hopeful ogling eyes.

She fingered a spool of black thread and then a leather pouch of hair ribbons. Both items were beyond her means at this point. If any mending needed to be done, she would salvage one of her threadbare skirts. And hair ribbons? Glory, they were only a fanciful thought of childhood so very long ago.

Her necessaries were dumped to the counter, and she stepped back to pay for them. A sack of flour, a quarter loaf of brown sugar, two scoops of salt, and a small can of coffee would have to do. She was pleased to see the sugar and salt wrapped in old newsprint. That was almost better than buying the hair ribbons.

Hank loaded the supplies in both horses' saddlebags and lifted her aboard her horse. But instead of mounting himself, he led both animals off. A particular pair of Indians, both toothless and hair generously smeared with bear grease, paused to assess her and then approached. Maggie caught her breath and tugged her hood over her hair.

But they called out a greeting to Hank in their native language and to Maggie's surprise, Hank answered in similar fashion. They murmured a bit and gestured toward her. But Hank shook his head and kept walking.

Despite vowing not to speak to him, she couldn't seem to stop herself. "What was that about?"

He kept walking until he came alongside the blacksmith's shack a stone's throw away. Then he paused and secured the reins on an iron ring near the open doorway. He turned a quirky smile to her.

"They wanted to barter for you."

She gasped. "Barter—you mean *buy* me?"

Hank shrugged, but his grin grew wider.

Maggie whipped her head back, but the two were gone. Only a group of men trudged through the muddy pathway from the post to a couple other buildings collected in this small area.

"What did you tell them?"

Hank tipped the brim of his hat back and caught her eyes. "I told them you were my woman."

"How dare you?" she hissed.

Then he was there, beside her leg, his hand on her mount's bridle. "Don't get your dander up. If they think you're mine, no one in the vicinity will bother you."

Before she could think, he ducked under the other horse's head and disappeared into the ramshackle hovel. If he thought she would allow him—what were they doing here anyway? Her curiosity snapped one thought in half with another. Did one of the horses need a shoe? Exactly what was he up to now? Only one way to find out.

Glancing around to make sure the area was cleared of any other male characters, she swung her leg over her horse. Once her skirts were in rights, she snuck around the mare. Standing in the doorway might be too obvious, but she'd noticed a window of sorts on the other side of the shack. She sidled along the tumble of logs that made

up the side of the shed-like building and paused at the edge of the window.

Perfect. If that confounded blacksmith would quit pounding iron long enough for her to hear…ah. That was better.

"Nope. Ain't got no news for you. Even Bellmira ain't had nobody through."

Hank's voice filtered to her ear. "Is that so?"

The blacksmith's laugh came low and deep. "Yep. Just visited Bellmira's place the night before."

Bellmira? Maggie searched her memory bank. The same who owned Bellmira's Parlour House? A fancified name, but whispered none too quietly as the Bawdy House. The profitable two-story clapboard house lay just to the north. The woman, Bellmira Zimmerman, was known as a Mormon Madame who chose to make her fortune the old-fashioned way rather than hitch up as one of many wives to one man.

Maggie shuddered. She never thought she'd see the day when Hank showed an interest in a place that exploited women, given his mother had carried on a one-woman version of it in her own home. Hank's voice came again, guarded, soft.

"Keep your eyes open."

The blacksmith harrumphed. "'Twill be a pleasure, sure."

A coarse laugh popped from the man's throat as Maggie quickly high-stepped it back to the horses. When her companion appeared through the door, Hank's brows puckered as he studied her, no doubt wondering why she'd dismounted.

She shrugged. "I needed to stretch my legs."

In silence he bellied up to her mount to swing her aboard. Despite her determined disfavor toward her childhood crush, a quiver of delight rippled through her to feel his strong hands upon her waist. What a pathetic silly woman she was.

Maggie clenched her jaw, determined her logic would overpower these giddy, girlish emotions. It made no sense to yearn for a criminal. And that was final. Surely her heart would get the message.

Eventually.

Chapter Six

The temptation to run with Maggie thrummed through him. Her son Corbin gone, she would have nothing to return for, would she? With Maggie by his side, did he even need to finish the mission? A few hours of hard riding would give them a good start.

He glanced at Maggie. My, but it was tempting. But living on the run would never do. Soon Maggie would resent him even more than she did now. And she was already in enough danger, let alone living a life running from a savage bunch of men. A heaviness settled on him as he turned them both south, back to the gang's camp.

He let a burr of frustration hum in his throat. Unfortunately, his grunt was so loud, it caught Maggie's attention plodding alongside him. No need to alert her on his thoughts of desertion. He had to escort her back. He had no option.

The whole reason he'd originally left years ago still hung over his head like a noose for a condemned man. That overwhelming need to feel worthy of Maggie had driven him away. So, this time, he was here to stay. Leaving had only paved the way for another man to take what he'd yearned would be his.

"The fur trader wrapped the goods in old newspaper. At least we'll have something to read when we get back."

We'll? Her guarded tone and deliberate gaze on him melted away the pleasure of her more intimate reference. "Yep."

"I haven't had much opportunity to stay in touch with happenings. How about you?"

Hank kept his gaze to the road. She was fishing, using that soft, gentle tone to weasel out information. "Nope."

A quick huff of air told Hank he'd struck a nerve.

"Really, Hank. You are the limit."

The pathway curved up a steep slope ahead. All too soon they would be back. "In what way?"

"I've already expressed the way," she snapped off a reply.

He pulled his horse to a stop, and she did the same, her face furrowed. A blonde, wayward lock of hair blew across Maggie's face.

"Why are we stopping?" she demanded, yet uncertainty softened her tone.

He pulled his mount beside hers and reached out to grip her forearm. Her eyes flew to his, wide and bewildered. "I want you to know, I will protect you, Maggie. Don't fret. If anything happens…call for me. God willing, I won't leave you."

Her mouth parted and a sparkle of moisture glinted in her eyes. She looked so incredibly kissable, so vulnerable, it smote his heart. How he wanted to snatch her from her horse, tug her to his lap, and kiss her until she lost her breath. Hold her, keep her. *Marry her*.

He let go a deep sigh and shoved down the intense longing. He stroked her delicate jaw. Yet, his voice came thick. "I'll give my life to save you."

God grant he be there when she needed him. No matter what, he would not abandon her ever again. If she only knew how easy it was to make that vow. For without Maggie, his life was as meaningless as dirt.

Hank took a wad of papers from Maggie's outstretched hand, the crumpled newsprint carefully pressed to allow reading. Should he tell her he'd already read this edition? Naw. That would be opening Maggie's Pandora box of questions. Instead he took it with a nod of gratitude.

The bench below him surely had become permanently attached to his rear-end, but he refused to leave his post for longer than a few minutes of necessity. Maggie, dressed in a worn brown dress, stood beside him for a moment, hands on her hips, cloak out like bat wings. The day was nippy but bearable. She'd holed up for several days since their trip to the outpost, only making an appearance to put the red and white cow out of her misery. Seeing her on the porch lifted his spirits more than a little.

"Thought you'd like to read that."

"Obliged."

Hank turned his head to the paper, but kept his eyes on the woman pursuing the naked trees in the distance. He yanked his eyes to the words before him when she pivoted to scowl at him.

"Are those lowlifes still about? Seems quieter the last couple of days."

It burned him that he'd been assigned to interrogate her, and instead, she seemed to be the one constantly looking for information. As much as he wanted to come clean and confess that most of the Moats's gang engaged themselves with what Hank suspected was a quick heist in Iowa before returning to sulk about the cabin, he couldn't. The desire to confide in her still ran deep.

Maggie probably had a few more days of respite as he figured the gang would stop at Bellmira's place on their return. It had become a common stopover for the restless gang members. But no matter what loyalty he still harbored with Maggie, he had to keep his cards close to his chest. Both for his protection and Maggie's, too.

"I reckon."

She snugged her arms around her middle and settled on the top step. "I think you're misleading me, Hank."

He grunted. "That's what outlaws do."

Her gaze raked him long and hard, her eyes chips of ice. Her tone deepened. "I suppose."

The article before him *Jesse James Claims Innocence* caught his attention. Oh, yes, the Northfield, Minnesota robbery. Hank had read about that a week after the story had broken. The entire gang had met their match in the vigilante townsfolk. As a matter of fact, half the James-Younger Gang had been captured. But Jesse and his brother

had escaped. Hank had been on a scouting trip for Moats, trying to prove his loyalty. Instead, he'd linked up with his contact and received new directives. Hence, the reason they'd migrated here.

Hank's determination steeled over. He had to get any information he could to capture the James brothers. And that meant extracting information from Maggie. The sooner he managed that, he could pursue what was really important—Maggie. "Like the James-Younger gang here. You read this?"

Maggie took a long breath. "Yes."

"They nearly caught him. Reckon he'll stay close or run?"

Long seconds ticked by as his companion huddled beneath her cloak. "I wouldn't know. Nor do I care."

"Ax ever run with them?"

Maggie stood from her perch on the porch, setting her feet on the dirt. "Hank, listen. Ax never discussed his plans with me. Have I ever met Jesse James? No. I believe I've seen him near the house a time or two. I overheard conversations about Pick and Ax meeting up with them, but never details."

She spun and stabbed him with wounded eyes. "The fact is, I didn't want to know. My husband was a criminal, Hank. I thought I married an upstanding man who'd care for me and see me through a dire time. Instead, it took all my strength to survive that relationship, protect my child, and see to our needs."

Maggie stomped up the stairs to the porch and Hank rose. As she veered to scoot past him, he caught her by the arm. He hated seeing the anguish written across her face. "Maggie...If I could, I'd—"

She tugged from him. "Don't. I have to be hard. I must survive. Corbin's counting on me. And that's all that matters."

With a swirl of skirts, she slipped through the cabin door.

Maggie bent to pull the needle through the hem of the worn cotton material of Corbin's pants. Soon she'd have to light the lantern, and she loathed to do that. Thinking on Hank's pathetic attempt today to interrogate her about Jesse James had brought on a fit of angry tears that had wasted away her complete afternoon. Breaking that cycle could only be solved by planning for the future.

She would survive, oh, yes, she would. And so would Corbin. Therefore, she would prepare. The next time she saw her son—a gulp rose in her throat—he'd need longer britches. Maggie would be ready. Besides, the task kept her hands and mind occupied. The less she thought about Hank, the better.

Shots echoed outside and she tensed, shrinking from the window. Now what? She plopped the fabric onto the table and fell to the hardwood floor. Several more rounds pierced the air, and Maggie huddled in a fetal ball, pressing her eyes closed. Had Moats returned from wherever? Was her time up? Would the door come crashing down and her worst nightmare come true?

But no one stomped to her porch. Only distant yells and raucous laughter could be heard. It seemed her unwanted wardens had returned. A shuffle brought her back to high alert. Hank. He seemed to do that every so often, whether to put her mind at ease or merely to stretch from his vigil, she couldn't know. Nevertheless, his vow of protecting her swirled in her mind.

Never had she known him to break his promises. *Except once.* And he'd abandoned her when she'd needed him the most. How could she ever forget that? No, trusting Hank was like trying to hold sand in your fingers. She had to depend only on herself.

Maggie slithered across the puncheon floor and tugged the kitchen knife from beneath the mended mattress. Pressing her back against the base of the bed, Maggie pulled her legs up and tucked her skirt under her stockinged feet. They would not take her. She'd fight to the death.

Several minutes ticked by, and Maggie's breathing returned to normal. Feet scuffled across the porch and then she heard the soft thuds of footsteps growing softer. Just as she had suspected. Already, Hank had left her. Left her open for attack. The miserable fiend.

But the thuds returned and then tramped across the porch. The sharp knock on her door drew a gasp from her throat.

"It's me, Maggie."

Hank. But who else? With the fire banked low and the room awash in darkness, she rose as quietly as she could. If only the lone window didn't face the backyard. Boots shifted on the porch boards. It seemed to be only one set.

"Open up. I'm alone."

She gripped the knife handle as she eased the bar from the door. Sweeping the door open, she realized having a lantern might have been an asset, for all she could make out was a vague silhouette of a large man. Still, she held up the knife.

"What are you sitting in the dark for?"

Sitting? More like cowering, but she wouldn't tell him that. Instead she tromped over to the table, struck a match, and lifted the hurricane glass. "What is so important that you had to distur—"

She gave a cry at the bloody wad of fur in his hand. The knife she still carried tumbled to the floor.

"Sorry. Didn't have a pan to put it in. Here."

When she didn't take it, he stepped across the threshold and pushed the door closed. "It's just some fresh venison, Maggie, not a dead body. And fetch that knife before you get hurt."

She whirled around to snatch the offending blade from the floorboards and thrust it back beneath the mattress. Then she set the lantern on the table and grabbed her Dutch oven off the shelf. He slid the roast into the pan, as she eyed the door.

"Don't get your apron in a wad, they've all settled for the night.

She gritted her teeth. "Might I remind you there were shots not ten minutes ago?"

"Yeah." His voice seemed weary. "Merely celebratory ones."

"Humph," she grunted, none too lady-like. "Your *friends* have an odd way of celebrating."

She quickly rinsed the meat, set a lid on the pan, and placed it near the banked coals. Her stomach churned in anticipation. She'd only eaten a little dried meat today. While wiping her hands on a towel, she cleared her throat. "Ummm, thank you. For the roast that is."

Hank inclined his head. My, he looked exhausted.

"You need to keep your strength up. You're dropping weight."

"Really?" Maggie flopped her hands to her hips. "I can't imagine why that might be. Can you?"

He tugged his hat from his head, his too-long hair mussed in an adorable way. Maggie pressed her lips tight to keep the threads of his bungling charm from stitching into her heart.

"Don't start, Mag. You need to eat."

"Preparing the fatted calf, are we? Moats must have put you up to it. Impressive how you care for *his woman*."

The last two words came in a growl despite her attempt to remain coolly in charge. In the dim lantern light, Hank's Adam's apple bobbed. He stared at his hat as he rotated it in his big hands. Then he turned and sauntered back to the door.

"The only way that will happen is if I'm dead."

He tugged something from his canvas jacket and tossed it to the bed. "For the kid."

Her gaze glued to the handkerchief-covered package on the quilt. The door slid closed, and she was alone once more. She tugged her attention from the gift and barred the door with more than a bit of reluctance, wishing he could have stayed a little longer. Long enough for her to soften, long enough for her to get her fill of looking at him.

Instead, she took a long shaky breath and reached for the bundle in Hank's white hanky. She perched on her bed and untied the knot. Out fell a perfectly formed wooden pony. A ragged sob scaled her throat with the speed of a galloping mustang. Every time she wanted to hate him, she couldn't.

Maggie scrubbed away the tears that wet her face and cradled the carving. The figure had been honed smooth and authentic. Hank

had fashioned a beautiful gift. She sniffed. Accepting it was foolish. Giving it back, unbearable. Corbin would treasure this little horse. Oh, how she missed her son.

She collapsed upon the bed, gripping the figurine tight beneath her chin. Just holding it shred her heart. The colt would forever remind her of the two people who meant the most to her in the whole world.

And both were beyond her reach.

Chapter Seven

Hank shivered and leaned against the tree in the darkness. Even with Ni'-da-wi's buffalo robe across his shoulders, his teeth chattered. The Missouri River had chilled to liquid ice, and he'd had the shakes ever since. Leaving Maggie defenseless tugged at his soul. He had to hurry this inconvenient appointment. Already, it would take several hours of hard riding to return to the river for his second dunking in the freezing water.

Being in Iowa was the last place he wanted to be. He squinted at the lone squat log lodge. It wasn't the cabin where he wished to be. Not by a long shot. He shoved away his preferences and focused.

Shadows crossed the flickers of light dancing across the window, indicating Stilts was not alone. Hank closed his eyes and pulled the heavy cloak tighter around his neck. A smattering of snow

slapped against his cheek. When this was over, he was going to sleep a solid week, inside a building—with a roaring fire.

Reality nosed in. Coercing information from Maggie proved to be a near impossibility. Not only did her mood swing faster than a gate in a gale-force wind, but his every attempt to begin a conversation turned into a bumbling circus act. Plus, shame seared him to mislead her. He loved her. He couldn't use her for his purposes.

The ever-present cutting breeze dropped the temperature, and a snowflake wedged in his lashes. *Please let this be over by winter.* There seemed no rest from the biting wind, the pretense, and Maggie's hatred. He dropped his head.

Maybe he wasn't cut out for this. Maggie's reluctance to talk of her former husband made it difficult to get any information about Ax's ties to Jesse James. Ever since Maggie had married that thug, he'd set his sight on being appointed U.S. Marshal. It had given his life a new direction and something to douse the searing fire burning for Maggie. Joining up with Stilts for undercover work had seemed his best avenue. But all attempts to accomplish his goal had failed, and the desire for the prestigious job waned. But the hunger for Maggie had quadrupled.

Now, the wheat-haired woman occupied his every thought. From his hiding spot behind a large cottonwood, Hank cut a glance back to the cabin, then to the small shed. At least the smaller building would offer some wind protection until the visitor left. *If* he left.

He secured the horse behind some scrub brush and picked his way across the frozen clearing to the shed. The door yielded, and he gratefully stepped in. His eyes searched the windowless interior with little luck. He dug a hand into his pocket and brought out a match and struck it.

The weak flickering light displayed shelves full of apothecary jars of varying sizes. The flame sputtered, burned his finger, and went out. With the second match, Hank located a candle on a work table next to a gray marbled mortar and pestle. He crept closer to the strange sight of glittering glass containers filled with grasses, liquids, and other dark substances. A skull leered at him from a low shelf.

His eyes flicked across the handwritten ivory labels: hog's lard, citric acid, Codeina, quinine and tar, calomel, silvol—the sound of a door closing jerked his attention back to the cabin. He blew out the candle and slid into darkness behind a tall cabinet with many small drawers. Voices floated to him, and he recognized the first one. Stilts. Hank clenched his fist when he distinguished the second. *Jeether Moats.*

The shed door creaked open. A dim light lit the space beyond Hank's hidden corner.

"I'll have you feeling dandy in no time," Stilts said as the pair trundled in.

"I'd rather feel nothing."

Stilts laughed. "That can be arranged too, my friend."

Shuffling ensued and Hank concentrated on breathing lightly, remaining completely still.

"Ah, here we go. Just the thing." A cork popped and paper rattled. I assure you that this little number will get your desired results."

A grunt answered him. "What about Sutter?"

A silence stretched, and Hank's body stiffened.

"He's useful for now. But his elimination is imminent."

"Understood."

The door opened once more and the two exited, their voices droning on in disappearing mumbles.

Hank took a deep breath, his ears strained for the creak of leather. Hard to distinguish with the breeze. Shame scalded his insides. There would be no further discussion of the mission. He'd been a fool to trust Stilts.

A good thirty minutes passed before Hank stepped from the shed. With great care, he picked his way back to his horse, the cold all but forgotten. He fumbled to pull his numb body into the saddle. It still stung to think Hank had gone undercover for a traitor—a lying, murderous traitor. He exhaled a deep puff of frozen air. He'd have to hurry to beat the second man back to Maggie's cabin. It was imperative that he arrive first.

Moats and Stilts were in cahoots. The moment Hank had heard Jeether Moats's voice, he'd known he'd been played.

One thing put him on his horse at a dead run. If they were so willing to dispose of him when his usefulness reached its end, Maggie's life would mean nothing to them.

Maggie lugged the huge bag of wool to the boiling kettle. Silly to be starting this task near dusk, but if she couldn't find gold, she'd just as well get on with the chores. Corbin needed a new wool coat to take him through the winter. She shivered. Why focus on the possibility that she might not ever see him again? Her chilled fingers pulled the grungy wool shreds from the muslin bag and tossed them into the hot water, bubbling with shaved soap.

With the big, wooden paddle, she pressed the thick material under the water to soak while her eyes scanned the yard. Not one of Moats's men had showed themselves today, not even Hank. She ran her tongue over her rough, chapped lips. Her heart squeezed with the jumble of emotions thundering in her heart. How was it possible for her to love Hank and hate him all at the same time?

It made her utter a low groan to admit she craved his presence. Despite the fact he was nothing more than an outlaw, she had a small snippet of peace when he was about. In her internal turmoil, some of the water sloshed out of the huge kettle, and the fire hissed in protest.

With a sigh she left the water to boil and returned to the shed to retrieve the carding paddles. She grabbed another empty flour sack, shoved the two brushes inside, and then gave a gasp. On the small milking stool in the recesses of the shed sat the dandy, dressed in black, nearly concealed by the dimness of the interior.

"Ah, Madame. Pleasant day for scalding wool."

A tremor quaked through her body, but she pressed her lips together and narrowed her eyes. Her pupils grew accustomed to the shadows, and she saw he once again wore a sleek suit, his legs

encased in knickers, pointed shoes and white socks. His cane rested across his lap and a crooked smile creased his waxy face.

"Cat got your tongue, young lass?"

Maggie filled her lungs with air, bursting to go at him and topple him from his perch. Instead, she snipped, "No. Merely wondering why a man of such substance continues to slink about my farm like a common criminal."

A soft chuckle lit the air. "My dear woman. A common criminal, I am not. Am I to presume that since you are about such menial tasks, that the trove of gold is still as yet unaccounted for?"

Her nostrils flared. Despite the fear that still had her limbs shaking, anger rose up at the boldness of the unwelcome scoundrel. "You seem to know more than I. Why do you waste my time asking for an answer that you already know?"

The man stood. He wasn't an overly large man, quite compact but still taller than she. He pressed his cane to the dirt floor then lifted it perpendicular as he took each step.

"Now, now. Let's not appear ungrateful for what I've done for you."

"What you've done for me is steal my mother's picture."

In the dim light, the smile that cut across the man's face sent a sliver of fear through her. "I beg to differ, gentle lady. I paid quite dearly for such a treasure. Now, with the boy gone, perhaps you feel a little safer, hmmm?"

Maggie tilted her head up. She'd feel much safer if she knew beyond a shadow of a doubt that Hank was perched on the porch.

But he wasn't. He'd said to call. Well, her cry for help would go unheeded.

The dandy stepped closer, raised his hand, and ran his finger under her chin. She jerked away. The mongrel. How dare he lay his filthy hand on her?

Another soft rumble of laughter escaped Dr. Stills, but she refused to step back. "Quite feisty. I think it will work within your captor's plans to have the boy far from this place. Less complications when his mother begins to scream."

Thankfully, her anger fed her audacity. Fear be cursed. She crossed her arms and stood tall. "I'm sure you're very concerned for my well-being."

His black eyes picked up the light from outside as his face loomed closer to hers. The pungent odor of Macassar oil surrounded her. "More than you know. But let us get to our dealings. Gold."

Maggie tamped down the desire to slap his smug face. "What is it you desire now? A lock of my hair?"

He tapped his cane against the pitchfork leaning against the wall. "You are closer than you think. No, no. I want the ring."

She rubbed her hands down her arms at the sudden chill. "What...ring?"

His greasy mustache lifted on one side of his mouth. "The cameo."

She gasped.

"And being as I will be leaving you a large chunk of change, I'll take the watch fob as well."

Maggie swallowed. "How? How do you know about these things? Those were my mother's personal items. No one knows about them. No one but—"

"You and her." He stroked a thumb down the underside of his lapel. "And...I."

She clenched her hands behind her back to hide the trembling. "I can't—"

"You can and you will." His voice whipped harsh and the cane smacked against the pitchfork handle, sending it tumbling across the space. "Do we understand one another?"

Maggie turned and shut her eyes for a moment. What choice was there? If only Hank were here—

"I won't ask again." His voice barked in a low growl.

She spun. "Or what? You've gone through my possessions. What more can you do?"

He glared at her. Then he lifted his foot and struck a match to the sole of his shoe. The flame flared as he held it to his face. His pale, oily skin shone, his eyes mirroring the flame.

"Don't tempt me, fair damsel. There are a sundry of things I could do to terrify and discomfort you. Many things, indeed. My mind whirls now of the possibilities."

He pressed the matchstick to his pale, cheesy cheek, and in a hiss, the light went out. Maggie took a quivering breath and stumbled back.

"Bring them. *Now*."

In a flurry of skirts, Maggie fled to the cabin.

Hank pressed himself against the dirt bank as the shadows left Maggie's shed near the cabin. If only he'd returned from checking in on his blacksmith informer an hour earlier, he could have clearly identified the figure with Maggie.

Couldn't be Moats. The figure was too small. Maggie's figure disappeared behind the cabin's silloette. As much as he wanted to join her, he forced himself to follow the unidentified hurrying form instead. He counted to five, sure by that point Maggie had slammed the bar into place. At least he had that much to be thankful for. She was locked in.

The crisp leaves impeded his attempt to follow too closely. But it was a familiar trail that Hank had trod many times. He gave a sigh as the man moved onto the ferry and heard the muffle of conversation. The stranger merged into the mass of people, and Hank squinted in the darkness to separate the shapes, but to no avail.

His eyes traced the odd pattern of clustered riders across the swirling, dark waters. He snorted. Quite a marshal he'd make. Not only had he joined forces with a madman disguising himself as a federal law officer, he couldn't even tail a possible perpetrator.

Since he was not yet shed of his mythical law duties, perhaps it would've been better to tackle the stranger and demand some answers. It stuck in his craw that this stranger emerged from Maggie's cabin. Was he a friend? A co-conspirator? Or an...admirer?

He stretched his neck, first one side and then the other. Maggie would probably never be his, yet seeing her with someone else weighted his shoulders with regret. With a grunt he walked up the

slope to set up vigil on the cabin's porch. Nothing else could be done but be here and doze away his nightly guard duty.

In the cabin the next morning, Hank had to check his jaw drop. Maggie tossed two bags to the floorboards at Moats's feet. When he gestured for one of the lackeys to investigate, streams of gold twenty-dollar pieces clattered from the bag, sprawling across the rough, grooved floor.

Heartrending curiosity burned in Hank's gut where regret had set up house. He studied her, standing defiant before Moats. Her threadbare navy dress highlighted her pale face. Maggie's dropped gaze tugged at him so, he had to look away. The gang's leader pivoted, spewing threats anew, and Hank gratefully stepped outside the cabin door with relief. The coins jingled as Leonard and young Mort Worthy gleefully gathered the booty.

"Watch her, you hear me, Sutter? She's getting that gold from somewhere. And I want it all." Moats turned on his heel and huffed off toward their camp.

As soon as Leonard and Worthy had scrambled from the cabin, the door slammed shut. The successive scraping noises sent sorrow through his heart. She was so terrified, it took several tries to set the bar.

Hank settled on the thin bench next to the front door of the cabin. Did the late night visitor have something to do with the gold? He could tell Maggie's resistance wore thin, and her vulnerability unnerved him. Protectiveness thundered to the forefront.

A U.S. Marshal couldn't allow personal feelings to interfere with the case, yet all he wanted to do was barge through her door,

demand answers, and then bust Moats in the face. U.S. Marshal, be durned. He'd been duped anyway. Now all he cared about was Maggie's safety. He clenched his hands. Knowing Moats conspired with Stilts, made the whole gold coins appearance suspect. Why, it could have even been Stilts who'd snuck from Maggie's cabin. So what was really going on?

Hank rubbed his whiskered face. So what was his next move? Maggie was in a perilous position. *He* was in a perilous position. And what of the boy? Who knew where he was but Maggie. Helplessness, an unwanted companion, swirled in his bowels.

Maggie perched on the edge of the bed while tears squeezed between her eyelids. She missed Corbin. She absolutely ached to have him in her arms. Moats would never be satisfied, and this stranger scared her more than she cared to confess. Her eyes went to the wooden box on the bottom shelf of the bookcase. That monster had demanded her mother's cameo ring that contained a tiny lock of mother's hair and the newly-found watch fob. How many times had she held the ring and reminisced of her mother?

Hank's face filled her thoughts. She'd clutched that very box the day their lips had met. The day she'd tasted his mouth on hers. Maggie stood and paced. There in the dimness of the springhouse she had her first kiss. *Think. Stop remembering his lips on yours.*

Her pace slowed. Why had Mother wanted the box thrown in the river? The inscription on the cameo band burned in her brain. Forever yours, R.S. She'd always assumed the initials were her

father's, Reuben Saddler. Yet, why would her mother destroy such a treasure?

She strode forward and reached for the rough wooden box on the bottom shelf. Her mother's diary lay inside, locked and wrapped in silk and sewn closed. Maggie hadn't been able to open it since her mother's death. Breaking the latch distressed her, but as she reminisced over the dark lock of hair contained within the face of the cameo ring, Maggie knew it was time to expose her mother's most personal thoughts.

Her hands fumbled with the coarse outer crate, and then she carefully pulled out the sleek rosewood box with the mother of pearl inlays in floral patterns about the lid. With a shaky breath, she glanced toward the window before stepping to the darker area near the bed, grabbing the lantern as she went. She pulled the keys that hung about her neck and gripped the smallest to insert it into the keyhole.

She peered at the silk-encased journal resting within the red velvet. Such expensive items and so out of order with the rest of Mother's things. Carefully, under the light of the lantern, Maggie slit the stitches to reveal a simple red-leather volume, sealed with a tiny brass lock. She wet her lips. None of the keys in her possession fit the small opening.

With trembling hands, she wedged a knife point into the keyhole.

Chapter Eight

Maggie's eyes ran over the flowing script. Emotion choked her throat at the familiarity of the slanted writing. The date indicated her mother neared her sixteenth birthday.

Mother feels Rupert is the perfect fit for me. He is always so finely dressed and his manners are impeccable. It would be lovely to ride under the leather top of his park Phaeton and lean back in the leather seat. He's the most exotic man I've ever known.

Rupert? Her father's name was Reuben. Maggie searched the rest of the page and flipped to the next.

Tonight Rupert held my hand. He promised to ask Father's permission to court me, and Victoria is so jealous. He's is the best catch in Nebraska. I can't help but dream of the house we'll live in. Rupert says perhaps we'll have a servant. I feel like a princess!

Flipping through several pages of her mother's teenaged gushing, Maggie's soul ever grew more and more dismayed. In all the heart-to-heart talks she and her mother had, never had this romance been mentioned. But she recalled Mother's face that day in the attic when she'd discovered this box.

"Take this down to the river and pitch it in. Nothing but molded flour sacks. Pity. They had value at one time." Her mother's hands shook as she pressed it into Maggie's hands. Promise me you'll dispose of it. Quickly."

Maggie remembered nodding and hurrying to the door. But at fourteen, her curiosity raised at her mother's reaction, Maggie took a shortcut to the river near the spring house. There she'd found her mother's youthful daguerreotype framed in cherry, the cameo ring, the watch fob, and the journal. Hank had appeared at the spring house door.

Maggie sighed. She shared her find with him and then she and Hank had hidden the box. And then…that kiss. She pulled her thoughts to the journal at hand.

Father agreed. Rupert will court me. We shall take a buggy ride after church today, just the two of us. Oh, such romantic notions run through my mind, my heart trembles. He, almost ten years older, seems so worldly and wise. Why, he knows nearly all the names of the local plants and their healing properties. I do hope he finds me interesting, for I can barely hold a thought in my head. In just a few hours' time, I shall be alone with him.

Maggie pressed the journal to the rough table top. She stood and paced, stopping only to dip a drink from the bucket. Her mother had

lied to her about the contents of the box. Now, what else had she hidden from her? Maggie wrung her hands together and stared at the book. Fear pierced her heart. How could Mother have kept such things from her?

Goosebumps broke across her arms as she seated herself at the table and took up the journal again. There was only one way to find out.

Hank drew a deep breath and opened his eyes. He sat up and pulled away from the cabin wall. The wool blanket did little to block the freezing temperature on the open porch. He grunted and scanned the frosted yard and woods. What woke him? Merely the cold?

A shuffle inside the cabin caught his attention, and he leaned his head toward the door. Muffled sounds brought him to his feet.

"Maggie?" His hoarse voice barely made a sound.

More scuffles followed. Hank grabbed the leather handle, but the door wouldn't budge. He tossed the blanket to the bench and sprinted around the cabin to the back door. There the handle yielded,. and he stepped inside. In the shadows, two forms wrestled on the bed. Maggie let out a stifled squeal.

Hank pulled the Peacemaker from his belt, strode to the bed, and pressed the barrel against the temple of the assailant. A sickening click froze the gyrations on the quilt.

"Stand up." Hank demanded.

The figure obeyed with his hands up.

"Light the lamp, Maggie."

She gave a strangled cry and lurched from the bed to the table behind him. When the room lightened, Olin Leonard, lone suspender hanging loose, stood before him. The man grinned when he saw Hank.

"Share and share alike, Sutter. I'll go first, then you. No sense in Moats hogging the goods."

The smile melted from his face when Hank straightened his gun arm for dead-on aim. "You touch her again, and I'll share this bullet with you. Now get out."

Leonard flipped his limp suspender to his shoulder and headed for the door, eyeing Hank. As he slid through the door, he said, "You better watch your back, Sutter."

"I already am," Hank's reply fell on the closed door.

Maggie's body hit his back full force, her arms encircling him in a vice. Her body quaked all over. "Thank you, Hank. Oh thank you, thank you..."

He eased her arms from him and turned to embrace her as she continued to mumble her gratefulness. The scent of her hair rose up to meet him, and he squeezed her closer, laying his face against the top of her head.

"He...he just barged in and started talking. Said he wanted to help me find the gold. And then, he grabbed me and pulled me to the bed. I couldn't stop him, Hank. I couldn't."

"Shhh. You're safe now."

"He was just...too strong." A sob escaped her, and he massaged her back.

A tiny seed of fear spiraled within him. What if he hadn't awakened? Would he be here to stop it the next time? He clenched his teeth. Oh, God help him, he'd be here if he had to sleep on her doorstep every night. A prayer left him as Maggie quieted in his arms.

She loosened her grip enough to wipe her eyes. Hank brought the handkerchief from his pocket, and she clenched it gratefully.

His eyes strayed to the back door. "Why didn't you bar the door?"

When she caught her breath, his eyes narrowed. His voice dropped a notch, searching her tear-splotched face. "Maggie?"

Her eyes captured his, and he cocked his head in awareness. Even with a blotchy face and hair askew, her helpless expression tugged at his heart. He took a deep breath and clenched his hands. His lack of resistance to her charisma roughened his voice. "The door?"

She licked her lips, drawing his gaze, and he jerked his chin to the left before fastening his gaze on hers.

"I…" Her gaze fell. He cupped her chin and then gently lifted it.

Her parted lips and eyes shimmering with tears nearly undid him. "Spill it."

"Sometimes I have late-night visitors."

His heart dropped to his toes. Memories of his mother entertaining late-night male guests while shoving him from the cabin washed over him. Bitterness and hate scraped at his heart. He grabbed her shoulders and gave her a shake. "What are you saying?"

"Hank," she wailed, "stop it."

His hands gentled, but his rage escalated. She stepped back, fear lighting her eyes. His gaze bore into hers. "Who comes, Maggie?"

She blinked, as if seeing him for the first time. "White Moon."

He turned and paced, running his hand through his hair. For once she stayed silent, and if he hadn't been so worked up, he would've pondered her reaction. Instead, he stopped in front of her and pressed his forehead against hers.

"Tell me you don't have male visitors coming at all times of the night." His voice was but a groan.

Maggie's hands came up to warm his tight cheeks. "Not like that, Hank. Not like your—"

Hank closed his eyes. *His mother.* That's what she meant. Relief poured through him like a waterfall.

"White Moon is an Indian child. A friend of Corbin's. But…there is a man." She gasped when he tightened his hold.

"Go on." His grip softened into a caress. Her touch on his face stirred him.

"He shows up, here in the cabin. And he trades things for bags of gold."

He stilled his hands stroking Maggie's shoulders. "What do you give him for the gold?"

Her eyes were pools of shimmering water. "Mother's picture. Then her cameo ring and her watch fob. He's an older man. Always in a suit, a bit of a dandy, with oiled hair and a cane."

Hank's hands dropped. "Rupert Stilts?"

She turned toward the fireplace and hugged her arms about her body. "He said his name is Dr. Stills. But, I'm not sure he's telling me the truth."

Maggie stared into the embers for a few moments and rubbed her arms. Hank fetched a couple of logs and affixed them into the andirons. With the poker he prodded the ashes to let the coals bloom hot and red around the fresh wood.

"I don't know who to trust anymore, Hank. This horrible man— that dandy. Why does he want my mother's things? And why are you with bank robbers? Is Corbin safe? I think of Corbin all the time. And if that is not enough, I'm in constant fear that Jeether will burst through the door and demand payment for the missing gold." She pressed a fist to her mouth.

He stood. "You can trust me, Maggie."

"I want to, but I've discovered I couldn't even trust my own mother." She picked up the journal and slapped it to the tabletop. "She had some fling with a man before my father, and she doesn't even explain who. Or why."

Hank pulled her into his arms once more. "I'll be here for you this time, Maggie. I will."

"You feel cold." She ran her hands up to his neck and tilted her chin up.

Hank studied her face for several minutes. Her body trembled.

She gave a small laugh then sobered. "I must look a mess."

"Uh-huh," he murmured, "a beautiful mess."

Her hand touched his cheek, her face growing softer in the dim, flickering light. "Stay here tonight, Hank."

He nodded. "You bar the door and I'll be right outside."

The mussed wheat colored curls shook. "No. Stay...*in* here."

Something mighty moved within him, and he straightened. "I can't do that, Maggie."

Her lashes fell to her cheeks. "Please, Hank."

He pressed his lips to her forehead and squinted back his desire. "I'll be on the porch."

Her hands pulled his head closer. "You could protect me. If Moats thinks I'm your woman, he—"

"He'd kill me." The temptation made him groan the answer, and he leaned away from her.

"No. Don't let go yet." She stepped closer and nuzzled his neck, giving a sigh.

Thoughts of coming home to her, raising a family and crops clapped him into a frozen statue, pondering the fanciful paradise. He'd give it all up for a chance of such a life. His arms tightened around her, and he nosed her hair to inhale her scent.

Her fingers splayed into the hair at the nape of his neck, and he pulled his head up to peruse her face beneath heavy lids.

"Please, Hank."

He'd lost track of what she pleaded for, and instead of mulling it, he lowered his head to join his pulsing mouth to hers. She melted into him, and Hank dug his hand into her heavy hair. Desire scintillated between them as his mouth searched her parted lips. She murmured his name when he trailed kisses to her ear. His lips teased her earlobe and she gasped.

He groaned and returned to her mouth with renewed urgency. She matched his passion with each kiss until he emitted a growl, forcing his lips to separate from hers. But his rebel hand caressed the small of her back as he fought to control the building voracity inside him.

Her voice came in a breathless whisper. "Hank?"

"Be still, Maggie."

"But—"

"Woman, you're one step from needing protection from me."

She tilted her chin up. "I don't want to be protected from you."

He fixed his eyes on the far corner of the cabin and jerked his head to push away the aching hunger. With reluctance, he settled his hands on her shoulders and set her from him. He firmed his jaw when his gaze met her pleading one.

"If I ever get a chance to—" he cleared his throat and searched her face, "if I do, it won't be in a flash of emotion. You'll be my wife, Maggie. Mine. To protect and cherish. I promised myself I'd never take advantage of a woman. Never take that gift from her unless I was joined to her before God and man. Never."

Maggie surveyed the intense face before her. So strong, so passionate. He could coax her into a heated rush of ecstasy by his mere nearness. She drew in a long breath. How could he do that? Her reaction frightened her a bit. All reason became an unwanted notion.

Even now, she only wanted, no yearned, to be back in his arms, for his lips to be exploring hers, her neck, her shoulders. Closing her eyes, she imagined unbuttoning the bodice of her shirtwaist and

watching the desire jump in his dark eyes. That unobtrusive silent man so lost in undeniable desire for her. She shivered at the power of their ardor, and longed to give herself to him, to discover the full reward of his passion and to experience his love.

Never had she known such an overwhelming onslaught of emotion, such a depth of adoration. She blinked when he murmured her name and fought to keep the torrid fervor burning within from showing in her eyes. She examined his buttons in front of her and ran her fingers down the front of his leather coat.

He caught her hands and brought them to his mouth to kiss each one. Passion flared once more in his pupils, and Maggie knew if she only pushed, they'd soon be tangled up in each other atop her bed. No, she wouldn't do that to him. As much as she craved the comfort of his body, she'd seen the torture in his eyes when she'd mentioned her nighttime visitors. His mother's profession still haunted him, and to push her need upon him would only cause him more remorse.

She exhaled, stepped back, and then spun to pull a quilt from the chest. "I'll make a pallet for you by the fireplace."

"Maggie—"

She clicked the lid closed and shook her head at him. "Hush, Hank, and bar the door."

Chapter Nine

In the low morning light of the fire, Maggie rolled over, her eyes going first to the pallet on the floor. But it was gone. Instead the blankets were folded nicely on the trunk. Her gaze snagged on a big form huddled on the fireplace hearth. Her heart skipped a beat until she realized who it was. Hank.

He leaned toward the coals, a rough-cut paper in his hands. Then he raised a stub of a pencil to add a scrawl. She pushed up on one arm and drew his attention.

"Good morning." She wouldn't dare spill how lovely it was to awaken with him in her cabin. For a moment, she let herself daydream, let herself believe they were man and wife. She imagined, just for a moment, that the marauding gang didn't hover just outside, ready to compromise and kill. A sigh escaped her throat.

Hank would rise, saunter to the bed, his eyes full of love and passion, and wrap her in his embrace, pressing her back onto the mattress, his hands would—

"It's not morning yet. Go back to sleep."

So much for that dream. Maggie swung her legs to the floor, careful to keep herself encased inside her day dress, which she had slept in. But it didn't matter. Hank's full attention centered on the paper he held. "What are you doing?"

"Writing."

She rolled her eyes. Perhaps her dream of dwelling with Hank had its flaws. She bounced to the floor. "I know that."

"Shhh."

Had he just shushed her? Clenching her teeth, she rubbed the sleep from her eyes and strutted to the fireplace. She stopped in front of him and parked her hands on her hips. "Hank Sutter, sometimes I just want to—"

"Maggie, hush." He reached up to tug her to the hearth next to him. "I don't have much time. Moats's men could already be lurking about."

She studied him in the firelight. Strong masculine face, slightly clefted chin. He needed a haircut, with the curls whipping out around his ears. But he was adorably mussed. The flared anger of moments before dissolved. She scooched closer. An early morning kiss would be enchanting.

"You're blocking my light."

Hank wedged away from her, peering at that silly paper. She reached up and swiped it from him.

"Wait—"

"What is so all fired-up important that you have to huddle here in silence?" Her eyes ran over the missive. Then her brows puckered. "Who's BB?"

Hank captured her wrist and clamped onto the note, but she refused to let go. "Tell me, Hank."

He let out a stream of air, let go of her hand, and stood. Then he paced to the bed and back. "Blacky Balch."

"Who?" Then it dawned on her. "That lewd blacksmith next to the fort?"

Hank nodded.

She returned her eyes to the note. "What information are you waiting for?"

"I don't suppose, none of your business would suffice?"

Maggie bounded to a standing position, her voice hardening over. "You got that right, buster."

He slung his head with an impatient sigh. "Can't we just let this go for now?"

She hiked to him and plastered the note against his chest. The firmness she found there put a bit more sarcasm in her reply. "Sure. Why not? You claim you care for me, yet you're covered in secrets and—criminalness," she struggled for a word, so angry at his caginess.

She threw her fists to her side with a growl. Truly this man had deranged her brain. "You know what I mean!"

"Whoa."

He suddenly was much closer, and his arms came around her. His lips dipped to her ear.

"Don't you know how much danger I'm in being in this cabin right now? And I don't dare leave you, even for a moment."

His whispered breath alone softened her angry reserve, and she felt herself melt toward his sturdy body.

"Listen, Maggie. The plans I've made have come unglued. So I've fallen back to searching."

"Searching? For what?" Surely whatever he sought didn't reside at Bellmira's bawdy house.

"My father."

She caught her breath and pulled back. "But I thought you didn't know. That your mother—"

"Don't say it, Maggie. I know he could be one of so many. But I...need to know."

For a moment, she let him hold her, her own hands snaking behind his head. But her gaze stayed on the far wall. "Why Hank? What's the point?"

He thrust her from him and glared at her. "I thought if anyone would understand, it'd be you."

Her mouth dropped. In his eyes she saw a little boy, desperate for connection...desperate for worthiness. After everything they'd gone through, he still groped for his own dignity. She reached up and stroked his whiskered face. "Oh, Hank. Don't you know that doesn't matter?"

His eyes burned into hers. "It matters to me."

Hank pressed the note into her hand. "You said you had an Indian child who visits. I need to get this message to Balch."

She nodded and took the wadded scrap. "If she comes, I'll pass it on."

He tipped his head and then grabbed his hat from the table. Her heart squeezed when he stepped to the back door. "Bar this when I leave. Understand?"

Maggie rushed forward and gripped his shirt. "Don't leave. Please. Stay."

He shook his head. "You know the danger in that. Besides," he detached her fingers from his clothing, "I'm nothing until I know."

And he slipped through the door.

Nothing. Nothing until I know. Those words hammered over and over through Maggie's skull as she fiddled with the wool in her hands. Finally getting a good twist started once more on the wool, she pumped the foot pedal and the spinning wheel spun with a comforting hum. She'd always known Hank's yearning to know the man that had spawned him, but given his mother had been visited by numerous men, she'd always thought he'd dropped the idea.

After all, could there be any good in knowing? A man who frequented a soiled dove for companionship didn't strike her as a person she'd like to be associated with. And why? Why did it seem so important to him? Was he seeking a heritage? A kinship? Or revenge?

Maggie snarled when she let the wool get too thin and broke. Her foot stilled the contraption. She was in no mood to deliver any

quality of thread. In a huff, she rose and paced the small room, binding her front with tightly crossed arms.

Think from a man's standpoint. A father would be…important, true. She thought of her own father, a man of integrity and hard work. He'd bounced her on his knee, showed her how to milk a cow, and how to wrestle a sheep. With a short laugh she stopped in the middle of the room. He'd roared with his head tilted back when she'd managed to catch that slippery lamb. She smiled now just thinking of it.

Yet, Hank was without childhood memories. At least, any good ones. No gentle hands took him and taught him the way of the world or stood beside him as he accomplished childish aspirations. He had only his mother, a woman of the night, and a boatload of rowdy gents parading through his life with no care whether he lived or died.

Indeed, it would've been quite a trial. Still, she couldn't for the life of her understand why he'd crave a connection with an immoral man. Her gaze slipped around the room and settled on the carved horse. *Corbin.* She paced to the nightstand and plucked up the figurine. Her son had an immoral man for a father. What long-term effects would manifest in Corbin? The questions caused her to shiver.

The hoot of an owl caused her to pause. Could it be? Maggie rushed to the door and waited. The short shadow that crossed her window had Maggie yanking the bar off the door. In glided a slip of a girl, black hair braided and shining in the lantern light.

"White Moon." Maggie reached for her, but the child flattened herself against the door.

"Light out."

With a nod, Maggie lifted the hurricane glass and blew out the flame. Then the small body lurched against hers. Maggie wrapped her in her arms, dismayed at the chill of the child's skin.

"You're cold."

White Moon shrugged.

"Where's Corbin? Is he here?"

The girl shook her head in the shadowed room and hope plummeted in Maggie's heart.

"No. He safe. With uncle. But food low."

It pained her to think of the people, including Corbin, doing without the basics of life. "What of the government help?"

"White-face Gore say big Washington men say no."

Maggie gnawed her lip. Hank's and Corbin's fathers weren't the only immoral men that walked the earth. She feared the Indian Agent Jarvis Gore, not known as the most humane of men, might be lining his pockets with Indian annuities.

"Now, we farm. But Father...hunt."

Maggie jumped up and found a canvas bag on the shelf. "I can't do much, but I can help."

She grabbed the finished wool balls from the basket on the table and shoved them into the bag. Maggie scurried to her meager pantry and threw in the rest of the stores she had of salt and flour. At last she scraped the few coins from the chipped porcelain bowl hidden behind Corbin's books.

"I'm afraid it's all I can manage. But maybe it will be of some help." She pressed the bag into the girl's hands. "Oh, wait."

Maggie grabbed the jagged scrap of paper tied with a jute string. Then she knelt before the girl. "Listen, White Moon. I need a favor. My friend Hank needs this message delivered to a man named Blacky Balch. He's a blacksmith in Fortstown. Do you know him?"

At White Moon's nod, she continued. "And if there is a return message, please let me know. Can you do that?

"Father knows."

She patted the girl's shoulder and rose. "Please...tell Corbin I love him and that we'll be together soon."

"I bring him."

"What?"

"White-man Christmas come. I bring. Gift for you."

Maggie's breath came to a screeching halt and her hand crept to her throat. Christmas. How could she have forgotten that such a holiday approached? She dipped on one knee and ran an affectionate hand down White Moon's shiny braids. "Truly? It won't be too dangerous?"

"Omaha walk on feather feet. We come."

Sobs worked their way up Maggie's throat. She knew she should halt the treacherous plan, but she couldn't deny herself a few hours with her son. Instead, she clutched White Moon in a tight hug. The child patted her back.

"No sadness."

Pulling back, Maggie scrubbed the tears from her face and handed the folded paper to the child. Perhaps it was unwise to trust such a young girl with so much, but she knew the child possessed a

wisdom beyond her years. White Moon stepped back toward the door.

"You watch. We come."

Maggie wadded the yoke of the apron in her hand. "Please…be careful."

The sweet girl gave a small smile. "God guards feather feet."

Thick regret shivered over Maggie when the child slithered through the door. Just having the girl's presence had eased her sorrow. She pressed the bar in place and glanced back at the calendar hanging from the far wall. Today was the eighteenth. She had one week to worry and stew. But with a little luck, she would be embracing her son once again.

The slam of the cabin door lifted Hank's head. Keeping his eyes on Leonard and Gibbons circulating through the yard, he'd started the guise of hunting for a good branch for carving. Now the two had disappeared, and he stood some thirty feet from the cabin with a good stern aspen limb in his hand. Yet the sight of Maggie, covered in a cape and thick gloves on her hands, made him toss the treasured find. Now, what was up? Hank strode up the slope.

"I need supplies."

She wasted no time on hi-how-are-ya's. "Already?"

Hank pivoted his head toward the campfire lurking at the bottom of the hill and then turned back to her. Her chin lifted. That was not a good sign.

"Yes."

Blast. "Come on."

She followed him to the base of the hill. The campfire burned low, and Worthy flipped several eggs in the hanging cast iron pot. The matted hair around the kid's face didn't keep him from leering at Maggie. Great, Moats wasn't even up and around yet which was another bad sign.

With the expertise of a man used to fending for himself, Worthy flicked the three eggs into a tin pan. The yokes broke, bleeding yellow across the pan as steam rose. The smell of breakfast cramped Hank's gut.

"Just in time, Ma'am." The kid grinned, much like a fox at a rabbit hole, and held out the pan.

A small gasp slipped from Maggie, and she stepped behind Hank. If the kid was hankering for his fist for breakfast, he was heading the right direction. "She's not here for breakfast. Where's Moats?"

"Son of a—"

"Enough!" Hank held out his arm to shield Maggie huddled at his back, as if that could censor her ears.

"Biscuit-eater." Worthy grinned, but only hardness shone from his cold eyes. "I would toss you some eggs, Sutter. But I ain't wastin' my breakfast."

The kid chortled a high-pitched laugh. "You get tired of him, lady, look me up."

Maggie groaned against his back. Hank kept his eyes on the ill-dressed youth clothed in pants held up with a leather strip and a torn wool coat around his shoulders. Finally, the kid disappeared through the dried undergrowth. Hank let his muscles relax. Dang the kid's

hide. But Hank knew he had no worries from him. He could take the boy on a bad day with one arm tied to his boot.

Yet, if Leonard, Gibbons, and the boy consolidated their efforts—why that might have very different results. His eyes flicked to Maggie, and for the hundredth time, Hank prayed he could be there to keep her safe.

Even if it meant his own death.

Chapter Ten

Moats birthed his way through one of the dirty canvas tents held up with only a jute rope between two slender trees. The fur-faced man stretched a moment, clad in only wool britches and a long-underwear shirt. His suspenders hung at his sides. The gang leader cursed when he saw them.

"Don't want to hear nothing until I get some whisky. Leonard? Gibbons! Awww—" Another swear word let loose. "Sutter, find my bottle. Now."

The man slipped back into the tent. Hank spun to Maggie. But she had that determined look in her eye.

"You think I haven't heard those words before? Find his nasty liquor."

She stepped forward and grabbed the first saddle bag and riffled through it. Hank headed for the pack near the front of the tent. Pulling forth the flask did not inspire him. It was nearly empty. He held it up to cease Maggie's prodding through the packs scattered across the dried leaves. She crossed her arms in front of her and glared at him.

"Stay right there." Hank slipped inside the tent and handed the flask to Moats who had stretched back out on the buffalo hide. He tipped it back and then threw it out the door with a string of curses.

"Get me more hooch."

Well, that was permission if Hank had ever heard it. Hank ducked back out and motioned for Maggie to follow. In a whipstitch, he had the two horses saddled with Maggie aboard the mare. Before Moats could come to his senses, he mounted and kicked his horse into a quick trot, with the mare tethered behind.

"Remember when you used to come to our house on Christmas day? Ummm…the smells of roast turkey and cranberries? The pine of the tree." Maggie gave a heavy sigh. "I remember the feel of the tree's needles when we hung strings of popcorn, and the few precious wooden ornaments we had. Then on Christmas night, we'd light the candles waxed to the branches. It was so beautiful. Mama would always put out the gifts the night before, wrapped in scraps of wool and calico."

Maggie gave a heavy sigh before continuing, "It was never the same once Papa died."

They rode for several moments in silence through the desolate landscape, breath coming in puffs of fog.

"Hank, what's your best Christmas ever?"

His heart squeezed, noting her chipper voice had grown melancholy. Best Christmas? Had to be the ones he'd spent with her and her family, for the holiday had passed without much fanfare for the last ten or so years. "I reckon the one your Pa gave me that knife."

"Oh, yes. I remember. Weren't you about twelve?"

"Thirteen." He still owned it, used it. The tool had a bone handle with a folding blade. Hank still kept it bound in his right boot. Handy little thing.

"Do you remember what I gave you?"

He inclined his head. "Gloves."

A pleasant trickle of laughter lifted from her lips. "Weren't they horrible? My first attempt at handling wool from start to finish. All I remember is how the stitches were so uneven and bumpy. I'm sure you pitched them the first chance you got."

"I didn't pitch them." The woman might be lost for words if she knew he still carried them in his saddlebags. He'd worn them for a couple of years through the heavy cold snows. But once a hole had worn through one of the fingers, he stowed them amongst his dearest treasures.

"Anyway, I'd slaved over them for over a month to get them ready. At least you know I'd put forth my best effort at the time."

Hank maneuvered around a huge red oak, the horses' hooves crunching on the frost-covered leaves and debris. The numerous tree trunks blocked the view of the Missouri River which had only recently retreated to its normal banks. He turned north and headed

for Fortstown. They'd gone quite a way when Maggie spoke up again.

"Do you suppose we could visit the river before we ride back?"

With a shrug he replied, "I don't see why not."

At the trading post, Maggie made quick work of gathering basic supplies while Hank kept a vigil near the door. Mostly he kept his eyes on three half-breeds scooted up with their rears pressed near the pot-bellied stove dominating the center of the cramped room. When their glance fell on him, he reached down to adjust his side arm.

"Get outa here, ya durn oafs!"

The same rough character who'd manned the counter before, dressed in the same unwashed buckskins, shooed the stove squatters from the store with a wave of his rifle then grinned at Hank.

"Soakin' up my heat and don't spend a dime." He shook his head, the raccoon tail of his hat flung across his long beard. "Good fer nothings."

Maggie tried to ignore both the gun-slinging owner and the other tenants that hightailed out the door. All she could think of was Corbin. He would be home for Christmas. She had to have something special for him. Sure, she'd stitched a new shirt, knit sturdy socks and mittens, but what she really wanted was something to really express how special he was. How could basic clothing make his heart sing? Who knew how long it would be before she would lay eyes on him again? This Christmas had to be special.

Her eyes lit on a shelf littered with recreational notions—a leather bag of jacks, a set of checkers, and a red book, with gold

lettering. *Around the World in Eighty Days*. With joy cascading over her heart, she dared to pluck it from the shelf. Why, Corbin would be overjoyed. A new book would not only spark his interest, but keep him through the cold nights huddled about the Indian campfire in the chilly lodges. Yes, she simply had to have it.

She strode to the counter, her cheeks flushed triumphantly, and added four peppermint sticks to her purchase. And if she lifted her eyes with a bit more spark in them than was necessary, why that only made the filthy post owner scurry about all the quicker. He'd gathered her necessary purchases with a wink which she ignored. He totaled the items and now his eyes sparkled, not with joy, but greed. Now, came the point she had dreaded.

"Yes, well." She lowered her voice, willing Hank to stay at the doorway, just out of earshot. "I came to barter."

The buckskin-clad man ran a tongue over his blackened teeth and his eyes narrowed. "Nope, straight cash here."

Maggie held up a hand. "Please, hear me out. I'm sure you will be quite satisfied with the offer."

She pulled out her reticule and extracted a beaded pouch. With shaking fingers she fumbled inside. Giving up on grabbing the slippery little item, she flipped the bag upside down. A small band of gold bounced across the rough surface of the counter. Then, calling everyone's attention, the ring rattled to a halt.

The trading post proprietor grinned. "Girlie, we might have a deal after all."

The proprietor reached to swipe the band, but another large hand enclosed it first. Maggie lifted her eyes to the big man beside her. How could Hank move so quietly?

"Maggie?" Hank's gaze probed her inner thoughts.

She darted her eyes away. Instead of answering, she held out her hand. "Please, Hank. I need it."

Hank turned to the vendor. "What's the damages?"

Maggie tried to interrupt, but Hank motioned to the glass bottles behind the counter. "Throw in a whiskey and five cigars."

Then, he pitched cash on the counter."

"No, Hank, I—"

But Hank's finger rested across her lips, his eyes burning coals. "We'll discuss it later."

She should've been angry, angry as all get out. Yet a bubble of gratitude settled in her chest. Bartering away her mother's wedding ring would have left an ache in her soul.

Hank wasted no time packing up the items and lifting her to her seat aboard the mare. Then, like last time, he led her to the blacksmith's shop. Thunder, she'd failed to tell him she'd slipped his note to White Moon.

"Uh, Hank…"

He merely grunted a reply. She dug her hands into the mare's dark mane. "I—"

Her voice halted at the lack of activity at the tumbled-down shed. It was closed up tight, iron bar across the front, barricaded with a large padlock. Hank drew to a halt and glanced back to the only

other building in Fortstown, the saloon, such as it was. It was nothing more than a cabin with a lean-to room attached to the side for rent.

Only three buildings existed in Fortstown, set out in a U, the trading post, Balch's blacksmith shop, and the keeping house or saloon. Surely, Hank wouldn't dare step in there and leave her abandoned in the street.

"Hey, you."

Hank hailed two men, trappers from the looks of their fur-lined coats, coming in from the north. "What's up with Balch's?"

They pulled up their mounts. "Heard he'd holed up at Bellmira's. He'll be back in a day or two."

With a wave, Hank thanked the men and mounted up. With the speed at which he wove out of the village, she had little opportunity to speak. She clutched the saddle horn and leaned forward to avoid losing her seat.

"Hank—" His name jostled from her, but he'd cut from the trail to the right, through the trees. She held her peace, for she was sure he was winding them toward the river. He would have to stop eventually.

The huge expanse of water peaked through the trees, and it never failed to take her breath. At long last, he halted the horses. Her face burned from the rush of the cold air. She tugged her cloak about her as Hank sidled up to the mare and pulled her free of the saddle.

He cleared his throat as his gaze grazed her windburned face. "Sorry."

She tugged at his coat when he went to pull away. "Wait."

"Look, Maggie if this is about paying for your supplies, then don't. You can't give up your mother's ring."

He knew. He'd remembered. She blinked and circled her own plain brass ring around her left hand's third finger. She only wore it when she went into town, and not for the sake of being sentimental. Most certainly not. Wearing the despised ring was merely a feeble attempt to keep the wolves at bay.

Hank pulled her cold hands into his and fixed his eyes on the tarnished band. Then he raised his narrowed gaze to hers.

She shrugged, yanking on her gloves. "Not for love, I assure you."

He nodded.

"I sent your message, by the way."

This brought a sharper glare. "When?"

"A few nights ago. It'll reach him. One way or another."

He nodded, gathered the horse's reins, and then ambled to her to aid her descent. His big hands held her captive for a moment.

"Thanks for passing on my letter."

"Mmm-hmm." Funny how it was hard sometimes to speak. Did Hank feel this same hesitancy?

Hank stepped away and a loss shimmered through her. Then she shook her head. She was nothing but a fool. He ground tied the horses and threaded his way through the trees. She followed and soon the enormous expanse of water could be seen through the trunks and underbrush. The low thrum of its constant movement was mesmerizing. The Missouri River.

He paused and took a long sweeping gaze before stepping from the cover of the trees. She inhaled a long breath. Something about being near the water seemed to freshen the dead winter air, though the breeze cut more sharply down the expanse of open water.

"The river."

Hank announced with a voice that displayed a touch of strain, and she couldn't help but assess him. My, he stood tall in the late morning light, eyes ever searching, ever vigilant. Then he turned toward her.

"Why are we here?"

She smiled and tilted her head. "I'm looking for clay."

One of his brows rose, and he struck a casual pose, arms crossed with one hip relaxed. The charming masculinity of his stance made her inhale, and she pressed her gaze back to the soil.

"Clay," she confirmed, probing the soft bank for signs of the gray substance while giving herself some space from the captivating allure of her childhood love. Though if she were honest, completely bare-bones honest, there was nothing childish about the emotions washing over her at this very moment.

Over the next half an hour, they scoured the bank and located a long clump of clay some fifty feet south. She giggled as her boots skidded several inches toward the flowing water. Hank's hands encircled her waist as she bent to work a large glob from the soil. Maggie tugged the gloves off and scooped out a large gray lump, enough to fill both hands.

The clay proved quite resistant in the freezing air and quite bone-chillingly cold. Maggie's teeth chattered as they worked their

way back up the bank, Hank's arm about her waist to keep her from pitching back down toward the dark water.

Hank wouldn't, couldn't lie. She felt good in his hands. Real good. He gave his fingers permission to reposition and shift several times just to relish her womanly shape. The curve of her hip. He stifled the deep hum that wanted to crest his lips. My, to possess her would undo him. The suggestion rose up his throat—to take a little longer while collecting…dirt. Clay, rather. That substance that molded, much like Maggie when he pressed her against— He took a deep breath. If he didn't pause, he might lose it, tug her closer, and never to let go.

But, it was cold. Painfully so. He put his concentration on that and drew his chapped hands away from the scintillating arc of her waist. "Exactly why are you collecting that mess?"

"For Corbin. I'm going to make him a marble set."

"Collecting acorns would have been less dangerous and a lot less cold."

And, he hated to point out, she could have waited until the weather warmed a tad. He doubted that fact would comfort her, given the amount of time it would take for the weather to warm. Being without her son was taking a toll. He allowed himself to press a hand to her back and they ascended the moist bank.

She shook her head as they wove into the tree line toward the horses. "They aren't perfectly round and don't roll correctly. Don't you remember having them as a kid?"

He did and she was right. "Well, how are you going to store that dirty lump?"

If he knew Maggie, and he did, she was liable to cradle it in her hands all the way home.

She stopped short. "Oh, dear. I'm afraid I didn't think that far ahead."

His shoulders slumped. He did have something. But, man was it going to cause a fuss. "It's all right. I've got a way to store it."

He fumbled in his saddlebags and pulled out two wool gloves, poorly knitted. Her mouth fell open, and her eyes raised to his.

Chapter Eleven

"Hank?"

He ran a hand over his jaw, overgrown with whiskers. Exposing those simple gloves might have just bared his heart. "Promise to wash them once they've done their duty."

Hank had to give her credit. She only paused a moment or two searching his face. But he refused to meet her gaze. Instead, he surveyed the forest around them, giving what he hoped was an impression of checking the perimeter for safety.

Then, she glanced at the sopping blob in her hands. Maggie's stiff fingers worked the clay into two sizable balls and slid them into the old gloves. He returned them to the saddlebags.

"You kept them."

He cleared his throat. "Yep."

"Oh."

The sound came like a delicate groan, and he cocked his head to release the surge of awareness it brought within his gut. To dispel it, he spun and pulled another pouch from his pack. "Let's get your hands washed. I have a bit of pemmican and hardtack we can share."

Durn, if she didn't blink away moisture. That nearly tore a hole through him. Gently, he spun her by the shoulders and eased her forward, pressing his hand against that small hollow in her back.

Interestingly enough, she stayed silent as he escorted her to the edge of the river to rinse the mud from her hands. She came up chattering, flicking off the icy drops, and he captured her cold, wet hands in his and then rubbed them to bring back some warmth. She gave a small laugh, her chin quivering from the cold.

"Corbin's lucky. The things I do for my son. If I didn't love him to death—"

Her words screeched to a halt and her eyes, wide and alarmed, collided with his. This time, moisture welled up and tears spilled over.

"Oh, dear, Lord. I didn't mean to say it like that."

With a moan, he drew her into his arms, pressing his hands beneath her cape to draw her closer. She sniffed against his chest a few times, and he massaged her back, friction bringing some comforting heat.

Her pitiful whimpers made him close his eyes and lay his chilled cheek against the top of her head. Then he blinked and looked around. They were so exposed. Anyone could see them from quite a distance.

"Come on, Maggie. Let's get in the shelter of the trees."

She came so willingly it smote his heart a bit. A fierce protectiveness lit his insides as he ushered her to the shelter of the foliage. He swiped away a reaching bush and nearly carried her to a clearing. Her jaw still convulsively quivered, and he reluctantly let her go to seek his flint. The woman had caught a chill, and curse Moats if he thought he'd hurry her back for the sake of his whiskey.

He collected tinder and a few small branches and made short work of starting a fire. Maggie snuffled behind him.

"We don't have time for a fire, Hank." Her voice came in bursts of breaths as she chattered. "We should get back."

He ignored her and coaxed the smoke in his hands to blossom into a flame. Quickly he loaded the broken branches onto his burning coal. Maggie hunkered down and huddled against him, holding her hands out to the eager flames.

"Moats will keep." He handed her a wad of meat with a hunk of stale hardtack.

"Thanks. I think."

Her low chuckle brought a smile to his face.

Then she whispered. "Will this ever end?"

"What?" He was stalling for time, wanting to enjoy her nestled against his side. He might pay for it, but he'd gladly do that and more.

"Always feeling...hopeless."

He swung his arm around her shoulders and snugged her in tight. "It will be over before you know it. I promise."

The woman had a way of pushing out his assurances that he might never be able to fulfill. But he sure would do his darndest to make them come true. For Maggie was right. Living in strained conditions without the one you love felt…hopeless.

And he…knew exactly how she felt.

Maggie grinned as she wrapped the black gloves into the brown paper she'd saved from the many trips to the general store. Her gaze went to the old pair she had knitted so long ago, washed and dried on the table. She'd even mended the small hole on the third finger.

He kept them. Hank had actually kept that old pair of pitifully-pieced gloves. She calculated. Hank had carried them for nearly fifteen years—her little old gift. The depth of that devotion floored her.

And then it didn't. A bit of a chill crept into her heart. He'd kept the gloves and discarded her. She puckered her lips. This wasn't the time to be hating on Hank. She tied a strip of muslin around the package and laid it on the navy-and-green-squared quilt she'd pieced together in the last several weeks. She had thought to present it to him in the spirit of keeping him warm on the porch, but now, she'd rushed the job to ready it for Christmas.

She rose to set the two gifts next to the others. A book, shirt, and her clay marbles for Corbin, hand-knitted socks and a dark wool cape for White Moon. Indeed, Christmas had come despite the dire circumstance. A smile crept over her face.

A knock at the back door banished the warm fuzzies in her chest, and she gave a cry of surprise.

"It's me."

Hank's muffled voice stilled the panic shivers that crept through her limbs. She lowered the flame on the lamp, and unbarred the door.

Her breath caught in her throat as a bushy mass greeted her. She stepped back and the white pine tree entered with Hank right behind, a grin lighting his face.

"Brought you a gift." He eased his burden to the center of the room.

She pressed the door closed as she collected a long gulp of breath. "A tree!" His chuckle warmed her from her head to her toes. "Oh, my. Oh, my!"

She threw her arms around Hank and smacked his lips with hers. She yanked away from him to sidestep around the spindly evergreen. It wasn't terribly large, just a little over her height, and a bit pathetic. But to her, it was the most beautiful thing she'd seen in a passel of days.

She perched praying hands beneath her chin. "Oh, Hank. This is the best gift ever."

When he didn't answer, she slid her gaze to him, unable to wipe the silly grin from her face. But the solemnness of his features eased her smile into a pucker. "Hank?"

And then he seemed to shrug off the gloom, and his lips tugged a small smile. "Merry Christmas."

"Thank you."

He merely nodded. "Reckon I should move it."

"No. It's perfect here."

"Smack dab in the middle of the room?"

She grinned and jigged a couple of steps, unable to tamp down her excitement. "Yes."

He shrugged and she stepped closer. Maggie gnawed her lips a moment as they stared at one another. "I have a secret."

That furrowed his brow. "Hmmm?"

She crept closer to whisper near his ear. He leaned forward, his hand pressed against her back. "Corbin's coming for Christmas."

Both of his big hands landed on her hips, and then he tugged her back to stare at her, his face thunderstruck.

"What?"

She set her hands lightly on his as they rested against her, fighting the feelings that bubbled up. "White Moon is bringing him."

Hank spun away and strode to the fireplace before he turned. "You can't do that. He'll get stopped. She'll be captured. Then, we'll be in an even bigger mess."

Maggie blinked, and her mouth firmed. "No. It will work. It's all arranged. And I want you to come, too."

He rolled his eyes and tossed his head. "Maggie, that's plain crazy. There's no way two children can creep into this cabin and me be missing from my post without stirring up a lot of commotion from Moats's gang."

"It will work." She rushed forward and pressed her hands against his chest. "It will."

He covered her hands with his, but she pulled from him. Being close to Hank was dangerous territory. But he was right. He couldn't be gone from his spot on the porch again tonight without alerting the sentries. She hurried to the trunk and pulled out a pair of worn pants

and shirt. Then she tugged the smashed hat from under a pile of quilts.

"I can make a decoy. It'll be simple."

"Maggie."

The annoyance in his voice lit a spark of anger. "Stop ruining my Christmas, Hank. Get back to the porch, and I'll get this done in no time. By Christmas Day tomorrow, I'll have everything ready."

She threw the clothes down and pushed him toward the door. "Go. We don't need them seeing you gone tonight as well."

Hank's groan did nothing to dissuade her. Nor did the stern face he shot her when she eased the door shut.

Nope. Nothing would stop this. Corbin would come. White Moon would stay. Hank would attend with grumpy bells jingling on his heels if he so chose, but he would come. And it would be a blessed deliverance in a time of terror. She breathed in the pine scent that enveloped the room. She smiled. A tiny tick of joy amped up the anticipation blooming in her chest.

Oh, yes. Christmas would happen.

Maggie dripped the melted wax onto the sturdy branch and then pressed the candle stub into the cooling goo. She blew gently on the hardening wax until it held. Then she stepped back to survey her creation.

The gangly tree, now covered in home baked treats of gingerbread shapes and ropes of popcorn, sported six stubby candles. When she lighted them, the entire tree would glow. She reached her

shears up and clipped a little more of the branch directly above the candle she had just affixed to the tree. Better safe than sorry.

She hummed as she wrapped the bottom of the tree with one of her best quilts. Then one by one, her excitement bordering on reckless, she plopped and adjusted the gifts below the tree. Then she breezed over to the fireplace and checked the cotton stockings. She'd quickly stitched up two more to match her and Corbin's stockings.

Biscuits, nuts, berries, cookies, and a stick of peppermint lay nestled inside each one. A bit of her eager starch dissolved when she remembered that Hank had actually paid for the peppermints and Corbin's book. She shook her head. Paying Hank back would happen after the holidays, and not before. Though how she would pay that debt was beyond her. But, she would worry over that later.

With a spin she gulped in frightened surprise. Then she let out a giddy giggle. The scarecrow she'd assembled to take Hank's place on the porch perched convincingly on the trunk, complete with his stew pot head and a crushed hat to complete the look. She hoped Moats's men were as fooled.

Maggie scurried to press her nose against the window pane. The sun had long ago hidden itself behind the trees to the west. Soon, it would be time. The smell of split pea soup perfumed the air, the pot resting just close enough to the flames to keep it hot. Maggie added another log and threw the rest of the pine sprigs into the fire. She had one last thing to prepare…cornbread.

Her humming had bloomed into a full-blown Christmas Carol by the time she had the cornmeal whipped up and slathered in a pan. She shored up the dutch oven into the coals and spun.

It was dark. Time to begin.

She dragged the scarecrow to the front door. Hank, wrapped in a wool blanket, turned to appraise her.

"What are you doing?"

"Shhh. Stand up."

She pivoted the life-sized figure and positioned it on the bench.

"Are you kidding me?"

Maggie had to press her lips together to stem the giggle. She scurried back for the boots. Once she had everything set in place, she pulled the blanket from his shoulders and wrapped it around the figure. She grabbed his hand and tugged him inside and barred the door.

Oh. Hank almost groaned. Inside was just this side of heaven. The cabin almost throbbed with warmth and coziness. Smells of ham-flavored soup, bread, and pine filled the air. Hank took a deep breath and closed his eyes. He'd swear he'd never smelled anything so good in his whole life.

He blinked his eyes open to Maggie grinning, lighting the candles on the tree. Then she scurried over to check the heavy quilt hanging across the only window. With a soft laugh, she spun in a circle and then threw her arms out.

"Merry Christmas, Hank!"

He reached up and scratched the nape of his neck. "Merry...Christmas."

Oh, did she know she was setting herself up for all kinds of hurt? The tree, the stockings, the food. What if Moats caught wind of

what was occurring inside the cabin? The place wasn't soundproof or smell proof.

And the myth that Corbin would soon arrive? Yeesh. And he had a front-row seat to the misery when everything fell through.

"The cornbread's almost done. They'll be here any time now."

Her skirt twirled when she spun to remove the pots from the fire.

"Yeah, about that, Maggie. Did they give you a time? I mean...it's going to be pretty difficult for two children to arrive for a Christmas dinner given the circumstances."

"White Moon can do it. She has her father and his people to help." She motioned to a chair. "Come on, sit down."

This was not a good idea. He sat.

The wooden chest was pulled to the table to form more seating, and four plates indicated the place for each to sit. With the two large pots, there was barely room for silverware and a cloth napkin. It was nearly the finest table he'd ever bellied up to. Maggie finally plopped into the chair across from him and pulled it in before he could even rise to assist.

"I'm sorry for the simple fare," her words came in a rush, her grin alight like fairy dust, "but on such short notice, it was the best I could do."

"It smells wonderful."

That earned him a million-dollar smile. He rubbed his chin. At least he'd taken time to shave. She tapped her finger on the table and peeked behind the quilt-covered curtain.

"If you want to warm up by the fire until they get here, that's fine."

He cleared his throat and fingered the spoon beside his plate. "I'm warm enough."

She nodded. "I hope you don't mind, but I wrapped your carving for Corbin. He'll be so excited."

Hank crossed his arms and leaned back in the chair. "I'm sure he will be."

But not tonight. He wanted to groan with the futility of it all.

A scraping noise at the back door made Maggie bolt to her feet. The sheer glee on her face shone like the candles on the tree. She tiptoed to the door and whispered.

"They're here."

Chapter Twelve

Hank rose, his hand to his gun. Maggie seemed to have forgotten the need for secrecy and yanked the bar from the door, making all kinds of racket.

When the door swung open, nothing but cold air greeted them. That, and a fat raccoon staring with bold eyes.

"Oh."

The disappointment in that one breathy word stabbed Hank's heart. He pressed his hands to her shoulders. "Let's sit awhile."

But she leaned from him and stuck her head out the door, looking for a long time to the right and then the left. The comforting heat inside the cabin quickly diffused tepid by the time she swung the door shut. Her tongue took a swipe over her lips. Then she bit down on her bottom lip with a shrug.

"Guess I'm just a touch overanxious."

"I reckon."

She returned to her chair and sat with a stiff back. The disillusionment on her face was hard to look at, so he took his seat and stared at the banked fire. Eventually, she rose to pick up her needlework. She adjusted her skirt as she sat, and then scooted the chair a bit toward the fire. Maggie took up the hoop, sat a few minutes, listening before gripping the needle in her fingers. Her hand rhythmically tugged the thread in and out. In and out. Pause. Listen. In and out. Pause. Listen. The clock ticked on to the rhythm.

Soon, the candles on the tree grew too short to continue to burn, and Maggie rose to blow them out. The wind gusted against the window, only reminding both of them of the absence of the expected guests.

Hank's eyes went to her timepiece on the mantle. Nearly nine o'clock. The soup had long gone cold. Maggie stood to collect the pans and pressed them near the banked fire.

"They're just…running late."

But her voice contained no true hope. "I'm sure they are."

She rose and spun. "You don't believe they're coming."

He stared at her then. Maybe it was best or the only option for her to pull out that temper. Either way, he'd be the one to face it. And he'd do that and more. Hank cleared his throat. "It's not that, Maggie. I—"

"They're coming. They are." She snapped her head away and took in a long shuddering breath. She clasped her hands at her waist and stood stiffly for a few moments. Then, as if melting, her

shoulders fell, and she crept forward. Her liquid eyes sought his. "You don't think they've been…caught, do you?"

He shook his head. "I honestly think it was too dangerous. Since we haven't heard any commotion, I believe they're safe."

Maggie snugged her arms at her breast. "I suppose."

The next hour was filled with slurping unwanted soup despite the fact it was quite tasty, though thick. Plus, the cornbread had gone quite hard by the time Maggie scooped a piece on his plate. He slathered butter on it to help it slide down his throat. It didn't improve matters to watch Maggie toss the contents of her bowl in different swirling patterns. Rarely, she touched the spoon to her tongue.

In silence, Maggie heated water and continued the chore of washing up. Hank grabbed a towel and dried the few items. When finished, she wadded her hands in her apron skirt.

"I suppose we should turn in." She let out a sigh, her whole body sagging with what he suspected was heartbreak rather than exhaustion. "I'm a fool."

Her words proved his suspicions. Hank gripped her shoulders and gave a gentle shake. "You're not a fool, Maggie. Just…hopeful."

She tossed the towel to the table. "A lot of good that did me."

Maggie pulled the blankets from the chest and folded a couple to spread near the fireplace. "I'm afraid I'm bushed. Please stay and enjoy the heat. The scarecrow will surely fill your post at least until sunrise. Good night, Hank."

She circled the tree, stepped from her shoes, and pulled the quilt down on the bed. Without much ceremony, she snuggled into the mattress, her back to him. The quilt flew up and covered her head.

Everything within him wanted to gather her in his arms to stroke the sorrow away. But he knew that wouldn't be wise or wanted. It was bad enough to consider sleeping on the pallet yet another night. Yet the heat of the room and the gnawing disappointment had zapped him, too.

He removed his gun belt and set it near the pillow, but he left his boots on—just in case. With much on his mind, he reclined with his hands behind his head. The thick quilt warmed his body as well as the glow from the fireplace.

Well, Maggie had asked what had been his favorite Christmas, but she hadn't asked his worst. This was definitely one of the worst. He drifted off thinking of the many depressing holidays he'd spent in the lean-to while his mother…turned her tricks. Bad memories every one, until Maggie's family had started including him in their festivities.

But this was the first time he'd experienced a foul Christmas when Maggie was involved. A sad day indeed…

Shuffling woke him from a dead sleep. Maggie tottered across the floor, trying to slip her shoes on. A hoot owl's mournful sound drifted through the night air. Hank struggled to a sitting position. "What is it?"

She didn't answer, but the sound of the door bar being eased from its stays brought him to his feet. He grabbed the gun from the

holster on the floor. His eyes squinted at the clock. Two-forty. Smack dab in the middle of the night. "Wait, Maggie."

But she already had the door cracked open. In tiptoed two small figures. Maggie collapsed against them, soft sobs filling the room.

"Mama, Mama." Soft muttering carried a gut-wrenching joy.

Hank took a deep breath. By jove they'd done it. Two young children had pierced the darkness and the hedge of the formidable gang.

"Let me light the lantern. I have to see you—"

"No. Much danger. Only have short time."

The whispered voice could only belong to White Moon.

"Then come closer to the fireplace. Please."

Two buckskin-covered children neared the banked hearth. It didn't afford much light. But it was enough.

"Oh, Mama. A tree."

Corbin's whispered voice carried such elation, something shifted in Hank. Suddenly he was glad he'd listened to that inner voice and chopped that small evergreen, no matter how ridiculous it'd seemed at the time. The children both gasped at the gifts Maggie laid in their laps.

Hank marveled at the muted quilt she'd slid into his arms and he studied the new, neatly knitted gloves. A sure improvement over his originals, though he'd always cherish them. Then the stockings came down. Nuts, gingerbread, peppermints. Why, he was almost as enamored with his own stocking as the children were with theirs.

He'd been wrong—so, so wrong. This wasn't the worst Christmas ever. It was the best, especially when Maggie found the

pouch hidden deep in the tree's quilt. The last thing he'd done before sleep had truly claimed him just a few hours ago.

While the children pressed their heads together on the hearth, whispering words of wonder and delight, Maggie pulled the porcelain trinket box from the canvas. Her eyes lit on his in the dim light.

"When?"

A grin tugged at Hank's mouth. "It's a Christmas miracle."

She reached a hand up from her spot on the floor and grasped his hand. Sparkles glittered from her eyes.

"Thank you, Hank. Thank you for...everything."

He wanted to bask in her gratitude, tell her his heart, and dang it, yank her into his embrace despite the company of children. But a shadow stood next to his chair. The delicate Native child stood there, a somber look upon her shadowed face.

"Must go. Must go now."

The strangled coo Maggie emitted sounded much like a dying dove. The woman shook her head only a fraction of a second before she dropped her head and rose to fetch a swath of muslin. Once she'd tied the gifts into two bundles, she knelt in front of her forlorn son. Corbin huddled into Maggie's arms. Mother and son hugged long and fierce, with huffs and sniffs. Then, the two slipped through the door, and Maggie pressed her face against the wood with a low moan.

Hank slid the bar in place, caught Maggie before she crumpled to the floor, and carried her to his chair. There he nestled her in his

lap, her wet face against his neck. As she wept out her sorrow, he crooned to her until she fell into a fitful rest.

Holding her in the middle of the night was pure heavenly torture. As a matter of fact, that described the whole night. What was it Charles Dickens had written? Ah yes, "It was the best of times, it was the worst of times…"

Sadly, so it was.

A strident clanging brought Maggie's head up with a sharp intake. Arms tightened around her and then suddenly she was set on her feet.

"What was that?"

Hank hurried to the front porch. With a yank of the door, the source of the noise lay at his feet. Scarecrow's stewing pot head had tumbled from its perch.

"Quick. Dispose of this."

Hank tossed the body of the scarecrow at her and swiped the hat and pot from the porch floorboards. Maggie grappled with the items he thrust at her and the door shut. "Hank?"

The door cracked open, his face near hers. "Hurry, Maggie. If we heard this racket, you can be sure Moats did, too."

Fear sliced through her. "The children. They'll find them!"

Hank's jaw firmed. "Pray they don't. Bar the door."

"But—" The door snapped her protest in half. With shaking hands, she settled the wood in its place. Already there were men's voices crying out. Sounds of running feet surrounded the cabin. She

glanced to the curtain. Still dark. How she hoped she'd been asleep longer than she feared.

Grabbing the scarecrow, she hurried to the mantle clock. It only neared four a.m. Had the children had enough time to escape? Stomping startled her as someone scurried across the porch boards. Hank? Or someone else?

With a small cry she shredded the limp figure in her hands and stuffed the clothing into the chest. She retrieved the pot and hat from the table and returned each to its proper place. Once she'd thunked the trunk's lid closed, the scarecrow was as if he had never been.

Agitated voices drifted to her from the porch and then more thumping boots. She backed away from the door and scrambled beneath the quilt, clutching it at her chin.

Please don't let them find the children. Please.

Calming under the quilt, her muscles felt restless. So Maggie rose and spent the next hour pacing. Then she stopped and set her hands on her hips. Outside had long gone quiet. The only thing she could surmise is that Moats's gang had given chase. A shiver raced through her, and she clenched her eyelids closed.

This dangerous hostage situation would end by finding the gold—the elusive…no, the mythical gold. A sob broke loose as she stood in the middle of the room. Well, there was nothing to be done now, and she refused to sit and fret over what could or could not be happening. Chores always helped her work through an unworkable problem.

She stomped over and whipped Hank's quilt from the floor. It settled her nerves to be about the business of tidying, not that her

tears agreed as they continued to wet her cheeks. Maggie stuffed the quilt into the trunk but saved the Hank-scented pillow and tossed it to the bed. Next, she spun back to straighten the chairs and table.

An exclamation squeaked from her. Hank had left his gun on his chair. She pivoted. Hadn't he had a holster as well? Her eyes searched the floor, the hearth, the mantle, anywhere she thought he might have absently stuck his gun-toting belt. But it was nowhere. Just...the gun.

Letting out a breath, she reached for it. It was stone cold in her hand, but not unfamiliar. Ax had left a firearm or two about the cabin at one time, but she'd never fired one. But that didn't mean she didn't know where the bullets went and how to pull the trigger.

She flipped open the loading gate. The bullets' rims glinted at her. Six of them. Maggie pressed down a swallow. Had Hank left it on purpose? Whether he had or not, she would hold on to it until he asked for it, and even then, he might have to wrangle it from her stiff fingers.

With hurried steps, she treaded across the room to the bed. She lifted the quilt and sheet to reveal the mended mattress. The added pocket she'd inserted now held her kitchen knife with the dented handle. Hopefully, there would be enough room for the Colt to join it.

By layering the gun on top of the knife, both weapons fit nicely into the space. She yanked down the extra cotton panel that concealed the hole and tucked it in gently. Yet, the distant sound of thundering horse hooves made her snatch the gun from its new hiding place.

She perched on the bed, gun cradled in both hands. Her eyes darted about the cabin, listening and feeling the reverberations grow louder and louder. The noises indicated several horses. Voices implied some men halted near the cabin while yet more hoof thumps indicted a few had ridden beyond the yard.

Stomps on the porch floor drew a soft cry from her throat. And even though she expected it, the loud pounding on the door jerked her to the floor.

"Open up."

She shook her head. Not again. Maggie licked her lips and set both thumbs on the hammer. Would it matter if she kept silent? The monster had threatened to chop the door down before, he surely wouldn't let it intimidate him this time either.

One hand clutching the gun, she reached with her free hand and flipped the thick post from the stays. It thudded to the floor, partially blocking it. The leather string pulled tight and lifted the wooden latch. She grabbed the gun with both hands and flung the weapon out straight armed. Leonard's filthy face and greasy hair tumbling from his hat appeared in the crack.

With a shove, the door popped open. Leonard, Gibbons, Moats, and Hank froze in the doorway.

"What do you want?" Already her arms grew heavy, but Maggie had growled out in her gruffest voice. Moats shouldered ahead of the other three.

"Put that gun down."

The gang leader's harsh demand only stiffened her resolve. "You've got no business in here. Get out."

Moats's arrogant step forward halted with the hammer click of her gun. "I may not be a deadeye shot who can take out all four of you. But I can guarantee you, Jeether Moats, I can lay you dead where you stand."

The man's eyes narrowed, his next words peppered with obscenities. "—Where'd you get that—confounded gun?"

"You take another step, and you can ask Saint Peter yourself."

"Mrs. Robbins, you ain't been nothing but trouble from the get-go. I don't know what just happened around here, but I want you to know one thing. If I don't have the gold heist in one week, that little six-shooter you got there won't mean a blame thing."

She took a small step forward…and then another, lifting the gun up to his chin. With a tilt of her head, Maggie squinted her left eye to fix her aim down the blade of the barrel's sight. "You come in my house again uninvited, and you can tell both Mr. Blame and St. Pete your sentiments about my gun. Until then, get your sorry behinds out of my cabin!"

Chapter Thirteen

Maggie took a deep breath and opened her eyes. She pulled the quilt back from her face to fix her gaze on the gun balanced on the small table next to the bed. Once Moats had retreated and she'd secured the door, she'd collapsed on the bed. It hadn't taken long for exhaustion and trauma of the uninvited guests to take a toll on her. She'd snoozed away the morning.

She drew her hands up to cover her face. What was her next move? Maggie was trapped like a mouse in a corner. Well, at least this mouse had a loaded gun. Yet, how to get out? And was it true Corbin and White Moon were safe?

If only she could locate this fabled gold. Moats had laid down one last threat. A week. She had a paltry week. And for some reason, Maggie knew this was her last chance.

Pray.

The inaudible nudge seemed to whisk across the room, and she caught her breath, half-expecting the dandy to be sitting at the table.

But the chairs were empty. She shook her head and rolled to her side. What use was praying? Hadn't she done that when Mother was sick? Hadn't she pleaded with the Almighty to save her mother's life? Maggie bunched the fabric of the pillow's corner in her hands. And Axel, using her and discarding her amidst his plundering escapades. Where had God been then?

Then the hoppers came and cleared their meager fields and her garden in a matter of hours. Now, Jeether Moats breathed down her neck, demanding a fortune in gold that may not even exist. Things had gone from bad to…disastrous.

Her gaze settled on her mother's journal, still resting on the mantle. All of mother's journal entries had abruptly ended a few months after courting Rupert. Several entries aroused Maggie's suspicions. Mother wrote of his anger when the carriage wheel had broken and her concern over his physical advances. Yet, she continued to mention his wealth, as if that solved all his character flaws.

So many questions, so little answers. Maggie flipped to stare at the ceiling, glared at it, wishing she were face to face with God.

"You know the answers, don't You?" she whispered, her bottom lip quivering. "Yet You keep them to Yourself while the rest of us suffer down here in misery."

Her breath came in a sob. This is what had kept her prayers silent—her anger, her bitterness, her resentment. There, she'd confessed it. She'd felt cheated by the One who supposedly had everything bound up in His immeasurable, benevolent hands. The very One who'd allowed Axel, the hoppers, and Jeether Moats to devastate her life.

Yet...there was...Corbin. And...this cabin. Years of joy...with her family, growing up, surrounded by love. Her health, her grit, that same determination that, only this morning, had run Jeether Moats from her cabin with his tail between his legs.

And there was...Hank...

She let a puff of air whoosh from her lips. One by one the blessings of her life swirled around her brain. But still that angry ball swelled inside her chest.

"Fine. You want me to pray? Then I will. I've had to send my son away, and I miss him. The few stolen moments with him last night was not near enough. I have bandits outside just waiting to hurt or kill me. I've a strange man who shows up to threaten me and take my possessions. I'm alone and I'm not even sure I can trust Hank."

Her childhood love's handsome face intruded, and she pushed it away. "I'm supposed to find gold to exchange for my freedom. But. There. *IS*. No. Gold."

She pushed to a sitting position and pointed her finger at the tongue and groove boards above her. "And You let my mother die, and I had to marry that horrid man. That *horrid, horrid* man."

Tears streamed down her face, and Maggie struggled to keep her voice down. "Oh, why did You let her die? Why? I needed her. I needed Hank. I'm so tired of battling alone."

She wept into her hands for several minutes before movements on the porch quieted her sorrow. But nothing further alerted her to danger, and she wiped her face. It was only Hank, back to his lookout spot.

What an absolute idiot she was praying to the empty heavens.

From the window, a stream of sunlight crept through a crack where the quilt hadn't quite covered. The ray of weak light lit the dust motes drifting down from the ceiling. Her eyes tracked up and searched the boards above her and stopped on the attic trap door.

The hatch was perfectly camouflaged, the climbing pegs removed and stored in the trunk. Small wooden plugs disguised the diagonal peg holes that led to the sealed opening. One might not even know a room existed up there. After all, it was nailed shut like always when Ax had vamoosed on a raid. She pulled her hanky from beneath her pillow and wiped her nose. She hadn't even bothered to go up there since his death.

Not that she'd ever been allowed. Oh, she'd stuck her head up there plenty of times for Ax to yell a command to fetch something or to cook something. Her husband and father-in-law usually sat at a rickety table in the center of the eaves poring over papers. And after the hoppers, Ax had stored wheat up there in the far corner in case the insects returned.

She worried her bottom lip with her teeth. Why hadn't she gone up there to the mighty bank robbers den? She swung her legs to the floor. Fine. After the chores were finished this evening, she'd bring the crowbar from the shed, and she would step into the forbidden

loft. Perhaps something up there would give her a hint of the trail of gold. If nothing else, she could retrieve some of the wheat.

Hank fingered the side arm's handle holstered at his side. He didn't much care for his extra saddlebag gun. But he'd left his good one for Maggie. And she'd been nothing short of a feisty feminine fortress. Squaring up to Moats, barrel trained on his Adam's apple, and banishing him from her house took a barn full of gumption.

His lips twitched at the thought. She was one gutsy gal, that was for sure. Still, her bravery wouldn't have stopped Leonard from violating her a few nights back if Hank hadn't brought a stop to it. He released the barrel of his gun, spun it, and settled it into the one empty chamber. Yep. He'd be glad to sight in his second gun. One glance of Leonard nearing the cabin again and target practice was on.

Hank took a deep breath, and eyed the milk bucket he'd set by the front door earlier in the day. It neared time for the evening chores, and Maggie hadn't even shown herself to fetch the cow's morning donation. Where was that woman?

As if summoned, Maggie opened the door behind him.

"Goodness, Hank. Why are you sitting right in the doorway?"

He stood and spun. His gaze swept over her tired features. "You know why."

Was she kidding? First, Leonard had sprawled her across the bed, and then Moats constantly threatened to chop the door down— likely to finish exactly what Leonard had in mind. The thought made his stomach go rancid.

She leaned a hand against the lintel and sighed. The kitchen knife flashed in her hand while the gun took up residence tucked into her skirt's waist.

"Hmm. There's plenty of base men about, but this repeater evens out the odds a little."

He nodded at the gratefulness written on her face and then motioned to the bucket. Then he repositioned the bench next to the doorway, and fell into step next to her. She stopped.

"Ah, yes." She cleared her throat. "Thanks for tending the cow this morning."

She set out across the porch and hopped to the weary winter grass, heading for the barn. "You don't have to follow my every move."

"Probably best if I do."

She placed her hand on his arm and nodded. "Thanks, Hank. I'll admit the last couple of days have been nerve-racking. And the night that ruffian had crept into the cabin was a close one."

Hank swallowed. Two close ones, if they were counting himself. His mind dwelled on how near he'd been to sharing her bed. Would she have welcomed him in? He feared he knew the answer, which disconcerted him not a little. Maybe he was no different than Leonard and Moats.

His lips tightened as she turned away. Maybe Maggie had more to fear from…him. They walked the rest of the way to the barn, and she paused at the door.

"Why don't you just settle here and let me do the chores?"

He shook his head. Was the woman crazy? The barn was the perfect place for Leonard to ambush her. "I'll go in with you."

He searched the small space, looking in places no grown man could've ever maneuvered into, until he stepped back, allowing her to start the feeding and milking. Maggie yanked the bucket from beneath the leaching barrel first and dumped it back in the top, and then settled behind the cow with a fresh pail.

The squirts of milk accompanied his thoughts. If only he could get into town and alert the sheriff. Of course, what clout did he have anyway? He'd been part of the gang for months, trying to infiltrate for a man who was an impostor. No one would believe him at this point.

He moved to the door of the barn and looked out. No, he'd have to take care of this alone. Well, maybe not alone. *Lord, I need you to get Maggie out of this situation. Even if you have to kill me in the process, just keep her safe and send someone to be good to her, to take care of her.*

The cold air bit his lungs while he searched the frozen yard. How he wished he could turn back time. He should've never left Maggie those many years back, even if he'd had nothing to give. Well, live and learn. He wouldn't leave her now.

Not ever.

Maggie caught a shadow from Corbin's secret spot and caught her breath. Someone was in there. She swallowed. Was it Leonard just waiting to jump out and attack her? Her eyes went to Hank's

back at the doorway. She grabbed the knife from the crate and scooped a bucketful of grain from a barrel with her other hand.

The cow gobbled the cracked corn eagerly, and Maggie tiptoed to the loose boards as she gripped the knife handle. But White Moon's head peeked out, and Maggie nearly swooned with relief. She motioned for the girl to come out. They snuck behind the cow's large body.

"What are you doing here?"

The girl shrugged. "Forgot note."

Maggie shot a glance at Hank over the cow's back. "Is Corbin safe? Did you have trouble escaping?"

The dark-eyed girl shook her head, keeping one eye on Hank pacing the front of the shed. "Safe. Bad men slow."

"You said you had a note?"

"Listen. Mother very sick. Father done hunting. He moves in for the kill."

Maggie shook her head. "What? I don't understa—"

They both froze and crouched when Moats's voice addressed Hank. Maggie pressed a finger to her lips and eyed White Moon. "You need to leave."

The Indian child with such light skin shook her head. "Much danger."

Maggie laid her hand on White Moon's cheek. "I'm sorry to hear about your mother. Here, take this. Just in case."

Maggie pushed the dented knife handle into the child's hand.

"No worry. Corbin safe with my people. Soon, also you will be safe."

Maggie's face puckered, and tears filled her eyes. "I wish it were so."

The child's wide gaze never wavered. "Lord say so."

Maggie cupped White Moon's face with both hands. "I hope you are right."

The young girl nodded. "You will know. You will see." The girl shoved a paper in her hand and with the grace and silence of a deer, White Moon turned, studied the gentlemen at the door and crept back to her hiding spot.

Maggie stood, gripping the note in her hands as Moats stalked off. She laid a hand to the red and white cow's back, stroking it. Hopefully, neither man would be aware she'd exchanged the knife for a message.

She unfolded the crumpled paper that looked suspiciously familiar. Beneath Hank's handwriting a short-worded message looped in feminine hand. In the dim light, she could barely make out the words. *Come to Bellmira's Parlour for the answers you seek.*

<u>Chapter Fourteen</u>

Maggie inhaled a deep breath. Hank summoned to the bawdy house? A shiver ricocheted down her body. No, she would not deliver this message. It could be nothing but a trick…or turning a trick? She shook her head. She could not do it.

Yet, what if the answers Hank sought were there? Would they turn him toward the right? Would this information pull him from this horrible gang and set him on an honorable path once more?

She glanced toward the secret place where White Moon hid. Was she still inside? Perhaps the girl had already crept away. Maggie couldn't begin to understand how the child moved about as if invisible.

But she couldn't dwell on that now. Moats had disappeared and Hank now paced and then halted, arms crossed and legs wide, setting up a guarding stance. A small moan oozed from her. She had no right to keep the message. He'd been here. Yes, he was part of an atrocious gang, but he had rescued and guarded her with his life. She knew what she had to do.

Maggie picked up the bucket and strode forward. Snow freckled the air as she emerged from the shadows of the shed. When she paused, Hank turned his dark, enigmatic eyes on her. She blinked and puzzlement glinted in his gaze. He leaned forward and took the heavy bucket of milk from her. Her hand stilled him from striding away.

"For...you."

His brow tightened, and then he flicked his gaze to the note and back to her eyes.

She nodded. "You need to go. Find out. Settle your heart. I'll be fine."

Maggie scurried toward the house, leaving him to untangle her words with the feminine script tucked inside the note.

Her hand had touched the leather loop to unlatch the door, when Hank called her name. He tramped closer and set the pail down on the porch.

"I can't go. I won't leave you."

She tugged the Colt from the waist of her skirt. "You've left me well protected. And I've seven days of safety. If Moats chops down the door, I'll shoot him dead. Him and any of the other five that dare step through. I've got six bullets, Hank. I'll use them well."

Hank rested his hand high on the door and leaned in, his breath a tickle of awareness against her neck.

"Maggie, you need—"

She spun and pressed her hand against his chest which might have been a mistake. The warmth beneath her palm made her want to beg him to stay. Instead, she swallowed and shored up courage. "Go, Hank. Find your answers. You won't be whole until you do."

He stood, his face growing nearer, making her ache to feel the stubble of his chin against her cheek, her lips. The short coo that squeezed from her seemed to ignite a realization that she needed to flee, and flee now. If she didn't, her resolution to let him go where he shouldn't would turn into pulling him into the cabin, a place where he also shouldn't go.

"Maggie."

His husky voice spurned her into jerky movements. She bent, snatched up the buckets, and charged through the door. The latch fell into place and she threw the bar into the stays, not trusting him not to come through nor herself to rush back.

Oh, heavens. She loved him. Hank Sutter, thief and member of a malevolent, immoral gang that plundered and murdered. And what was worse, she'd always loved him. Always. How could she have been so unaware of her own emotions?

Sobs billowed up, and she cupped her hand over her mouth to smother them. Hank probably stood right where she'd left him, indecision warring in his mind. She slid to the floor and let the pails' metal handle clink to the top of the buckets.

Not only had she married a thief out of desperate naiveté, the love of her very soul also was a thief…if for no other reason than he had stolen her heart.

She huddled into a fetal ball on the cold floorboards. The mangled, depraved existence she'd survived before had only been a taste of the anguish she now felt. Corbin gone. White Moon treading through a shadowed evil valley of enemies. And…Hank. *Oh, Hank.*

"Help me, Oh, help me."

Whimpers interrupted the hissed words that came from her mouth. She scrubbed at the salty tears on her face, knowing if words continued to tumble from her, Hank would be breaking down the door. She squeezed her eyes shut and pressed her hands against her face to block her weeping sounds.

There was no one to help. No one but the…Almighty. And he knew her tortured prayers even if they weren't spoken. Didn't He?

Lord…keep White Moon safe. And Corbin. And…Hank.

Maggie pried the corner of the attic trap door while balancing on the tiny pegs now holding fast in the chinked logs. Sweat collected on her forehead and ran a rivulet down onto the bridge of her nose. She gritted her teeth and repositioned the crowbar on the one last stubborn nail.

It gave a screech, and she halted. No worries in alerting Hank. She'd heard his feet leave the porch some time ago. But the others? Who knew which brute might have his filthy head pressed to the door? Thankfully the oafs probably couldn't scale the porch's tongue and groove planks without cuing her into their movements. Praise God for squeaky boards.

Her hand checked the gun stuck in the back of her shirt waist. She would go nowhere without her handy-dandy pepperbox. With a

determined set to her jaw, Maggie, as quietly as possible, yanked the crowbar with enough force to ease the nail from its hole.

The door flopped open, gaping wide, while dust and bits of straw rained to the floor. She shook her head and closed her eyes, all the while trying to suppress a cough. Once the air cleared, she fetched the lantern and clambered back up the short pegs to the second story.

The room appeared ghostly in the meager light and she shivered. Unwanted memories of Ax and her father-in- law glaring at her from the table nosed in. Fear shimmied across her skin.

They're not here. They'll never be here again. Moats had shot them both dead—stone-cold dead. She grasped the floorboards and pulled herself into the small space. The rafters prevented standing so she crawled to the center space near the table. Here she could stand, but barely.

Maggie surveyed the tight, shadowed room, assuring herself no demons from the past resided here any longer. The lantern flame sputtered adding an eerie glow to the small space.

Dust coated the few papers on the table, and she grabbed them first. A rude map filled out the first page. Names and dates scattered across a second in hurried writing. The third contained columns of figures, added and re-added. With a shaky breath, she pressed the lantern and the papers to the table.

A pile of wheat sheaves filled the far corner all the way to the eaves, the seeded ends dropping towards her. The seeds that had let go of their mooring scattered across the floor. Plenty to fill a large bowl. Why had she not thought to come up here? Once she had

winnowed the seeds from the bundles and ground them, she'd have quite a pile of flour.

She eyed the stack. What a waste. The bundles could have remained here for years, a hidden treasure trove of food. What an imbecile Ax had been. He'd wasted his life and nearly this pile of fine wheat. Just thinking of Ax had her glancing around again. She'd grown so accustomed to him popping up unexpectedly, uneasiness gripped her. A few pants flew from her mouth as she calmed herself. It was nothing but a table and a wasting pile of wheat sheaves.

Her eyes swung back to the enormous pile. There had to be hundreds of them. Curious why Ax hadn't just winnowed the wheat from the straw and stored it in bags. It required much less space. But then, work had never appealed to him. He was much more interested in the easy pickings of thievery.

Bitterness rose up as she strolled closer to the golden mountain of wheat. Thoughts of Ax invaded, though she tried to fend them off. Her arms crossed her breast, feeling a need to protect herself from his cruelty even now.

Oh, Ax had been so sugary sweet when Mother ailed. And perhaps a few weeks thereafter. But it had been like a dive into a freezing pond when his true personality had come to light. Then his occupation had left her in fear for months—no—years. Years and years of more waste. Wasted years of sorrow and misery.

Her lips trembled and then tightened against the anger that built inside. He'd violated her over and over—even offered her to his father. She closed her eyes. Thank God her father-in-law had declined.

Her eyes flew open. Thank God? Yes, who else could she have thanked? It could've been worse, she realized now. She'd made her choice. Ax Robbins had charmed her, and she'd failed to recognize the signs, the anger, the physical advances.

Her mother's journal came to mind, and she caught her breath. They'd both been duped. Understanding bloomed through her chest. Mother had been fooled as well. How painful it must have been—too painful to tell of it. Just like the agony she'd suffered at Ax's hands.

"I wished I'd never met you, Axel Robbins." Her hand flew to her mouth at the whispered utterance. *Corbin* . Without Ax, there was no Corbin. Even in suffering, she'd been given the most precious gift…her son.

How stupid she'd been. How unwise her choices. Yet God had blessed her even so, and she'd cut Him from her life.

"I'm nothing but a trusting idiot." She drew back and kicked the wheat bundle nearest her. A clink stalled all thought. Her brow wrinkled. What had made that sound?

She knelt and wrenched the eighteen inch bundle from the bottom of the stack. For a bundle of wheat, it was terribly heavy. Three strips of twine encircled the wheat stems from top to bottom. Her fingers clawed at the strings and slipped them free from the sheave. The long stems separated, revealing a narrow white bag in the center. She gasped and pulled the hefty package from its nest of straw.

Her heart thundered as she tugged at the drawstring. The clinking inside couldn't have prepared her for what tumbled out. Gold twenty-dollar pieces slid from the opening. Her hands flew to

her mouth as she stared at them. She shoved them from her skirt and stood, the coins tumbling to the dirty floorboards, jangling and spinning. One by one the coins settled, the last vibrating to a stunning stop with a metallic quiver. Shivers raced up and down Maggie's spine and she shot a glance to the open hatch. Had anyone heard the clatter of the coins?

After several minutes, no footsteps could be heard and no one pounded on her door. She drew a few calming breaths and rose to fetch the lantern from the table. Legs shaking, she knelt back down to collect and deposit the scattered coins back into the bag.

Her eyes drifted to the huge pile of sheaves next to her, and she lifted the lantern. The wheat seeds alone would provide a treasure trove of flour. And if—*if* there were this many coins in even half of those sheaves, there was a whole lot more than a treasure trove of flour. There would virtually be a fortune of gold beneath the eaves. Heaven help her. It wasn't just a fortune of gold. It was a fortune of *stolen* gold.

With shaking hands, she poured the coins back out and counted them. Seventy-five. That was…her mind calculated. Fifteen hundred dollars! *In her lap.* With a small cry she dumped the coin bag on the table and grabbed the next couple of shocks from the top of the pile. Empty. But the third felt solid.

The next five she opened contained the same as the first. Her stomach tossed. Nine thousand dollars littered the table. Exactly how much money *was* here? Did it matter? Was it even important that it was stolen? Fear evaporated and her heart sang. She'd found it, she'd finally discovered the gold. Now, she and Corbin would be free.

Her brows drew together, and her hands paused on the next wheat bundle. But what about the dandy? What would happen once the Moats's gang left, if they left, and Corbin was safely ensconced in the cabin once again? Would she be free of this ominous stranger? Would she be free once the authorities caught scent of this stolen bankroll? Or would they jail her with the rest? Suddenly, the piercing fear ricocheted inside her chest once more.

And what about Hank? Would he leave—again? Where the gang went, he went, especially if the news he now hunted gave him no satisfaction. Her heart lurched. Could she bear life without him? A sob rose up her throat.

"Oh, God. What do I do?" Tears bit her eyes as she surveyed the mound of wheat bundles. Reason returned. First things first.

Get the gold from the straw.

Chapter Fifteen

Leaving at dark was the absolute stupidest thing to do. Yet, Maggie had told him to go. No…she'd insisted. And here he was, plodding through the forest slopes wishing he were back at the cabin. He turned his head and a crack of bones rippled up his neck. Remember, he wasn't leaving, he was merely on an errand. With a little smile from upstairs, Maggie would sleep like a baby through the night and he'd be back by first light.

Even from far off, the piano music drifted to his ears. As he grew closer, women's voices and men's laughter grew louder. By the time the two-story clapboard house, the best building in a ten mile radius, came into view, the entire downstairs poured out light through the gauzy curtains. The upstairs, however, remained suspiciously dark.

Curtains wafted out the small openings of the windows to let in a bit of air. The filmy material moved like ghostly apparitions, making him set a hand to the gun at his hip. He shook off the uneasiness. No doubt that many hot bodies could heat up a place. Hank grunted. He'd give a hundred bucks not to have to step inside.

He threaded his horse among the others. Near on twenty mounts shifted in the frosty air. B.B. had better have news—real news. Hank looped the reins around the long wooden hitch and stepped out to stare at the front.

Even the shadows through the curtains made him pause. The outline of a man with a woman in his lap laughed, throwing his head back. Couples made fainter outlines, dancing. He supposed that was dancing. They were dipping and such. Maybe not. This close to the door, the laughter and loud conversations would overshadow his entrance.

His Adam's apple bounced as he climbed the stairs and set his palm against the brass knob. Then he hesitated. Did one knock on a bawdy house door or barge right in? Hank opted for the second considering no one was likely to hear him if he pounded on the door with a hammer.

The uproar inside quieted only a little with faces turning to investigate the newcomer. The woman at the piano, shoulders bared in a frothy gown, leg exposed sporting a garter belt, never ceased pounding the keys. Then, the painted ladies captured the attention of their escorts and the whole laughing, dancing, sitting-in-laps thing went right back to business. Hank grunted and glanced around. B.B. had to be here somewhere, right?

A more mature tart stepped away from a bearded man with a gold tooth and sauntered toward Hank, a coquettish yet keenly assessing look in her eyes. She carried a bit of extra weight, dark hair piled high, curled and jeweled, and decked in the most flamboyant shade of red he'd ever seen. The woman tilted her head and a hard smile crossed her full lips, well outlined in the same color as her dress.

Her eyes caught one's attention, a startling blue against the mounds of kohl on her lashes. Her coffee-washed-in-cream skin simply glowed with the light of so many lanterns and candleholders spread about the room. The closer she grew, the more he realized the dip of her bodice.

So, this was Bellmira. He'd heard the woman was a looker, but she was more than that. She commanded the room. The red dress drew closer and she fluttered her hands to the necklace hanging low at her neck, drawing his eyes once more where they didn't want to be. He cut his gaze back to hers. He would have to be careful. Bellmira was full of tricks.

"What do we have here?" The woman batted her lashes and half circled him. She tittered a throaty laugh before stopping to assess him from boots to hat. "The full moon brings in all kinds."

Hank cleared his throat. "I'm looking for B.B."

One perfectly darkened brow rose. "Are you now? Well, I am sure we can accommodate you."

Lifting her hand, dripping with diamonds, she tapped a finger down each of his shirt's buttons. Hank's jaw tightened. Knowing he stood there, filling the same position of the men who'd used his

mother, made him want to swat her hand away. But he refused to give her that much power.

"Just B.B, if you please."

The woman leaned her head back. "Daleetha, come entertain our new guest. Perhaps you'd like a beverage?"

She motioned to what he would have assumed to be the kitchen doorway, but a tall countertop with stools blocked the way. Behind the bar, shelves lined the walls filled with bottles of the varying color of amber. Hank collided gazes with the bartender holding court at the counter, a stout figure, trimmed beard, arms outstretched to full length like a bulldog protecting puppies. The man's gaze didn't invite company. Ah, the muscle.

Hank took in the rest of the room. A large space sported several settees lining the walls, covered in rich green velvet. Two other imposing chaises stood adjacent in front of a grand fireplace nearly big enough to step into. A glittering chandelier hung overhead, sporting at least fifty candles. Its many faceted crystal droplets magnified the feeble candles, making it glitter like a mother lode vein of diamonds highlighted by a dozen miners' hat lights. The rainbow sparkles swirled on the walls drawing Hank's attention to two ornate doorways.

Couples filed in and out of the two openings. They appeared to be lit, but not at the degree of the current parlor. The rattle of dice and cries of both excitement and dismay intertwined in a loud burst. Someone had won big, hence, someone else had lost equally. From the looks of the grandeur and the adult diversions, Hank could only

assume the entire bottom floor had been dedicated to the purpose of captivating and beguiling any man who dared to enter.

"No refreshment? Then perhaps the gaming tables?"

Bellmira motioned to the door on the left side of the fireplace, and as the area cleared, he could make out four tables. From his limited view, one rectangular table with bumpers corralled the thrown dice while the other circular table lay speckled with cards. From a business perspective, Bellmira had built the pinnacle of man's entertainment—alcohol, cards, dice, and women.

A young blond, who couldn't have been more than fifteen, sidled up beside Bellmira.

"Ah, Daleetha. You've arrived. This gentleman needs your attention. Make sure he feels at home."

A wink from Bellmira set Hank's teeth on edge, but thankfully the carnally-charged woman sauntered off with a wave. He glanced to the blond child at his elbow. Dressed in white, she was a vision, her delicate form catching male eyes all around the room. So, Bellmira had sicced her finest merchandise on him. Daleetha vined her fingers around his arm, her lashes fluttering a well-practiced flutter.

"Perhaps we might sit here?"

The girl motioned with her head, her hand gently easing him. He'd taken a step before he froze. "How old are you?"

For a moment, the kittenish veneer slipped from her face and her gingerbread-colored brown eyes dulled. Then a smile widened her pink lips, turning her features into a charming fay. "Old enough."

"Old enough for grammar school?"

Annoyance rippled across her brow. "Certainly not. Perhaps—"

"Just escort me through the rooms. I'll look myself." He couldn't bear for her to run through her practiced line again. She pulled at his sleeve, a little more urgently this time.

"But we could—"

"Nope. Look," he leaned toward her, confusion winking in her eyes, "I'll make it worth your while. Just circulate me."

A small sigh puffed through her lips. Then she lifted her chin. "Very well." She headed through the left door. While the fire in the outer room had allowed a bit of a reprieve from the smell of dirty men, at the door of the gaming room, the sour smell of unwashed humans hit him in the face. He groaned and turned his face a bit. But there was no escaping it. The room was actually stuffed with four tables surrounded by both card sharps and voluptuous women dressed in a rainbow of colors, smiling and winking, taking slaps and gropes from the men they served.

The narrow pathway through the middle of the room made Hank turn sideways and scoot as he scanned the faces. He recognized a few men from Fortstown, but thankfully, none of Moats's men were present, at least not tonight.

The next room held only a few stiff chairs and benches along the wall.

"This is the ballroom," the young strumpet at his side volunteered.

Yes, there were couples swaying in the center of the room, but more of the oscillating, fondling, ravishing sort of way. Apparently the "ballroom" was merely the warm up room before the main attraction. As he stared, one dark-haired floozy spun and yanked her customer from the room toward the back stairway.

As revolting as it was, Hank ignored the tightening of his gut and ran his gaze over the ten to fifteen couples before settling on a man on the far-bench. B.B. had a lapful of woman, his head bent to investigate the exposed flesh at her neck. Hank peeled the girl's fingers from his arm and strode toward them, zig-zagging through the canoodling couples.

"B.B."

Blacky Balch rolled his head back to glance at him. "Not now."

The woman blinked prettily at him and giggled. When B.B. went back to gobbling her neck, she stretched her head back, allowing him full access. B.B. wandered lower.

"I need to talk to you."

This time B.B. tugged his furry head from her flesh and swore. His bloodshot eyes swung to his. "Sutter, you interrupt me again and I'll kill ya."

At that, B.B. swayed to a standing position, tugging the woman with him. He staggered toward the stairs with a swipe. "Tomorrow, then."

By now, the blond sprite had stepped in front of him, her hands exploring Hank's upper body.

"Looks like we've got plenty of time now."

Hank loosened the girl's grip on his arm and stepped away. The laughter from the other room kicked up a notch while his gaze stayed fixed on the darkened hall where B.B. had disappeared up the stairs.

A couple, engrossed in heavy petting bumped into him. Revulsion rose like bile up his throat.

He'd been conceived in this type of environment. Raised dodging the same clientele that circulated around him, warming up their trollops for the conquest that wasn't a conquest at all. Hank backed away from Daleetha who set a hand to her hip and held out the other.

"You said you'd make it worth my while."

Hank yanked three Liberty coins from his pocket and pitched them into her hand. Her narrow look let him know he'd undersold her. Nevertheless, he was sure she had time to make up for the shortfall by midnight.

He spun and stormed toward the front door. At first light he'd be back and he'd break down the front door if he had to. B.B. might be currently occupied. But tomorrow morning, he'd answer to him or find Hank's fingers wrapped around his neck with his second best Colt pressed against his jaw.

For now, he'd back away—just far enough to keep his sights trained on the front door where any horse moving from Bellmira's hitching rail would rouse him. Without Maggie's cabin to his back, a long night of bitter cold awaited him.

Hank gritted his teeth, spun his horse away from the hitching post, and urged his horse toward the woods. This had better be worth it. Recovering what little heritage he possessed would at least allow him to put the past to rest…and focus on his future.

Maggie's head twitched to the left and she froze underneath her quilt. She swore she'd heard a snap. Her eyes darted first to Hank's gun on the small table next to her bed and then to the front door before shifting to the back one. Even in the banked firelight, she could picture the thick bars she'd laid in place and checked numerous times before settling into bed.

Huddled under a mound of blankets, she tapped her pointer finger to the faint ticks from the mantle clock. The last time she'd peeled the blankets back and padded to the fireplace, the gingerbread clock's face had shown a bit past one. That had been a long time ago.

She squinted to see the hands on the round outline of the clock, but it was no use. Besides, did she really want to know what she already knew? Hank would not be back tonight. A snuffle worked its way up her throat. He'd chosen to stay at the bawdy house. He'd been pulled right back into the one thing he'd sworn he'd never do.

Pinching her eyes shut to cease the moisture that begged to gather, she let anger mount instead. Yes, let the fury rise. Even counterfeit rage would do. Anything to stem the wreckage Hank now wrought on her heart.

The wind whistled an ominous high-pitched keening sound as if the ghosts of the deep had gathered to mourn a great passing. Her body tightened into a ball. Seldom did the noise from the roofline make such a racket, but it always disconcerted her when the wind blew just right. But why tonight of all nights? The night Hank would be absent from his post?

Maggie plugged her ears with her fingers, then tugged them back out. Hiding from the eerie wailing would keep her from hearing

anything else approaching the cabin. The window rattled and she tensed. The wind now had isolated the only way to get inside her home. Perhaps if she stuffed some more wool scraps in the window crevice, it would take care not only of the rattle, but the icy wisps of air as well.

She slid from the bed and padded to her basket of wool scraps. Grabbing a handful, the wind shrieked so loud she tensed her shoulders. The sooner she got this task done, the sooner she could huddle back in bed. She lit the lantern and turned it down low. Surely this would only take a minute or two. Maggie snatched back the curtain and gave a gasp.

A face pressed against the pane of glass.

Chapter Sixteeen

The egg-cooking, long-haired, greasy, grimy, slimy— Maggie cut her list of the man-boy's horrible attributes in half—gang member leered at her through the glass. No, wait. It was a different one. He resembled the egg cooker with his grungy mane. Glory, had the vermin multiplied?

He had one finger pried into a hole in the corner of the window frame while his face smirked at her. Was his name Leonard? No, that was the egg-cooking assailant from a few weeks ago. Perhaps Worthy? Why this seemed important in a time like this was beyond her. When his eyes lit on hers, a sickly grin vined across his face. He jostled the wooden edges of the casement.

With a cry, she grabbed a butter knife from the table and whacked at his lone finger poking through the bottom corner like an invading snake. He growled and shook the sash harder. That sent her

scurrying back to the small table near her bed to snatch up Hank's gun.

"You get away." She tapped the gun on the glass right in front of his face.

He dropped down out of sight, but his hands came back wielding a knife that he pried into the bottom of the window. Maggie cocked back the hammer but hesitated.

If she shot, she'd shatter the window. Then he'd have clear access to enter. If she waited, he might pry the window from the frame. Her eyes grazed the door. Stepping out also gave him entrance, yet she could shoot him without damaging the window. Her breath now came in short gasps, her arms trembling as she clenched the gun handle. How dead a shot was she, especially as her body quaked? What to do?

Something thudded against the outside wall of the cabin. The hands and knife disappeared. Then she heard a shuffle and murmurs. Thumping ensued. Worthy came into view, grappling with the arms of someone she couldn't see. Then a fist connected with his face and down the scoundrel went. Maggie pressed her face against the pane to try to see more, but the closer she got, the more she blocked the light.

The muffled sounds of the scuffle stopped. Time ticked by. Maggie held up the lantern and angled it from one side of the window to other. But only darkness met her eyes. She lifted the hurricane lamp and puffed the flame out.

As her eyes adjusted, she could make out the stars, but little else. The cloud-covered moon made it difficult to see much of

anything. She tightened her grip on the curtain edge and gave a start when a tapping came on the back door.

"Maggie?"

Hank! With a sharp breath, she dashed toward the back door and unbarred it. His unmistakable shadow stood there. She reached out and yanked him in and quickly secured the door.

"You came. You were here."

Hank gave only a nod, hat dipping only slightly. With unsure fingers, she relit the lamp. His hand pulled a hanky from his pocket and touched it to his face.

"Are you hurt?" Maggie rushed forward, urging him into a chair. With unsure fingers, she relit the lamp. Indeed his face showed worse for wear for her rescue. His read swollen eye and bloody mouth and nose drew a gasp from her. "Oh, Hank."

A short grunt disguised as a chuckle slipped from his lips. "You're harder to guard than a single peppermint stick at a kid's Christmas party."

His rumble of laughter made her want to crawl into his lap and hug him tight. But she kept her attention on the split in his eyebrow and the blood pumping from his nose and lip.

"What happened to the boy?"

"Boy? Worthy may look young, but he's got plenty of…experience."

Hank's hesitation sent a quiver through her middle. He was right. The kid might be young, but he was strong and had little moral fiber. As she knew first hand, those attributes were a dangerous

combination. From the dry sink's pitcher, she fetched a bit of water in a bowl, wet the hanky, and dabbed at Hank's battered face.

"That's a sad, sad testimony."

Hank merely inclined his head. She rested her hand beneath his chin to tip it towards the light. His cool skin warmed beneath her fingers. Hank didn't flinch when she wiped the slash at his brow. Despite her ministrations, gentle yet firm, his eyes stayed on her. The now familiar sensation of Hank's allure tried to set up shop in her chest. She clamped her bottom lip in her teeth to stifle the sensations Hank could render in a mere glance.

Maggie blinked and concentrated her thoughts away from her emotions. Hank had saved her from another close call. How he managed to show up just in time niggled at her. "I thought you were at Bellmira's."

"I was. Felt the need to return."

She pulled the cloth from his brow. "Why? Feeling guilty?"

His head recoiled a bit at her words. "Guilty? Maybe. But only about leaving you."

Only one thought hammered in Maggie's brain. He'd come back like he'd promised. She tried to swallow the swell in her throat and spun to toss the water into the fireplace coals. The hiss added to the wail of the wind as it lit the side of the house. Her gaze wandered to the clock. Seemed they had a pattern of late-night visits. Yet he'd set off for Bellmira's some time ago. Long enough to… Suddenly she spun.

"How long were you outside?"

Hank shrugged. "An hour or so, I guess."

"Just an hour?"

Hank stood, making her sidestep him. "Now, before you get all het up—"

"Whyever would I get het up, Hank?" She fisted her hands and threw the cloth on the table. "Because you're ashamed of shirking your promise to keep me safe or ashamed of what you'd done in the last few hours?"

"You know me better than that."

"Do I?" she spat.

It only made sense, didn't it? Would she have ever guessed Hank Sutter to be involved in a thieving gang? No. Never. Yet here he was, involved in Moats's little plan of recovering the stolen gold. Her eyes darted to the ceiling where she'd nailed the drop-down door back into place. Hank, gold-stealing thief. Protector? Doubtful.

Her breathing grew as rough as the moment she'd discovered Worthy plastered against the window but for a totally different reason. Was he really any different than that piece of rubbish that had tried to claw his way through her window?

So, Hank felt guilty, did he? Probably on more levels than one. But tonight, it was obvious why. It wasn't because he'd aligned with a lawless gang and not because he'd left his post of protection. No, his guilt, if he truly had any, sprang from staying at the bawdy house enjoying its wares. For why else would a man spend several hours at Bellmira's? There was only one answer. He interrupted her runaway thoughts.

"Listen to me—"

"No. You're just like all the rest. Scrabbling around for your opportunity." She pointed to the door. "Get out."

"Maggie, I didn't—"

"Out!"

For a moment he just stood there and breathed, his shoulders riding up and down. Then he swiped a hand across his chin and he bobbed his head. "Fine."

He tugged the door open and dropped down the steps, but he held a hand up to keep her from shutting the door. His face came in and out in the flicking lamp light.

"Remember. Trust is an important thing."

Her teeth clenched while tears knocked at her lashes. "Yes. It is."

With all her strength, she slammed the door and buckled the bar into place. Despite her surging fury, that blamed moisture dampened her lashes. She wiped it away with a sling of her hand. It was obvious Hank failed to understand one thing.

Trust was a two-way street.

Hank shoved up in the unfamiliar, yet familiar man's face. "You got no right to batter a woman."

Why he'd stepped in front of Bellmira's muscle man to stop the patron from assaulting the young brunette tart, he had no idea. Just learning that this degenerate was his uncle, his mother's youngest brother, shifted everything sideways in his gut. That, and being thrown out by Maggie. Hank had shown up at dawn, thundering for a fight.

"She ain't no woman. She's a tramp. And she done stole my gold poke."

Despite the fact that the man's eyes and chin threw Hank in mind of his mother, he drew back a fist and connected it with the sleepy, inebriated man's jaw. His "uncle" went down like a lamp, his head bouncing on Bellmira's hardwood parlor floor. Only then did Hank look up. An assemblage of women, dressed only in chemises, huddled near the doorway, Bellmira their first line of defense, with her hands on her hips. The bouncer stood near, sleepy-eyed, but sleeves shoved up his forearms, ready for the next wave of violence.

Hank stepped back, his eyes going to the woman on the chaise lounge, black eye and swollen face. Some kind of stock he'd come from.

B.B. pushed through the gaggle of girls, buttoning his fur vest, hair askew. "What's going on here?"

His words were as unsteady as his gait. He stumbled to a stop when he saw Hank. "You get the message I left—"

Oh, Hank had gotten the message tacked on the door all right. Then he'd found the very man he'd thought he'd been looking for, busy pounding the woman he'd hired, in the front room. The blacksmith only now seemed to absorb the man laid flat on the floor.

"Huh. Well, that's him." B.B. motioned to the prone man, who now rubbed the back of his head with a moan. "Your kin. Ain't that what you were looking for?"

"Most certainly not." Hank spun and strode to the door. Soft hands encased his and he paused at the door.

"You come round anytime, Cowboy. No charge." Bellmira winked at him.

He shook his head and gritted his teeth. "I'm not a cowboy. And I won't be back."

The sun lightened the trees on his long trip back to Maggie's cabin, not that she wanted him there. Now more than ever, so much stood between them. And it had to end, somehow.

He shrugged, dead tired, and tied his horse up in the shelter of Maggie's lean-to. He'd weather her wrath to give his horse some break from the ever-present frosty wind. He rubbed the faithful horse down and served up a scoop of feed. Shoot, even Moats would be ready to slice his neck for boarding his horse within the shed. But did it matter? The gang's leader would cut him down without a thought when it became convenient.

As for him, he was through—through chasing after being a marshal, through digging amongst dirt to find some kind of heritage, and through with his connection with Moats. He would stay for one thing and one thing only—for Maggie.

He grabbed the scratchy wool blanket from his saddle, quietly trod up on the porch of the cabin, and snatched up the bench. Tonight, he'd camp on Maggie's back door near the window even though his new post would bring him in contact with that incessant wind with the will to freeze every living creature exposed on the land. And tonight, it would be him.

He settled the bench dead center of the back door. Then he eased his weary body down and covered himself with the blanket. To block the wind, he tugged down the brim of his hat. Not cozy by any

stretch, even with Maggie's new Christmas quilt, but maybe he could grab a few hours of sleep.

Hank's neck snapped forward, and he roused himself, moving slightly on the hard bench. The temperature had to be close to zero, and it was terribly hard to get comfortable for any stretch of time. He breathed slowly, watching the fog of his breath in the misty morning. What he wouldn't give to be inside the cabin on the pallet in front of the fireplace...with Maggie.

A dog barked in the distance, and he jerked his head up once more. *God help me to rest. I've got to protect Maggie.* He shook under the leather coat and wool blanket. His beard sported frozen droplets, and he ducked his chin into his collar to thaw the ice crystals.

A muffled sound brought him awake again. His weary eyes searched the landscape. Something seemed afoot. Hank's eyelids slid shut once more. Again the howl and his eyes opened to survey the area. Nothing, yet something. He took a deep breath and leaned his head forward once more.

The next thing he knew the door behind him swung open. Hank jumped up with his Peacemaker drawn, only to meet Maggie's shocked face.

"I—sorry."

Her hand fluttered to her throat. "I would think."

He tossed the scratchy blanket aside and moved the bench from blocking the door.

Her eyes widened. "What in Heaven's name are you doing back here?"

A rooster crowed near the barn, and Hank reached up a hand to massage his stiff neck. "My job."

She set her hands on her hips. "You look like death."

Was that a snatch of sympathy in her eyes? "You really need to get some rest."

He grunted. "No place to lay my head, or something like that."

Maggie sniffed and pulled the wool cape closer. "You? Quoting Bible verses? My, a special treat, especially knowing where you spent several hours last night."

Maggie flounced through the door, swathed in her thick wool cape, her chin held high. Enough. He grabbed her arm and spun her around.

"I didn't do what you think I did."

Surprise, then annoyance, rippled across her brow. "I know exactly—"

"Stop talking, Maggie, and listen. I went to find B.B. but he was busy, so I camped outside to wait for daybreak. Only, I couldn't sleep so I rode back here. That's when I saw Worthy."

"You didn't…" She blinked, snowflakes falling and snagging in her lashes. Her eyes grew a bit too shiny. Not a good sign.

Maggie trembled. Her voice came in a hoarse whisper. "Tell me right now, Hank Tobias Sutter. Did you or did you not engage one of the bawdy house girls?"

Chapter Seventeen

"Maggie," Hank shook her arms. "Don't you know me? Don't you know me at all? After all of our years together? My mother raised me while doing those exact things, immoral things, and I hated it. It made me sick. I grew up with a deep sense of worthlessness as a son of a twisted man who'd used a woman for his own purposes and then disappeared."

He stepped away and assessed her, her soft lips agape, her small hands clutching at her cape. "So to answer your questions plainly, I didn't lie with one of Bellmira's women. And I won't ever."

Snow thickened as it fell across the yard. Hank dropped his head and pulled a small volume from his pocket. He'd practically forgotten the presence of the thin New Testament. It had comforted him in the last several years. As he stared at it, a dawning bloomed.

He did have a Father, an everlasting One who was holy and true. One who loved him with an everlasting love, who called Hank His child. Why had he been searching for kin for so long, especially when what he found was less than his expectation?

Hank took a deep breath. So many years he'd wasted trying to find something he already had—a loving righteous Father. Something deep and marvelous solidified in him. He raised his eyes to the only woman he'd ever loved. Suddenly, the future held hope.

He pressed the testament into Maggie's hands. "Something I picked up while hunting buffalo for the train men. I think I'm just now beginning to understand its true meaning."

Her brows rose, but she took the book from him and flipped through it. "I see."

Her gaze searched the planes of his face, as if she looked to verify his claim of innocence. She must have found the truth in his eyes for she pressed the testament back against his chest and whirled to stride to the shed. Hank prayed she'd seen more than just the truth about last night.

He slid the Bible in his jacket pocket and started after her. He trailed her while she plucked the eggs from beneath the chickens and set them in her basket. Her cloak transformed her into a mythical figure in the near darkness of the shed. A strange urge to share his realization of a loving Father rose in him, but her chilly demeanor put him off.

"After the chores, I'll be staying in. I'm going to do some reading and resting. I didn't sleep much last night." She paused at the barn door and studied him. "Hank, I suggest you find a warm,

comfortable spot and get a nap in yourself. And I'm not saying my porch. You look like you could use a couple hours of uninterrupted sleep."

He nodded but kept silent, noticing she didn't offer the floor in front of her fireplace. The cow lowed as they entered the stall, and as the day before, Hank's eyes continued to search the entire building.

"Since Sugar is already sharing her spot with your horse, I'm sure she won't mind you napping here." Down Maggie plopped on the three-legged stool.

He had a strong desire to settle on the opposite side to help milk, but he didn't dare leave his post. Both Leonard and Worthy had tried their hand at getting to Maggie. It had to be circulating among the other men. As a matter of fact, most likely as soon as Moats awoke, he'd be looking him up. And Hank doubted he'd be in good spirits.

Hank shook his head to clear it. His head had a continuous buzzing and felt fuzzy from lack of sleep. Maybe he would tuck into a pile of fresh straw for a nap today if Maggie promised to stay put and bar the doors. "I might try catching forty winks."

Milk frothed into the bucket, steam rising, and Hank turned to pace the doorway. He stuck his head out and noticed the pink sky lighting to the east burning off the light mist from the early morning. None of Moats's men had yet shown their faces. They probably still huddled inside the makeshift tents in the woods. At least he'd hoped so.

Behind him, the bucket handle squeaked, alerting him that she'd finished. He turned to observe her progress as she patted the cow.

"Let me take the bucket." He grasped the wire handle and headed back to the door, but paused. "You coming?"

She shrugged. "Yeah. I've...been doing some thinking."

Hank straightened. That couldn't be good. "About?"

The cow pulled back from the stanchion, catching her head against the weathered wood. The animal twisted to gaze at them with big dark eyes. Maggie backtracked, loosed her, and led her to the door. "You're right. I mean...about this whole mess last night and me jumping to conclusions. I think I...overreacted and I'm sorry."

Hank kept his face still, not wanting to stir Maggie's wrath with any I-told-you-so quirks dancing across his face.

She raised her head and looked him dead in the eye. "I'm sort of in a corner. I have no one to trust. Not truly. Except...you."

He stepped closer, but she held up her hand. "But I have questions. So many, in fact. Like what's going to happen now?"

A flock of birds suddenly took flight outside, and Hank poked his head out to do a once-over sweep. When he turned back, Maggie's questioning eyes met his.

"Things will go back to normal, I guess." He firmed his voice.

"Normal? I don't even know what that means anymore. Will Corbin get to come back? Can we still live here? Will we ever be safe again?" She tucked her arms across her bosom and paced a couple of steps. "And what about you, Hank? What will you do? Where do...we stand?"

Her unreadable expression froze him. "I reckon I'll just pray on it and see."

She blinked and stared a long moment before she spoke. "That's it? Just we'll see?"

Hank let his shoulders slump. Now was not the time to reiterate the deep feelings he held for her. Everything was off and out of place. Besides, she'd brushed away his confession before. In her current state of turmoil, he doubted she'd cotton to his repeated affirmation. And all of her questions? He really had no answers.

But one thing was clear. If he had a future with Maggie, he had to somehow extricate himself from the gang without getting himself killed and eradicate the gang's presence here. And for the moment, he couldn't promise anything. "For now."

Maggie's pink lips compressed, her face suddenly as cold as the temperature. "Hmm. Fine. Excuse me. I think Sugar needs some air."

The cow seemed eager to exit and pushed through the door, leaving some of her red hair lodged in the splintery wood of the door facing. Maggie took off in a brisk hike, and Hank sauntered after them.

She never said another word. The cow lumbered free, and they walked up the hill to the cabin. At the back door she pulled the heavy bucket from his hand. Her features froze stiff as laundry hanging on a line in January.

"I'm going to churn, bake bread, read, and rest. I promise I won't leave the cabin, and I promise I'll bar the door. If someone comes to the window, I'll shoot his face straight through. Now, I know you have a hard time committing to anything, but please swear you'll return to the barn for some rest."

Unwilling to stir her up, he nodded. She hesitated and seemed to study him. Her expression didn't encourage conversation.

"Fine. Fine and dandy." Maggie stomped into the doorway and slammed the door shut.

Maggie, fueled by anger, completed the chores in a whipstitch then climbed the pegs to the loft. Muttering to herself about Hank's hardheadedness, she bagged all the gold she'd found inside the shocks, laid them on the floor in the corner, and piled the wheat on top. She climbed down and tapped the nails back in place, sealing the upstairs from any intruder's eyes.

If Hank had given her some indication of his intentions, she'd have spilled her guts about the gold. But no, he had to be all ambiguous and vague. She huffed and parked her hands on her hips. At least she was fairly confident he'd not indulged at Bellmira's.

Her eyes wandered up. She'd found fifty sheaves full of coins. Approximately seventy-five thousand dollars rested above her head. Anger drained from her weary body, and a shiver of fear slid up her spine. Maybe she should just hand it over and be done with it. It would certainly be a relief. And if she could trust the vile men to leave and never return, she'd dump it in Moats's lap and scurry back to the cabin. But she knew this gang would be forever a thorn in her side, not to mention the dandy who'd appeared.

She shuffled to the bed and collapsed. No, she had to find a way to expose the crooks to ensure the safety of her son and her land. With the willy-nilliness of Hank, she couldn't lean on him. And who was that dandy and why had he taken her mother's things?

Well, she would find that awful man and get her heirlooms back. Corbin wouldn't be safe until she discovered his hidden agenda. And she had to find where Hank's loyalty rested. What was his true allegiance? Gracious, she had to figure out Hank.

Her eyes drifted closed. From the slant of the light in the back window it was late afternoon. Perhaps she'd sleep until morning. She drew in a long chilly breath. But that would be unwise. Sugar had to be milked by evening. Her head grew hazy with sleep. Hank would do it. At least she could trust him to do that.

Thoughts came slower and slower, her eyelids heavier and heavier. Her last thought was a prayer for wisdom.

Crash! Maggie gasped awake at the noise. *Wham.* She bolted upright on the bed, her eyes darting to the tip of an axe through the front door. With a small cry she leaped up and ran for the back door. Through her sleep-muddled reality, her fingers fumbled with the bar.

The axe behind her shattered wood, and she whimpered. The gun. Why hadn't she snatched up Hank's gun? At last she pried the thick timber from the holds, but it was too late. Footsteps sounded behind her and hands seized her shoulders. A cloth muffled her scream.

Moats's leering face appeared inches from hers. "Well, my little lady. It's time to stop hiding."

More hands came around her head and secured a strip of cloth to keep the handkerchief firmly inside her mouth. Her tongue pushed at the nasty tasting wad of cloth but only managed to gag herself. A couple of men jerked her hands behind her. Leonard stepped up, a

smirk stretching his face. He grasped several lengths of hemp in his nubby hands. A rough rope scraped against the skin on her wrists.

Tears rushed to her eyes, and a sob strangled in her throat. This was it. They'd come for their pound of flesh. Maggie was at the mercy of several men, corrupt as politics. And where was Hank? She thrashed and kicked only to be rewarded by laughter.

Then, a man with a wide scar near his brow, grinned at her. "Say night night."

A cloth bag slid over her head. The smell of horse and filth filled her nose. Hands tightened around her ankles and she bucked for all she was worth. That only earned more grubby hands against her body, pressing her down, taking cheap gropes, grasping higher on her legs. Something pressed against the side of her head.

"Kicking only makes it hurt more," the same voice grunted in her ear.

Despite her battle, a rope tightened about her ankles. Sweat broke across her temples, panic like drowning water around her. She crumpled into several pairs of arms as tears wet the cloth encircling her head. She was done for. The reckoning had arrived. *Dear God, where was Hank?*

Carried now, she heard boots on her front porch, felt the jolts of being taken down the steps. Then the jostling continued. Where were they taking her?

"Right here, boys. Easy. Precious cargo."

Moats's voice. Scornful laughter surrounded her as she was released. Her body pressed against something solid. She bucked and kicked only to connect with something hard on all sides.

"Now we can't have that. Stuff the tent canvas around her."

Maggie sniffed in spasms as she felt the material being crammed against her body. Then something crashed above. Her eyes widened when she recognized nails being driven into the top of the container in which she now laid. Voices came in muffles.

"That should do it."

Leonard's voice.

"All right, load up." Moats this time.

Hysteria clutched her chest, and she began to thrash.

"You stop that, you hear? If I have to open that box, I'll be getting me a little sugar, Mrs. Robbins, and that's a fact."

Maggie sobbed silently, too frightened to even pray. She lay in the container for some time, trying to calm herself. Crying would do no good. It would soon clog her nostrils, her only way of getting oxygen. She had to keep alert. Think of a way to escape. Maggie screwed her eyes shut at the impossibility of that thought.

Footsteps approached. Then the box moved and rose. From the rhythm and the sway of movement, it seemed she was being carried by several men. They stopped and she felt the sickening sensation of being rotated. A grating beneath her indicated the box now slid into...something.

Soon, by the jostling motions plus the sounds of leather, she surmised she now traveled in the back of a wagon. The ride gave her time to speculate. The fact that Hank had been absent meant something horrible must have happened. Why, oh why had she sent him to the shed? Why hadn't she yanked him inside the cabin and let

him snooze by the fireplace? Then she wouldn't be trapped, fighting claustrophobia and dread of being ravished by a gang of men.

She could hear more voices now and the rocking wagon drew to a stop. Her breath sped up. Would they open the box? She strained to hear. Just odd sounds echoed to her amidst mumbled language. Then came a soft thunk and another. Was something being loaded—wait. There was something more...sloshing, like—water. *Water?*

She gulped with terror. Would they drop her into the Missouri River? Maggie shoved at the handkerchief with her tongue, trying to remove the soggy material that tasted like dirt and sweat. She had to get out. Now!

The ropes chaffed her skin as she squirmed this way and that, only managing to produce a warm stickiness. Blood. She huffed air through her nose. It was no use struggling. Her hands were fastened as solid as her feet. A hideous thought sliced through her. Which would be worse? Suffering at the hands of the gang's sadistic appetites or drowning in a box at the bottom of a cold river?

God, help me. Save me. The prayer came at last. She pleaded as the container lifted. To her relief the box slammed against something solid, nearly bursting her ears. Her muscles tensed and her head rang. Faint voices drifted around her, but there were so many she couldn't make them out. Everything remained still, and Maggie pondered where she might possibly be.

Some time later, Maggie tried to fathom how long she'd been encased. In her state of being where a few moments waxed an eternity, time seemed much, much longer. The box now floated from its perch, went airborne for just a moment, before slamming to the

ground. Maggie clenched her body as the box rolled. She ended up face down, her body smarting from slamming against the wooden sides. Someone swore.

"Flip that over. Ain't ya got no sense?"

The box rocked, and she fell once again against the bottom planks.

"Bring it over here."

She wedged her feet against the side of the box, cushioned with tent canvas, and did the same with her rear and head. If she was thrown again, perhaps she could at least break her fall. But the box eased down, and above her, the screeching sound indicated nails being removed.

She never thought she'd welcome those hands upon her body, but she could have cried when they pulled her from the box.

"Check her."

The bag whooshed from her head. Through her nostrils, she sucked the fresh crisp air into her lungs and gazed about with wide eyes in the dusky light. The woods surrounded them. She sat on the frozen earth with those ingrates surrounding her, two of which held each of her bound arms. She raised her head.

Moats stood before her.

Chapter Eighteen

Moats's nauseating smile soured Maggie's stomach. Now what?

"Perfect. Load her up."

Maggie shook her head, pleading with her eyes. They wouldn't put her in that terror-rendering sarcophagus again, would they? Oh, no. Not the box. Not again.

He grunted a laugh without a snatch of humor. "Did ya not care for the coffin? I'll admit, ain't the best way to travel. But it sure does a bang-up job of hiding a perty little lady."

The gang leader motioned to the others. "Get that mare ready. We'll let her ride for a while. If she behaves."

He winked then. If he'd have been closer, and her mouth unbound, she would have spit at his vile face. Instead, she made a

mumbling sound of wrath which only made Moats run a tongue around inside his mouth as he ogled her.

"Don't worry, little gal. You'll be delivered safe and sound."

And then what? The haunting question had no outlet, so she merely tried to relax her throat and breathe deeply.

In ten minutes they had her aboard a bay mare, Maggie's legs tied to the saddle's stirrups and belly cinch. When the scarred man approached toting that smelly bag, she shook her head and grunted over and over in gibberish mumbles. Moats eyed her a moment.

"Leave it off for now." He pointed at her with his hand-rolled soggy cigar stub. "You mind your manners, hear?"

She nodded. For now she had no choice. Even though dark encroached, she could see. And that was a small comfort.

The men mounted up, and she flicked her gaze around in the dark to count them. Four men plus Moats, including that opportunistic brute, Leonard. She'd have sworn there were more when they'd grabbed her. At the time it had seemed a virtual army.

Still, her heart sank. How could she overcome five men? Besides, with her hands tied to the saddle horn and her legs to the stirrups, she wasn't going anywhere without the bulky saddle beneath her.

What could they possibly be planning? Recalling the failed attempts of Leonard and Worthy, that vile egg-cooking man-boy, she feared she knew. An involuntary retch against the cloth in her mouth made her skin turn hot for just a moment. Then the wind and spitting snow froze over the momentary rise in body temperature. She shivered, pacifying her jerking throat and heaving stomach.

No matter what, she had to survive. She *had* to make it. Corbin depended upon her. Maggie sucked in long, cold breaths through her nose. She had to keep her wits and look for any opportunity to escape. But even a chance to flee seemed doomed. The snow descended with a vengeance, like thick curtains, reducing the visibility. Already, the horse shuffled through white fluff nearly a foot deep. Running and remaining alive in such weather seemed impossible.

She shivered under the smelly buffalo skin. Where were they going? She certainly hoped they had a good sense of direction, for not a thing was visible. Hank's face crossed her thoughts. His earnestness while they'd talked this morning made her want to weep. Had it only been a few hours ago?

Why hadn't she thrown her pride to the wayside and launched herself into his arms? Heaven help her, she may have lost her only chance to tell him how she really felt. To tell him of the hopes and dreams she secretly held of their future together. But instead, she'd been miffed by his put-off comment. And now, she may never lay eyes on him again.

He'd been so wholesome and bare-naked honest when he'd handed her that Bible. So…earnest and open. Oh, Hank. Dear, dear Hank. What had become of him? With dread, a verse crossed her mind and her eyes popped open. *Or else how can one enter into a strong man's house, and spoil his goods, except he first bind the strong man? And then he will spoil his house.*

The Bible quote came unbidden. Probably brought on by the remembrance of the New Testament Hank had pressed into her hand.

A whimper found its way around the gag. What had they done with him? Just as the Bible verse outlined, he wouldn't have allowed her to be kidnapped—not willingly anyway. That could only mean... Hank could be dead or dying. *Oh, dear God. Help Hank.*

The horses plowed through the snow for hours. Exhausted and lulled by the rocking motion of the horse's gait, Maggie's eyes drifted closed, and her body leaned forward. Icy crystals on the horse's mane dug into her cheek. She tried to care and attempted to revive. But her muscles grew slack, and her mind eased away from reality.

The sudden stop roused her for a moment. She opened her eyes and struggled to straighten her stiff joints. The lack of a moon rendered her sense of sight useless in the darkness. The shadows of tree trunks appeared and disappeared. Only the sounds of the horses' muffled hoofs and the creak of leather gave assurance that her predicament hadn't changed.

Were they lost? Suddenly, she didn't care. She was frozen, bruised, and exhausted. Low mutters indicated a discussion between the men. But it was too muffled and far away to make out any words. Then, the horse jerked back into motion. Maggie let her body bow forward and pressed her head once more against the horse's neck.

Time floated like bubbles in a tub of water. Maggie drifted in and out of sleep, aware, yet unaware. Then, the animal below her halted. Maggie hadn't even lifted her head before rough hands dragged her from the horse, and someone, likely that scarred man, shoved the cloth bag over her face again.

Somewhere, a cabin door opened, and warmth flooded the space around her. The heavy buffalo skin slid from her, and involuntary shivers rippled through her. The salty smell of beans caused her stomach to clench. Then she was shoved into a hard chair. Maggie took short breaths, wide awake now. Shadows danced through the dark material.

The bag yanked free with a few of her hairs, and she winced. Catty-corner from her a fireplace burned, and the strange dandy stepped into her line of vision. A sort of odd humor crossed his greasy, pale face, and anger mingled with fear lit Maggie's insides. It was him.

"Welcome, my dear, to my humble abode."

She glared at him.

"Remove the gag. This is certainly no way to treat a lady." The small smile on his face indicated otherwise.

Moats snorted. "You told us to bring her, not how."

Maggie heaved as Leonard thrust his fat finger in her cheek to pry the handkerchief free. She resisted the temptation to chomp down, only wishing to have her mouth be unobstructed. Maggie coughed and gagged once the cloth was removed. Then she sucked in a huge gasp of air. Her throat throbbed painfully but, praise Jesus, her windpipe was open.

The cabin door slammed shut as one of the lackeys exited. No doubt he'd went to tend the animals in the unforgiving weather. The three of the five men made short work of securing her limbs to the chair, despite her attempts to wound them in the process.

"Feisty thing, isn't she?" The greasy man laughed and brushed her chin with his finger. "I like that."

Moats removed a pot from the flames of the fireplace. "You have no idea."

The dandy cast a glance at him and mocked. "Yes, help yourself to anything you desire."

The gang leader's bear face split into a grin. "Don't mind if I do."

The suited man's face grew stiff, but he ignored Moats, turning his attention back to Maggie. She studied the small round scab on his cheesy cheek and remembered the night he'd extinguished the match against his skin. This man was a dangerous man to reckon with.

Her eyes glanced about the cabin. A small round table lay in the back corner where Moats and the three other rejects hovered around the pot of beans. A small cot lay directly opposite her against the wall. Except for a chest and the table's mismatched chairs, nothing else filled the cabin. Her eyes returned to her repugnant host's face.

"Perhaps the lady desires an entrée as well?"

Fury crested in her stomach. Food? She'd been abused and manhandled into a panicked state, and all he could offer was a bowl of beans? The leering man leaned forward and rage spiked. Maggie lunged and snapped her head forward. The impact of their heads colliding made Maggie see stars littered in a blast of white lightning. Her chair wobbled and then tumbled sideways. She grimaced as her knee struck the hardwood floor and then her upper arm. But she managed to keep her head safe from whacking against the planks.

The men, now seated at the table, laughed and slapped the wooden table.

"Need a little help there, boss?" Moats's voice split the air.

The dandy stomped one of his shiny shoes. "Remove this sorceress from the floor."

One of the men scurried behind her and everything shifted. The room spun for just a moment before righting. Her head throbbed. The only thing that gave her a smidgeon of satisfaction was the dribble of blood dripping from a small cut from the center of Dr. Stills' forehead.

His nostrils flared and his lips twitched. "Well played, milady. Well played. However, the penalty for your assault shall be the absence of sustenance. Perhaps starvation will entice you to constrain your passions."

With that, he spun on his heel and strode from the room. The slam of the door made her shudder. She clenched her eyes closed and breathed. Resolve hardened in her heart.

Let him starve her out. Didn't he realize her hopeless situation? She, a prisoner, Corbin gone, Hank most likely dead at this point—there was absolutely nothing to lose. Every ounce of her strength would be spent fighting the inevitable. The war may be lost, but she knew one thing was certain. God had given her a spirit of power. The deep-set fervor to fight and resist even unto death swelled within her.

The memory of Hank holding his New Testament, quoting what lay between its pages, brought both an indention to the dimple in her cheek and a tear to her eye. Die, she might. But on that journey, she would bite, scratch, kick, maim, crush, pummel, and ram her way to

defeat. And in that, even if she died, she'd win. For she would've done her best by her son and the man she loved. *God, help me be bold.* Her soul lifted just a shade.

Let the battle begin.

Hank woke with a gasp and blinked. A groan poured forth. Every muscle throbbed. His cheeks puffed out in an effort to control the searing pain that flogged his depleted body. With his head bowed, he only saw white. He blinked and focused, finding his gaze on his own booted feet— trussed and bound—planted in the deep snow. He was still in one piece, at least he thought so. Flexing his jaw, he rotated his head. Heaven help him, he hurt.

Breathing in a few deep breaths to fortify himself, he raised his head. *Woods*—he was somewhere deep amongst the trees. Snow covered his upright body and still tumbled down around him. He opened his hands, tightening and relaxing, to get some blood flowing. But when he attempted to move, he couldn't. Come to think of it, why had he been out cold—standing?

His bleary brain took slow inventory. His hands were fastened behind him, tight to something rough. Rotating and flexing were about the extent of his movements. Hank looked down. His feet also held fast against something round and immovable.

He blinked, shook his head, and lifted his chin to the sounds of an orchestra of pain. Naked branches swayed above while fat, white flakes landed on his face. Ugh. He was lashed to a tree. Not an overly large one, but a tree nonetheless. He waggled his head to

bring some comprehension—pain slashed through his skull at the movement. Oh, glory. *Now* he remembered.

He'd awakened in the barn and, still groggy, milked Maggie's cow. Then two of Moats's men jumped him as he exited the doorway. A swift blow to the head had erased the rest, and now, here he was. His gasps transformed into clouds of fog, and he hung his head to gather strength. He felt so cold, so tired.

The acrid smell of wood burning tickled his nose, and he lifted his eyes to search the tree canopy to gauge his location. Maggie's stone chimney peeked through the tree branches just to the right, and puffs of smoke poured out. Maggie? Was she safe?

He fought against the constraints of the hemp at his wrists and feet. The struggle didn't take long to exhaust him, and he sagged against the tree trunk and groaned. Of course, she wasn't safe. He'd been assaulted and tied to a tree.

Dear God. What had they done to her? Dread permeated his frozen nerves, and he strained to untangle himself once more. Pure terror fed his brain. What if they'd killed her? He stilled. What if they hadn't?

He writhed and thrashed until warm liquid trickled to his fingers. With a grunt, he sagged once more against the unyielding support behind him. Drops of sweat dripped from his head, and great puffs of air escaped his lungs. He was too late anyway. Judging by the amount of light, it was morning. He'd been strapped here all night.

He moaned. "God, help Maggie. Keep her safe."

Why hadn't he been able to protect her? How could he have been so stupid? Images of Moats's men pawing at Maggie filled his brain, her violet-blue eyes pleading and begging. He fought against the ropes once more. But for all his effort, he only exhausted himself further. At least he didn't notice the cold now.

The cabin door creaked in the morning air and laughter floated out. Hank's head shot up. Two men strode toward the tree. Fingers Stanley held an axe in one of his hands, his long dirty blond hair swinging beneath the sweat-marked hat on his head. The other—oh, great. Young Mort Worthy walked beside him.

Hank shook his head. Neither man proved to possess much compassion, but Worthy was the antitheses of his name, especially with his failed attempt to break into Maggie's cabin. Worse yet, the kid would be looking for revenge. The teenager continually shocked him with his brutality. It had taken several right hooks to fell the stubborn cuss that night in front of Maggie's window.

Maybe with Fingers, he would have a chance to talk his way out of this mess. Maybe not. After all, Hank's name was at the top of Stilts's hit list. And, of course, Moats factored into the whole scheme of robbing Maggie's husband's gold heist. At least they were both young and stick thin. He yanked at the restraints, hoping he'd managed to loosen them. Nope. Negotiation then?

Worthy stepped up, pulled up his hand, and smeared bear grease across Hank's face. "Hungry?"

Negotiations were not going well. Hank turned away from the putrid smell on his cheek, but kept his eyes on Worthy.

The kid cackled and bent to cleanse his hands in the snow. Both eyes were blackened and one swollen nearly shut. Hank had sure rung his bell. As much as Worthy deserved it, that did not help the situation he was in one bit.

Fingers chuckled, slinging the axe up on his shoulder, chewing on jerky. "I'm surprised you're still alive, Sutter."

Worthy flung the cold snow from his hands and smiled, displaying his uneven greenish teeth. "Well, we'll take care of that, now won't we, Fingers?"

"Where's Maggie?"

They both sniggered. "Not to worry none. That fine piece of woman is in good hands."

"Is she in the cabin? I want to see her."

Worthy wadded up and threw a hunk of snow at him. It made its mark just left of Hank's Adam's apple. From the sting, there must have been a rock embedded in the center. Worthy spewed a string of vile words, grinned, and kicked the snow in victory.

"You see my aim, Fingers? Shoot." Worthy's eyes froze over when he glanced back at Hank. "I ain't near done with you. And you ain't seeing nobody, numbskull."

The boy stepped up and, before Hank could blink, thrust a right hook to his temple. Hank's skull slammed against the tree trunk behind him. Reality spun in dizzying circles. He hung his head and then waggled it to keep unconsciousness at bay.

"I'm a-kill him right now. He done beat me down the other night, and I've got plenty of payback eating me alive."

Worthy's fists hammered until Hank felt sure he'd vomit. He clenched his eyes closed and stiffened his neck to ward off the strength of each impact. But unconsciousness edged in. Blood washed down his face, warming his skin.

"I think we can do better than that." The pounding ceased. Hank barely registered Fingers's voice. "I think we'll get our jollies first though. Go get the horse."

Hank watched the blood drip to the snow below him leaving little pink holes. Then, with some effort, he lifted his head. Blinking at them through a white haze, he could barely see Worthy shaking his head, an odd kind of leer on his lips. "Naw, I'll get that horse later. I gotta watch this first."

Fingers disappeared behind his back, and Hank twisted to see his intention. "Where's Maggie?"

Fingers snorted. "Not your concern. You got bigger fish to fry."

With that, a solid chop sent the tree shuddering. Fingers was right. He was about to be hacked or smashed, whichever came first.

This was not how Hank had ever planned to die.

Chapter Nineteen

H ank's head popped against the tree's trunk.

Worthy screeched in delight. "Cut his leg rope and watch him dance.

Another chunk behind him, and Hank's ankles slipped free of the bindings.

"You might want to lift your feet a little." Worthy's green eyes could barely contain his elation.

Chop after chop sounded behind him and Hank attempted to keep his legs clear of the flying axe. Then the six-inch trunk swayed.

"She's going, she's going," Worthy grinned in sadistic delight.

Hank sent a prayer skyward as the trunk tipped and fell forward yet lurched sideways into the snow. So this was it. This was the end. Maggie's face flashed in front of his eyes as the snow-covered landscape rose up to meet him.

Hank's face dipped into the thick layer of snow but didn't smash him as he expected. His hip dug into the hardened ground, but he was still alive. The tree rolled slightly but, thanks to the branches, didn't land on anything vital. Hank's body jerked against the cutting ropes as the tree settled against the ground. Only his left arm and cheek pressed into the snow. He turned his head to free his mouth from the cold fluff and sucked in several deep breaths. Worthy's gleeful yelps lit the frozen air around him.

"Get the horse, idjit." Fingers's voice came from somewhere above. "We got work to do.

Hank blinked the snow from his eyes and gritted his teeth. He heard nothing but his own breathing for several minutes. Then the two voices interchanged some distance above him.

"Pull it."

The tree shifted and began to move. And although the upper part of the tree gaped from the ground several inches, Hank's head still plowed through the foot of snow, his lower body scraping the ground. He kicked and pushed with his legs, but his torso stayed firmly attached to the trunk.

"I reckon he's thirsty," Worthy's voice floated back to him, "but don't you worry, now. You'll soon have plenty to drink."

Rumbles of the men's laughter could be heard above the ground rasping below him. Drink? Where were they taking him? Realization dawned. *The Big Muddy*. Hank thrashed like never before, but only earned a spot beneath the dragging tree. He ceased at last, turning his face to allow his cheek to take the brunt of the grazes from the snow and earth.

It seemed like they dragged him for hours. On and on. Hank kicked occasionally to ease the pain in his hip taking the bulk of the punishment. Hank swallowed and filled his lungs with air. The tree suddenly tilted, and he flipped sunny side up. The white sky stabbed his eyes.

Fingers appeared above. "Sorry, old buddy. But you were doomed from the start."

"Shove him over, shove him over." Worthy's face leered in, his dark, patchy stubble covered with frozen spittle.

Fingers straightened and pulled the gun from his holster, and Hank shut his eyes. *Here it comes.*

"Worthy, shut yer dang mouth."

But the kid laughed a bit maniacally. "Don't threaten me, Fingers. You gotta lay down some time."

"I'll kill you first if I have to."

Suddenly, the two were faced off above Hank. He blinked his eyes in the overwhelming brightness. Fingers held the gun at Worthy's chest.

The kid snorted. "Done seen the yellow streak down your back in Kansas City. You ain't got the brass to shoot nobody."

"Is that right?"

"Said it, didn't I?" Curses rang from the boy's lips, and a knife appeared in his hand. "You traitor. You think I can't—"

The gun exploded, and Worthy's face froze. Splatters hit Hank's cheek. Red bloomed below the boy's chin. He twitched a couple of times, and Fingers shot again, knocking his body backwards, and he disappeared from Hank's sight.

"Never did like him." Fingers holstered his pistol and glanced to Hank. The man's eyes lifted as he gazed out. The sound of rushing water filled Hank's ears.

"Let me go," Hank sputtered. "This ain't right, Fingers. Think about—"

"No can do, compadre." Fingers's gaze centered on his. "You know too much already. Blast, shoulda killed that lily-livered mouth after the tree was rolling."

Fingers disappeared from view, and the trunk lurched. As it tipped, Hank had one last glimpse of the cleared hill slope before him and, at the bottom—the river. Then the log rocked and rocked again. How many times could a guy almost die in one day? Yet Hank had a sinking feeling this was the one that would take him to the other side of eternity. His two passes were used up.

Hank felt the crest, the tree hesitating in that moment of weightlessness. Then like a stroke of lightning, the mass of branches shifted and the bulk twisted, taking him over the edge.

Everything spun. Light, dark, light dark, faster and faster. Stones flew, flesh tore, grunts exploded from his chest. Down, down his world tumbled, over, under, spinning around the trunk as it plummeted toward the muddy water. Hard dirt and rocks nicked and bruised him. In a fraction of a second he went airborne—an instant to gasp one last breath. Crash, splash, bubbling silence, the shock of the freezing water forced air to spew from Hank's nostrils into the silty water.

The tree rocked back and forth a few moments. Hank's face bobbled to the surface, and he gasped for one last breath before he

rotated beneath the trunk once more. Once submerged beneath the icy waters, Hank thrust his legs out to try to flip the tree. But nothing budged it. It bobbled a bit and allowed him to catch another breath.

Maggie. God, how he loved her. Flashes of his life burst across his brain in lightning speed. Hadn't he said he'd give his life to save Maggie? Yet he hadn't saved her. They had her. *God, God! Help.* It was the last thought before he slumped into unconsciousness.

Something pulled at his wrists. A shiver raked through him. A soft rushing noise lulled Hank at the brink of consciousness. Surely he slept? He jerked to find the wool blanket, but couldn't seem to reach it. Pure iciness permeated the very marrow of his bones. A cold like he'd never felt before enveloped him. Perhaps he dozed upon Maggie's porch? No—something wasn't right.

He slung his head, trying to clear his stupefied thoughts. Where was he? All he knew was cold—above him frosty air, below him liquid ice. He blinked. In the darkening light, he glimpsed at brown water rushing beside his cheek. His gaze focused up. Twilight. A few adjustments to the right, and he spotted spikes of naked tree branches. Oh, the cost of moving jolted through his body.

He was soaking wet, legs drifting in the current like a lifeless corpse. He sucked in a deep breath to revive. The tree rested on the opposite bank, caught on debris, and angled skyward, keeping his head out of the water. Something again tickled his wrists, something light and warm. Hank grappled his hands and fingers against it.

What felt like a small warm hand pressed against his palm, and he calmed. Several moments ticked by and the tight restraint on his

hands dissolved. He groaned as he extended his stiff arms. The ropes around his torso loosened and released. Hank grabbed a sturdy branch above him, gritted his teeth and forced his frozen muscles to comply. He painstakingly maneuvered himself out of the water and onto the precarious trunk. The cold set his teeth to chattering.

As muddy water continued to wash over his boots, Hank glanced to the bank behind him. There stood a small Indian child. The girl nodded when he gained his feet, and she backed up the slope, motioning him to follow. With a low groan he forced his bruised, weary body to jump to the bank and scale the slope in front of him.

Once he reached the edge of the woods, he paused and leaned against a tree trunk. His body was so cold he could hardly move. So bone weary. So beat. Pain cascaded through his body from so many sources it was hard to tell where it originated. A small hand slid into his, and he opened his eyes.

"Must go. Hurry. Warm fire."

Hank stumbled after the girl tugging him gently, trying to keep his brain from the fog that threatened to take him from consciousness once more. She led him some ways, weaving through the forest and then the flats until reaching the bottom of a high ridge. The side of the bluff towered nearly vertical. She pulled him toward the brush at the base and beneath a pile of trees resting against the steep, elevated slope. There a buffalo skin, covered with leaves and debris, hung from a branch, and she swiped it away.

Inside, dug into the bluff, emerged a large room. To the left, an old Indian woman stood near the fire that vented out the side wall. It was Ni'-da-wi, his old friend from long ago.

Another, an ancient Indian man, wrapped in deerskin sat beside the fire on an old leather stool, sipping from a pottery cup.

A cough sounded from the right corner, and Hank took in a mound of animal skins with a frail woman ensconced within. Ni'-da-wi muttered in her native language and went to the woman.

"Sit." The child indicated a crude bench on a cowhide next to the fire.

Ni'-da-wi pulled the blankets up to the woman's chin and then approached him with a wooden bowl of liquid. She held it to him.

"Drink. Kill pain."

Hank shook his head. He had to find Maggie. The woman pressed the container into his hands. The child scurried around and brought a heavy buffalo skin. She pressed it against his shoulders. A rush of warmth enveloped him.

"Thank you."

The girl nodded, kneeling to stir a pot hanging in a crude tripod over the fire.

"You are White Moon." His voice seemed as if it belonged to a stranger, containing both a tremor and a low gravel tone.

"Yes. Talk later." The young girl's solemn eyes lifted to his. "Drink."

He accepted the liquid before swallowing it in one gulp.

"Now, sleep." Ni'-da-wi indicated the skin-covered floor.

Hank struggled to stand. "No. I must—"

The room spun while the walls grew taller. The child scurried around moving the wooden bench. Suddenly pain radiated up his legs. He looked down and realized he'd fallen to his knees. Now, a warmth started inside his belly and seemed to expand.

"Sleep." Ni'-da-wi grunted.

Hank swayed. The blotched red and white cowhide rug rose to meet him. And then he knew no more.

Humming pulled Hank from his slumber. The monotonous noise grew louder as he became more aware. No, it wasn't quite humming. Rather Ni'-da-wi sang in her guttural Omaha language. Then a wail brought his eyes fluttering open. Hank shifted, every bone in his body ached. He pushed himself to a sitting position, throwing the heavy skin from this shoulder.

The socket of his left eye throbbed, and he fingered the painful orb which had swollen nearly shut. Guess he could thank Worthy for that. The late Worthy, blasted to kingdom come. If not for the grace of God, Hank would be facing eternity as well.

Raised weals stretched down both his cheeks. He slumped forward, wrapped his arms around his bent knees, and hung his head to gather his bearings. At least he was dry.

Once he looked up, White Moon stood before him with another bowl. He held up his hand and shook his head.

"No more sleep," he muttered.

She shook her head. "No sleep. Stew."

He studied her, noting the light shade of skin. But the eyes and hair were as dark as night. So, she was a half-breed. "You're Corbin's friend."

A ghost of a smile swept her face and she nodded.

Hank gestured to Ni'-da-wi. "Family?"

She nodded, then her head tilted as if thinking. "Great…Aunt. Poor Grandmother Mi'-wa-thon die. I named for her."

"Who's there?" He motioned toward the still, pale woman in the buffalo skin bed.

White Moon's face grew heavy. "My mother. Pacoosa. You say White Swan."

Hank's brows drew together, and he shot a glance as the singing and wailing commenced over the ailing woman. "She sick?"

White Moon shook her head, her luminous eyes empty by the light of the fire. "No. Ruined. Dying."

The girl pushed the bowl toward him, and he took it. "I'm…sorry. Who's the old man?"

"Red Feather. Brother of Great Aunt Ni'-da-wi."

He took a sip of the gamey soup, thankful for its warmth and its resuscitating qualities. "Thank you for rescuing me."

White Moon shrugged. "I leave soon. Mother die. Father mourn. Then Black Crow live no more."

Hank paused at his meal. His thoughts seemed to come so slowly. "Black Crow?"

She motioned to the corner where her mother lay. "Father of mother. Evil man. He…violate. Father say she die because her spirit broke. My father take…avenge, then hunt no more."

Avenge or revenge? He supposed it didn't matter. In his muddled brain, one was much like the other. He stared at her and then threw a glance back at the old man and woman. Thinking through the fog of pain and whatever had been in that first bowl proved quite a challenge. "I don't understand."

"Black Crow...you know, Man-Who-Cheats-Death. Black Crow with black hair, three legs, hair on lip. Bad medicine. You be careful."

Had she called Hank the Man-Who-Cheats-Death? He pushed the thought away. His brain couldn't handle more than one thing at a time. There was something more important here. He could feel it niggling in the back of his mind.

"Three legs?" Who in the world would have three legs?

White Moon stood and leaned over as if she had a cane and hobbled about.

"Rupert Stilts?"

From the corner, the rhythmic keening ceased. Ni'-da-wi pivoted and barked at the young girl.

White Moon turned to look at him with wide eyes. "Great Aunt say name is wicked. No say here."

Hank stood and staggered upright. White Moon's tiny hand clamped onto his forearm as if her small body could support him. Nevertheless, it made him mindful to steady himself. If Rupert Stilts was known among the Omaha, his reputation was more widespread than he'd first thought. And not a good one at that.

Hank stared at the old woman kneeling near the mounds of skins. He'd known her for many years, as far back as his boyhood.

She'd been friends with Old Polly. As much as he needed to talk with her and find out how Rupurt Stilts had connection here, he knew he had to respect her time of bereavement.

Had White Moon said Stilts had been her mother's father? He assessed the small girl beside him, still staring up at him. Thus explained the girl's light skin. "Then…this man. He would be your grandfath—"

"Never. White Moon is Omaha. Wicked Black Crow no family."

"But your mother is his daught—"

"No. He—" A hardness stiffened her childish features. Then she turned and spit on the lodge floor. "He force Grandmother and Mother. They both die broken. Ruined."

White Moon slipped her hand into his, perhaps needing comfort as much as the dying woman in the corner. Ni'-da-wi turned away from them, focused on the dying woman, and began her chanting dirge once more.

Force? As in raped? And both White Moon's mother and grandmother bore the dishonor. A violently conceived half-breed would not have been embraced by either culture. Perhaps this was the very reason she suffered onto death.

Bile gathered in the back of Hank's throat. His head pounded as he sorted through the bits of information. Hadn't Maggie mentioned a dandy who sounded much like Stilts? The same who'd taken various articles that had once belonged to Maggie's mother? His mind wandered back to the box he and Maggie had hidden in the

springhouse. Then her mother's journal had come to light from that very box.

If Stilts had violated White Moon's grandmother and mother, who was his very own daughter, concocted an entire hoax of being Hank's Pinkerton agent of contact, and gave instructions to have Hank killed when he no longer served the man's purpose, there was little the man wouldn't do.

"How long have I been here?"

"Two sleeps."

Dread swelled inside him. "I've got to go."

The girl nodded. "I fetch horse."

Hank wasn't about to ask which horse. He couldn't care less. He'd steal the first one available if he had to, and then face the wrath of the Indian brave for his wrong.

The urge to leave intensified. He followed the girl through the skin at the doorway to the cold air outside. He paused. It was dark, but at least he was dry and warmed. Two nights had passed since he'd set eyes on Maggie. Was she safe? Was she still alive? White Moon hurried further down the sheer bank and disappeared into the snowy slope. Oddly, she reappeared with his own horse, complete with his saddle. She handed him a buffalo robe and the reins.

"So cold. You take."

"When did my horse get here?"

The moon highlighted a ghost of a smile on White Moon's face. "Father. He hunts much."

He nodded, too much in a hurry to question the strange answer. "White Moon. If you are here, where is Corbin?"

"Reservation. He safe in lodge circle."

Hank mounted. "Thank you for all you did."

Her head bobbed. "God guard you, Man-Who-Cheats-Death."

Chapter Twenty

Maggie jerked awake. How she could have slept upright strapped in a chair only attested to the exhaustion weighing her down from the last two days. At least they hadn't touched her...yet.

Her head pulsated to the beat of her heart, sending waves of pain radiating down her neck. The soreness served not only as reminder of the skirmish the day before but of her resolution.

The room lay still, shrouded in darkness, with the banked fire the only light. She could make out Dr. Stills, or perhaps Rupert Stilts...strange how that name rang a bell...as Hank had referred to him, huddled on the cot, encased in a wool blanket. On the floor, the remaining gang members lay sprawled with their heads propped on their saddles, and their bodies covered over with thin buckskins and wool blankets.

She'd spent much of yesterday watching the men traipse in and out of the cabin, carrying wood and smelly tack from their horses. Besides the sour odor, she'd endured their coarse comments and fool jokes. The dandy had given up his attempts to force her to speak. She'd refused to answer his incessant questions and received several smacks to her head for her efforts. Still, she'd remained mute.

The thick, scarred man had been sent back to check on some other endeavor, as the oily man had called it. It occurred to her that might've involved Hank or even Corbin. But then, who could know? Unfortunately, Leonard had not been the one sent on the mysterious endeavor. Her skin still burned from his constant lecherous ogles. The only bright side? Now there were only four miscreants to deal with.

Her stomach rumbled, making her wish, just for a moment, that she hadn't refused the food offered yesterday. Her fingers tugged at a stray strand of hemp at her wrists. If only she could reach that blasted knot.

Moats rolled over and grunted. Great. They'd soon be all awakened as the window above the cot lightened. Then what? Maybe she should break her silence and confess she'd found the gold. She mulled that idea over in her head. After all, what had silence won her? A couple of nights strapped to a stiff chair? Her stomach rumbled and tightened as if agreeing with the hopeless plan.

Yes. Once they had that information, they'd recover the gold, and head on to the next vile scheme of ransacking the next innocent fool. Then, she could walk away—free. She and Corbin could live happily ever after like the tales she'd told her son to frighten away

the fear Axel Robbins had instilled into the very core of their lives. Perhaps…

She took an unsteady breath even as she lied to herself. *Happily ever after?* Ha. She almost felt ashamed for reading those confounded stories to Corbin, giving them both some false sense of hope. Hadn't the bitter turn of her own circumstances proved how wicked life could be?

And now, most likely Hank…was dead. A snuffled sob tried to work up her throat, and she pressed it down. No. Her jaws clamped down hard. She would not break.

Moats coughed and rose, dressed in only long underwear shirt and britches. Maggie didn't dare take her eyes from the degenerate despite his state of undress. His throaty hack and spit into the dying ember brought not only a sizzle from the hot coals, but an involuntary wave of nausea to Maggie's own empty stomach.

The shadow of the man hitched up the back of his wool trousers and staggered to the front door. Knowing where he headed only made the same need well up inside her. But she would wait until full light. Visiting the necessary accompanied by any one of these degenerates in the near dark must be avoided at all costs.

Several minutes ticked by and Moats returned. Soon the others stirred, and morning light filled the room. Moats milled around and collapsed into a wooden chair at the table next to Leonard. The last, a younger, knobby-jointed gent, flung a thick log on the fire and raked the coals to flare up.

To her relief, the room warmed, warding off the judders brought on by lack of movement and hunger. Leonard approached the fire

with the big pot of beans from yesterday, a piece of dried pemmican hanging from his teeth, making him look like a rabid dog circling her as his next meal. Maggie tightened her lips and dropped her eyes.

The doctor, or whoever he was, popped up from the cot, smoothed his trousers and pulled on his silk vest hanging from the peg.

"Ah, a good morning to you, Madame."

She puckered her lips into a tight bud.

He crossed the room to a dry sink and poured water into the bowl. Once he dipped his comb, he smoothed it through his hair. Then he applied some kind of grease paste from a tin and slicked it down flat. He took up a straight razor and leaned into the small oval mirror hanging on the wall.

"So, I see you have resolved to remain mute this morning as well. Madam, you are quite a tenacious woman."

As much as she wanted to remain silent, she knew this was going nowhere fast. "I've changed my mind."

The small man stiffened and twirled to survey her, half his face lathered and the other scraped clean. "Indeed?"

"Yes."

"Excellent." He made short work of rasping off the rest of the whiskers from his face. "Then, by all means, let's converse."

"I need to use the—facilities."

He threw his head back in a laugh. However, the sound he'd belted out appeared less motivated by humor and more fueled by victorious tyranny. The man motioned to Leonard. "You—tend her."

Not her first choice for an escort. Her mind didn't chase that thought, for the blessed relief of her hands and feet being released from their bonds made her want to moan aloud. She rubbed her aching wrists, her mind awhirl with possibilities of increasing her chances of escape.

Stills patted his jaw dry and leaned forward to remove his thin tie from a peg. He busied himself wrapping the strip of material around the short collar of his shirt. The blade which had rendered his chin smooth glinted at her. With a convincing stumble, she bumped the wood, and her hand slid the folded cut-throat razor from the table. With a faux cry of surprise, she concealed it in the folds of her skirt.

Once through the door, Leonard grabbed her arm. She tugged away and flipped the straight edge open. "Touch me again and I'll slice you to ribbons."

His beady eyes flared. "You little witch."

Her eyes flicked about the snowy banks. The wind whipped through the yard, sending frozen ice particles slashing against her cheek. A thick arm clamped on her wrist.

"Drop it."

She twisted and writhed, but Leonard's hand was like a vice. He squeezed and she cried out in pain. Tears bit her eyes as she sank to her knees. She would not—

A sickening, metallic click near her ear froze her.

"Drop it now or meet your maker."

Maggie heaved great fogs of air as Leonard pressed the barrel of his gun to her temple. With a cry she opened her fist, and he shoved

her back into the deep snow. For a moment, she just lay there, huffing in air and blinking at the brightness of the clouded sky. The mind-numbing iciness leached through the thin material of her dress. So much for her make-shift getaway. She'd already lost the first battle.

"Get up."

She struggled to her feet. Leonard made no move to help her, thankfully. She'd gladly thrash through a snowstorm to avoid that horrible man's touch. Maggie stumbled to the leaning outhouse.

Once back inside the cabin, Leonard held a gun to her head while the other man strapped her back to that infernal chair. She licked her lips at her failure. Why hadn't she slipped the stinking razor into her pocket and used it at a more opportune time?

No time to berate herself as the dandy rose from the table. He took one last sip from his mug, dabbed his face with his napkin, and sauntered back across the room. Maggie tensed when Leonard tossed the folded razor back to the shaving table.

Dr. Stills paused, cocked his head at her, and raised one eyebrow but said nothing. At his cot, he stepped into his shiny boots, licking his finger to remove a scuff near the toe. Then he grabbed up his cane.

"You're a diabolical prodigy I see. One who is extraordinary but not excessively efficacious. So, I'll be blunt with my ultimatums. I want the gold. I want the boy."

Maggie's brows furrowed. "Boy? What—you can't possibly be talking about Corbin?"

She nearly fell from her chair when he nodded.

"Corbin. Such an odd name. But it can be rectified to a more suitable moniker." Dr. Stills paced to the fireplace. "Not that such a thing is of great significance presently."

A fury like no other mounted in Maggie's chest. "You will *never* have my son."

He paused, extended his arm, and set the tip of his cane on the floor. "Tsk, tsk. It is my full recompense, and a reasonable one at that. But first, I must break my fast."

He spun and strolled to the table as if he'd just asked for a second helping of grits. She drew in a long breath. There was no sense in arguing with the buffoon.

The smell of beans wafted up, causing her anger to subside and her mouth to water. No, she would not partake of his food. She'd rather starve.

"Feed her."

Maggie clenched her teeth.

Stills settled at the table, pulled a cloth from the surface, and snapped the scrap of fabric into the air before settling it into his lap. Then he raised a hand and snapped his fingers. "Eggs. I require eggs and fresh fry bread."

A stillness fell over the room. All the other three men came to an abrupt halt and eyed the oily man at the table. Moats, hunkered over a dried piece of hardtack near the hearth, stopped chewing long enough to stare at him.

"You there. Eagins. Quickly. I've matters to attend."

"Name's Eakins."

"Mere technicality. Prepare my repast. With haste, my man."

The two other men looked to Moats who shrugged. Eakins. Now she had a name for the knobby-jointed gang member. The man, his hat tugged low, scurried around to snap eggs into a pan and sloshed them around. Soon, Stills had dined on his scrambled offering minus the fry bread.

Leonard approached Maggie with a bowl of burnt beans. She shot him a gaze chock full of loathing. He scooped a huge wad onto a spoon and stuck it near her nose. She twisted away.

"Enough of your incompetence." Stills's footsteps came nearer as he shooed him away. "Now, where were we, my headstrong hellion?"

Hate gurgled up her spine. "I believe we were discussing you taking my son."

"Yes, yes. Very good." He pulled a chair from the table and situated it in front of the fireplace, facing her. He sat, bringing his right foot up to rest his ankle on his other knee. "First, of utmost importance, the gold."

Maggie lifted her chin and narrowed her eyes. This might be her only bargaining chip. "Gold? You mean the seventy-five thousand dollars in gold pieces?"

The dandy leaned forward, the sick light of greed alive in his eyes. "Yes, yes. That's it, my dear. Reveal its location and you will be at liberty."

"And Corbin?"

"The deal is the gold and the boy. No other arrangement will suit." His face loomed closer, the bruised cut on his forehead and the cheek scar of the lit match accented on his pale, waxy face. "I want to make this abundantly clear. Your life for the gold...*and* the boy."

The monster. Maggie gathered the spittle in her mouth, drew back, and spat in his face. He flinched, instinctively blinking. The drool hung in a long strip mid-cheek, just below the black, healing scab. His eyes froze glacial as he stood, removed a silk cloth from his breast pocket, and dabbed his face.

"You will never have my son!"

Leonard stepped forward, a smirk on his face. "You need me, boss? I'd be glad to take the fight out of her."

Maggie's heart pounded. The dandy's nostrils flared in and out while his thin lips twitched. He reached forward to bury his hand in Maggie's hair. The backward jerk forced a squall from her and tears squeezed to her cheeks. The chair tipped back and hung precariously on the two rear legs. When her eyes blinked opened, he was mere inches from her face. He stroked her cheek.

"'Tis no problem. I'll enjoy taming the shrew."

He let her go and the chair tottered back to upright. She ran a quick tongue over her parched lips. Her scalp still pounded. That hadn't been wise. She had to start using her head. With squinted eyes, she trailed the dandy, who stomped a few laps from table to fireplace where her mother's daguerreotype rested on the mantel. Then the evil doctor snapped to attention in front of her. What she wouldn't give to have that photo in her hands as she ran from this cursed place.

Maggie's eyes narrowed when the dandy laid the tip of his cane to the base of her throat. Her body leaned back as the pressure grew

against her windpipe. The front legs of the chair left the wooden floor. Maggie closed her eyes as his voice cut into the silence.

"Quick medicinal lesson, my dear. A small hole here—" The sharp point of his cane dug into the flesh in the hollow of her neck. "—would still allow you to breathe. Then my compatriot could reposition the gag, thus silencing you. Hmmm. So tempting."

Maggie's eyes shot open, fearing the point had already pierced her. She shook her head, and the cane left the base of her throat. The chair pitched forward, and she gagged and choked. Whimpers escaped despite her best effort to swallow the pain shooting from her bruised esophagus.

"Then we understand one another?" The horrible man's black brows elevated.

Tears filled her eyes.

He chuckled and tapped the cane on the mantel near his head. "So like your mother."

Her head came up, her facial muscles stiffened. "How do you know my mother?"

His lips twisted. "Oh, I knew her well. *Quite* well."

"How?"

"You know me as Dr. Rumble Stills. But your mother knew me as her much revered beau, Rupert Stilts."

The very name Hank had mentioned. *Rupert Stilts?* The inscription inside the band beat at her brain. *Forever yours, R.S.* And Rupert? The very name in mother's journal? Could this horrid man be the one and the same? "You lie."

But he continued as if she hadn't spoken, settling on the hearth, nearly eye to eye. "I explored her lips and felt the swell of her body—ohhh. I could have dined on that voluptuous, curvaceous creature. And I did crave so much more, absolutely clamored for more—no, hungered for more of her sensual flesh. But she, at first flirtatious and wanton, spun a volte-face and jilted me. Denied me her hot, lustful lips, her—"

"Stop! You brute." She tightened her arms against the chair back and jumped, eager to pounce upon him and remove the mocking look from his face. All she succeeded doing was knocking her chair sideways to the floor once again. Sobs shook her body as she glared at his shiny shoes. If she could get loose, she'd squeeze the life from his scrawny neck.

A derisive humph sounded from Rupert Stilts's chest. His pale face gave away nothing, but in his dark eyes, something malevolent and carnal glinted. "She never told you about me, did she?"

"What's to know?" Maggie spat. "You were nothing. She married my father, Reuben Saddler."

His shoe tapped in front of her face. "Yes, the dirt farmer. If that Indian witch hadn't lied about my intentions, I... I would be your father."

Eakins lifted the chair from the floor and set Maggie upright.

"Two women for the price of one." Leonard snorted from the table.

Moats squatted near the pot of beans on the hearth to scoop a second helping into his bowl. "Reckon the squaw didn't lie, then."

"Indian woman squeezed out your half-breed kid, too. And ten years later, you help yourself to your own half-breed daughter." Leonard swore and shook his head. "Twisted."

"All in the family," Eakins cackled.

The suited man jumped to his feet. "I won't have you propitiating those lies."

"What's her name, Eakins?" Moats flung back from his position at the fireplace.

Maggie shot a glance to the table behind her where the other two played cards.

"Wha? Oh, White Bird? White Swan? Something white."

Laughter erupted. Moats toasted the dandy with his tinned cup and cackled. "Ironic, huh?"

Realization raked through Maggie. White Moon's mother was Rupert Stilts's own daughter. And the evil man had—

"You are never to speak of her." Stilts's face flushed to a deep red, his voice dry and strained. "Sutter's not the only one who's expendable."

Chairs scraped at the table, and men stood, pulling their side arms from their holsters. Moats grinned. "You may squeeze the life from a helpless woman, but me and my boys will skin you alive."

Stilts spun and strode across the room. From the corner of her eye, Maggie watched as he twirled a cape onto his shoulders. The door of the cabin slammed shut.

"Killjoy." Moats grinned. "Well, boys, I wouldn't eat anything Stilts offers from now on. He's witch brewing again."

The men chuckled and settled back into their chairs. Moats continued to stare at Maggie. "If Stilts had told me what a handsome woman you was, I'd have knocked off Robbins sooner."

She kept her face turned from him.

"You drink any of your mother's elixir?"

She swung her head to fix him with her stare, dread filling her stomach. "How do you know about my mother's medication?"

Chapter Twenty-One

Moats's boot shoved at her chair leg. "Did ya? If ya did, I reckon you were a might stronger since you're still alive."

"What are you saying?"

His glittering eyes watched her over the rolled rim of the cup. "Think about it."

Maggie tightened her lips. "You're touched in the head. A doctor recommended that elixir."

The cup came down, and a small smile lit his face. "Eakins, get over here."

The man with the low hat swore and threw his cards down. "Yeah, yeah, I'm losing anyway."

The small-framed man stepped to the fireplace.

"Take yer hat off." Moats commanded, never taking his gaze from Maggie's.

The man complied, showing unruly, red hair in need of a good cut.

"Slick it back like Doc Edwards."

Every blood vessel in Maggie's face drained as the man pulled his mane back. Even with the mussed, dirty clothes, she recognized the man who'd visited her house nearly every day until her mother's death. Maggie gave a strangled cry.

"Ah, I see you understand." He grinned, displaying his black, ragged teeth. "Stilts has been planning a good long while."

The four men chuckled amongst themselves. Maggie clenched the arms of the chair and held her breath. Fury and hatred collided inside until she screamed out.

"*You*. All of you. You killed my mother." She gasped at Eakins while reeling in pain. "You animals!"

The door exploded open, and the dandy stepped into the room, flung a flash of metal at Moats, still grinning near the fireplace. But he dove to the floor. The sharp instrument embedded in Eakins's temple, and after a horrible shock jolted his form still, he toppled to the floor. Both Moats's and Leonard's guns shuffled from holsters, clicked, pointed at the dandy. The dark greasy man's right cheek twitched into a devious half-smile.

"Yes, gentlemen, by all means. Shoot the only man who can administer the antidote to the cyanide beans you so rudely consumed. Won't that leave our lovely guest in quite a quandary?"

One by one the guns lowered. Stilts's smile stretched into a cunning grin. "Please, take your time. No rush to empty your stomachs full of poison. I'm sure my amyl nitrate will reverse the effects of suffocation, unless it's too far advanced, that is."

Stilts' laughter reverberated off the walls as both men scrambled to the back door. Then he strolled to the fireplace, clicking his cane as he went. He paused, stared at the body lying there, and then pulled the watch fob from his breast pocket. Maggie gritted her teeth when she recognized it as her mother's.

"Buffoons. Their mothers should have drowned them at birth." He kicked Eakins's leg.

"How could you?"

He turned to her. "What? Kill Eakins or poison the victuals?"

Maggie pulled her eyes from the pool of blood widening around Eakins's head where the surgical blade had buried deep. "Concoct an elaborate plan to kill my mother, you beast."

He flicked his wrist. "Oh, that. Quite simple. The harlot jilted me years ago, and I assured her I'd get even. A trusting fool, your mother."

She huffed several breaths. "I…*hate* you."

The dandy parked himself on the hearth. "Familiar phrase, from familiar genes. I'd materialized much sooner if you'd been a boy. Girls—worthless. When Ax and I planned your marriage, it was the perfect foil to settle the score."

The intertwining of the complex, lengthy scheme rendered her silent. Only Maggie's breathing permeated the space. Then with a howl, she wrestled the chair in a fit of rage. "You can't be serious?

Axel may have been in league with the likes of you, but my mother would've never involved herself with such an evil, twisted, pathetic creature as you."

He blinked his eyes with slowness and studied her with tilted head. "Remember R.S? Those initials are mine. I purchased this fob in Paris, the ring in Baltimore, and I commissioned this daguerreotype in Omaha. Oh, and the lock of hair inside the band of the cameo? It's mine."

"You lie." She screamed. "Those were gifts from my father."

He leaned his head back and laughed. "Your father? Pshaw. Your grandfather begged the dimwit to marry her to save face. Quite a shameful thing to break a courtship."

Blood coursed through her face as she struggled to pull free from the restraints.

"But don't worry, my dear. I had great hopes a son would be born, and so, he has. Your mother took procreation from me, and I'll steal it back. Your Corbin will make a fine apprentice. Quite intelligent, quite uncanny. I'll groom him as my amalgam assistant."

"You'll never have my son." Sobs broke from her throat.

His lips twitched. "Oh, I assure you, my dear. I will. You reneged on our deal. No gold? No son."

She hung her head and wept. Corbin. *Corbin. God protect him.* The door opened and the men stumbled in the back door, wiping their mouths with handkerchiefs. The malevolent at the fireplace rose with leisure.

"Give us the antidote." Moats's voice gargled.

The dandy ambled to the front door. "Antidote? Oh, dear no. I'll not waste any of my apothecaries on daft cretins who believe they've been poisoned from a perfectly good pot of beans."

Stilts paused at the door to survey their distressed postures. "However, future meals are free game."

Hank peered at the cabin through the early morning darkness. There was no way to tell if Maggie was inside, even if he slipped up unnoticed and looked through the windows. As dawn lightened the sky, he could make out a wrapped body on one of the horses. Fear slithered across his tightened muscles. But as the day brightened, it became clear the form was too large.

He crept around the cabin to the outhouse and set up surveillance behind the spikey bushes near the tree line. Whoever rested inside would need the facilities eventually. The foot and a half of snow drifted about the landscape revealed no new prints.

The cabin door creaked open and Hank slouched down. One of Moats's men plowed through the white fluff and headed straight for the outhouse. *Leonard.* Almost an hour went by as Moats and Stilts himself utilized the necessary. His heart sank until the door snapped open once more and a familiar defiant voice rang out.

"Kindly remove your gun from my spine, you low-down mongrel. I have little chance of escape in the backwoods of Iowa, especially with the lovely weather we're having."

Relief coursed through him. It was Maggie—in all her glory. *Thank God.* He raised his head just enough to watch her slap

Leonard across the face. He shoved her down and thrust her face first into the snow. Hank's hand quivered on the bone handle of his Colt.

She came up sputtering. "You imbecile. Don't you ever touch me again."

The hammer of Leonard's gun clicked, silencing Maggie's words. She struggled to stand, and then strutted to the outhouse. When they disappeared from view, Hank grabbed his horse and moved forward until he stood behind the structure. He crept around the corner. Leonard leaned his shoulder against the wood, and Hank raised the butt of his revolver. With one swift motion, he buried the gun's handle tip in Leonard's skull. His body crumpled silently to the carpet of white.

Hank yanked him behind the outhouse and returned to the door just as it opened. Maggie's mouth flew open. She gave a strangled cry and flung her arms around him.

"Oh, dear mighty God, thank you." Her voice rasped in his ear.

He tucked her against him, and let himself absorb the warmth of her vibrant body. The joy in finding her alive was cut short.

He pressed his lips to her ear. "Did they touch you?"

"No…I'm…fine."

"We gotta go. Now."

He swung her into his arms and plowed through the deep snow, sprinting, as much as he could given the circumstance, toward his horse. Although he wished he could have been more gentle, he tossed her aboard and mounted behind her. The horse seemed to comprehend his urgency and turned from the outhouse to lurch into a run.

Maggie's whispers of thanksgiving dissolved into sobs, and he wrapped his long coat around her, nestling her into his arms. They rode that way for over an hour before Hank felt safe enough to stop. He dismounted, and she nearly fell on top of him.

"I thought they'd killed you." She buried her face against his chest. "Oh, dear God, I thought you were dead."

She clutched at him, her tears wetting his chest.

He took a deep breath and pulled her closer. "They tried. God had other plans."

A quivering coo brought on more tears and Maggie laid her cold hands on his face, tracing the tracks of cuts and scrapes. Then she gently circled his wounded eye. "Praise Jesus you're safe."

Then she shoved from him. "Oh Hank. He's after Corbin. That horrible man, Rupert Stilts." She yanked at the lapels of his coat. "This has all been a massive plan of revenge. My mother's death, my marriage, the gold. Now—Corbin. We have to find him. He could be in danger."

"He's safe, Maggie, at the Omaha reservation."

She shook her head, face red from the cold and her tears. "No, Hank. That man's a maniac. He killed my mother with an elixir because she broke their engagement. My mother, Hank. Then he set up Axel to court me, just to produce Corbin."

Hank put his hands on her shoulders and rubbed her tense muscles. "Calm down, now."

She pulled away with fire in her eyes. "Listen to me. He killed one of Moats's men with a surgical knife right in front of my eyes, Hank. He'll find Corbin. We have to get to him first."

He hesitated. Could this elaborate story be true? Had Maggie's whole life been set up?

She stepped toward the horse and swung aboard. "I'm going with or without you. What's your choice?"

He grabbed the reins before she dug her heels into the horse's flanks. "With."

New tears glistened in her eyes. "There's something else you should know."

"What?"

She sniffed, and he groped for a clean handkerchief.

"There's seventy-five thousand dollars in gold in my attic."

His arm froze in midair.

She pulled the cloth from his hand. "We can use it to pay off Stilts."

"It's not yours, Maggie. You need to hand it over to the sheriff."

Her eyes narrowed. "You're not making a very convincing bank robber, Hank Sutter."

"I'm not a thief. I thought I was undercover for the U.S. Marshal. Stilts was my contact."

She sighed and dropped her head. "Why didn't you tell me that before?"

He pulled the wool blanket from his saddlebag and swung aboard. "A man don't like to announce he's been played for a fool."

She turned her head, and he fastened his gaze on her profile. "If it's any consolation, neither does a woman."

They both were still for a moment. Then Hank spoke. "Are you okay, Maggie? Did they…hurt you at all?"

She shook her head. "Other than my heart, no."

With gentle hands he draped the blanket around her, and she settled back against his chest. He closed his eyes for a moment, pressing his mouth against her hair while thanking the Lord for her safety. "I met White Moon."

She caught her breath. "Where?"

A laugh popped out. "At the bank of the Missouri River. You might say I was a little tied up."

"Hank, you better not mean literally."

"Unfortunately, yes."

He relayed the tale as they rode on and, by the end, she clenched his sleeves and wept.

"How have we gotten ourselves in so much trouble? What if they come after us or get Corbin before we do?"

With the reins against his mount's neck, Hank wrapped his arms about her, praying aloud. Her body relaxed against him. He caressed her hands and whispered in her ear. "We must trust, Maggie. Trust God to dig us out."

She nodded against him. "I wish things could've been different, Hank."

"We must live with what we've been dealt."

The horse kicked through the snow for a moment or two before she spoke, her voice hushed. "I love you, Hank Sutter. I always have."

His arms tightened around her, and he pressed his lips against her cool neck until it warmed. "Good to know, my love. And sometime soon, I wanna discuss it further. But for now, we better git."

He couldn't stop the surge of pleasure welling inside as he kicked his mount to a canter. She was his. Finally. After all these years. His chest ached. She always had been. But he pigeonholed the blissful knowledge with a slight grin. He grabbed the reins with renewed strength as they flew through the snow.

The deep drifts and frigid air made travel slow and agonizing. Maggie gripped the saddle horn, thankful for Hank's strong arms encircling her. She'd long ceased peeking behind them and tried instead to keep her face inside her cloak. Her arms and legs were numb, and she wondered how Hank hadn't frozen solid with his back exposed to the elements.

Snow started to fall in tiny flakes and grew in size as time ticked by. The dark horse beneath her slowed the pace and ceased blowing great puffs of vapor, but frozen froth gathered on its neck and shoulder while small icicles formed on his rough winter hair. The gray day darkened early causing Maggie to search the landscape, wondering where they would weather the night. Ahead, she spotted a thickening in the trees.

She stretched against the muscle cramps in her thighs. "What's up there?"

"Glenwood." The handkerchief muffled Hank's hoarse voice. His hat nearly covered his eyes.

Her body grew taut, and she twisted around. "We've gone the wrong way."

"Sit still, Maggie, please. We'll discuss it when we stop."

A tremor shot through the man behind her, and fear licked at her insides. Exposure. He was right. They needed to get inside. The unending wind dipped the temperatures below zero, and while she had his arms about her, he bore the brunt of the weather. She tucked her face into the neck of her cloak.

How much farther? Her heart plummeted. Panic swelled. *Trust.* Hank's advice thawed her alarm. *God, Hank says I'm supposed to trust you. You showed me the gold. Now, please get us to a warm place.*

It seemed an eon until they hit the edge of town. The snow seemed deeper here and small bits of ice popped against the blanket that surrounded Maggie. The few buildings of Glenwood were shut up tight, and only the saloon showed signs of life with light spilling from the window. Tinny piano music wafted through the clapboard siding. Ironically, the sheriff's office across the street appeared dark and empty.

Hank nudged the horse between the buildings to ward off some of the wind and then stiffly slid to the snow-covered ground. His dark eyes looked dull as he lifted his hands to pull her from the horse. When he steadied her on the uneven ground, she reached up and touched the small strip of his red, exposed skin.

"Are you all right?"

He hesitated before he nodded. Then he pressed his lips against her ear. "I'm sorry. This is the only place in town."

Her fingers snugged the hood around her head. "It'll do."

Chapter Twenty-Two

Hank fastened the horse to the hitching rails, grabbed her hand, and waded the shin-high snow to the front door around the corner. They stumbled up the stair steps to the drifted wooden walkway. A mound of white blocked the door, and Hank cleared it with his boot enough to yank the door open.

The thin man with a black garter around the white sleeve of his button-up shirt sat at the piano. He abruptly stopped torturing the instrument when the door shut. All eyes drew to them. The place held a relative crowd for such a nasty night. Hank pressed a hand to her back, urging her to the bar counter.

"Hep ya?" The thick, pock-faced man stepped closer, drying a shot glass. He clunked it down in front of Hank.

Odd thing to say given they had just survived a harrowing ride in a blizzard, and were covered with ice. The bartender acted as if all they required were a stiff drink and a window seat to sit back and enjoy the scenery. Maggie brushed at the frozen droplets at the neck of her cape.

Hank waved off the bartender's offer. "Need a couple rooms."

The bartender shook his head. "No can do, partner. Filled up."

"Not even one?" Hank's voice sounded desperate, even to her ears.

"Nope."

"Listen, all we need is a corner. Anything just to be out of the weather. The lady needs shelter."

The glass squeaked as he continued the rhythmic toweling. Then he picked up another small glass. "Well, there's the loft. But I only rent it when the weather agrees. No heat, low roof. Got just enough room for a mattress."

Hank grunted, and Maggie cowered closer to his side. Then he nodded. "We'll take it."

He made the arrangements while she took in the smoky interior and its occupants, feeling the stares of most of the rawboned gentlemen. Even the sheriff partook of the card game by the window. She shrank into her cape, forcing the hood to drop over her face, and spun to the counter.

"Turn right at the top of the stairs. Go all the way to the end of the hall. The last door on the left leads up to the third floor."

"Thanks." Hank draped his arm around her shoulders and hustled her toward the stairs.

They gained the second floor and peals of muffled laughter made her draw up her shoulders. Obviously, a whole lot more was going on in this place than hunkering down to weather a blizzard. Hank hastened her toward the last door and pushed it open. The stairs listed to the left, rising up single file, and Hank positioned her ahead of him, but stayed close to her back as she reached the landing.

She gasped as her head came through the floor of their room. Just a loft was an understatement. It boasted no door, and the ceiling, at its topmost point above the bed, measured four foot at best. True to the saloon keeper's word, not much filled the room but a mattress. Well, there was one bit of good news. At least the bed bugs wouldn't be able to survive the freezing temperature of the room.

Her eyes shot down the stairs beyond Hank's form. Still, it didn't seem very secure. Anyone could lumber up here.

Hank stood on the third step down where he could stand upright and let out a long breath. "I'm sorry, Maggie. Tell you what. You stay up here and I'll tend the horse. Then I'll bed up in front of the doorway at the bottom of the stairs in the hallway—"

"You'll do no such thing, Hank Sutter." She straightened and thumped her head on the ceiling. With a grimace she rubbed the sore spot. "I'm not sleeping up here by myself."

He rubbed his hands together. "I'll just be right there, at the base of the steps."

She clenched her teeth. "No. You'll stay up here."

His head bowed and shook. "Can't do it, Maggie. Ain't proper."

"I'd think we'd be past that. Besides, it can't be avoided. As cold as it is, we need each other's warmth."

241

Even as she said it in such logical terms, embarrassment lit a fuse on her cheeks.

He tucked his hands beneath his armpits. "Maggie, for the love of God, don't argue with me on this."

"Fine." She strutted to the stairway and wedged past him. "Let's go."

"Maggie, stop."

After slipping past his grip, she hurried her pace while he sputtered behind her. If she knew Hank, and she did, he would soon be hot on her heels. She raced down the last flight of stairs in a jumble of thuds and hurried into the room toward the window. Hank's voice trailed her and so did the sound of his boots. Maggie ignored the pointed looks of the patrons in the barroom and strutted right up to the game of poker. The sheriff looked up as she approached.

Hank slipped up beside her. "Maggie, be reasonable."

She shot him a glare. "I am. Sheriff, I'm Maggie Robbins, and this is Hank Sutter. We want to be married—now."

Hank gaped at her. Maggie tilted her chin up. This would certainly take care of the impropriety of sleeping together. And if it wasn't for her jaw being hardened in determination, she could have grinned at Hank's shocked face.

The sheriff, rotund as he was tall, stood, his gaze just a few inches above hers. His crinkled eyes narrowed as amusement lit his lips below his mustache. "Why, this is a privilege indeed. I'm Sheriff Cal Hokum. Robbins, you say? You wouldn't be related to…"

"Yes, yes. I'm Axel Robbins's widow." Another perfect reason to wed this very instant. She couldn't wait to be shed of that name. "Pardon the rush and the lack of sentimental tears over that thieving man's death, but we need to tie the knot right quick, if you have the time."

She huffed, drew herself up to her small height, and stomped one boot, hoping to press the man into action. The astonishment would soon lose its effect on Hank, and she wanted to press into the vows before he gained any momentum to deny her.

Sheriff Hokum's lips twitched, and he twirled the right side of his graying blond handlebar mustache. The man raised his eyes to Hank's. "Right smart filly ya got there."

"Excuse us." Hank spanned her waist and picked her up.

She struggled. He hushed her until he'd pressed her into a small alcove beneath the stairs. "Put me down, Hank, and let's be done with it."

His face, red from cold and anger, lowered to hers. "Stop this nonsense right now, Maggie. I'm near froze to death, and I still have to see to the horse."

She raised her brows and crossed her arms. "Are you saying you don't want to marry me?"

He shook his head with a growl. "I'm saying no such thing."

"Good." She slipped beneath his arm and stalked back into the dining room, Hank in hot pursuit.

The lawman had taken his seat again and glanced at her above the fan of cards. "Get it worked out?"

"Yes."

"No."

Both of their replies interlinked. She sneered at Hank and then grabbed his hand. "Commence, Sheriff."

The man grinned and shoved his chair back. "Reckon we don't have much problem with witnesses, do we, boys?"

The men in the room chuckled, and several shook their heads. One old timer, his lips puckered for the lack of teeth, shot a hand in the air.

"If'n the gent don't want 'er, I'll fill in."

More laughter filled the room, along with several me too's. Hank's arm came around her to snug her closer to him, and she wanted to spout a laugh. She could have hugged every man in the room for helping to encourage Hank to her side of the argument.

"Ya got several offers. Still looking to keep the one you got?"

Maggie gave a firm nod.

"Good. I take it you'd be satisfied with the short version?"

She bobbed her head.

"Maggie—"

She grabbed at Hank's hand at her waist to cut off whatever trivial words he had to insert. The officer stood before them, glancing from Hank to her, amusement dancing in his eyes.

Maggie nodded "Please continue."

Sheriff Hokum clapped his hands. "And we're off. Do you, Maggie Robbins, take this man, Hank..."

Maggie nudged him, and Hank stuttered out his last name to the waiting official.

"Yes, that's right, Sutter." The Sheriff winked at Maggie. "He's warming up to the idea."

More snickers tittered across the room.

"As your lawfully wedded husband?"

"I do." She bobbed her head firmly.

The man's brow danced. "And do you, Hank Sutter, take this woman, Maggie Robbins, as your lawfully wedded wife?"

Maggie could feel Hank's stare. She ignored him and yanked his hand.

"I…do."

"Then I pronounce you a wedded couple in sight of these good people, the law, and God Almighty. You oughta peck her just for good measure."

Maggie turned, planted her hands on Hanks's weather-roughened cheeks, and tugged his head down to hers until their mouths met. Guffaws and slaps lit the room around them.

"Well, well. Congratulations. I'll leave the official document with Ralph," he motioned to the man behind the counter and then pointed to the stairs," and you can be on your way."

Maggie felt her face flame at the snickers, but she set her jaw. "No, sir. I'm going to stay right here next to you while my husband tends his horse. Then we'll retire to our room."

With that, she grabbed an empty chair, scraped it across the dinged hardwood floor, and plopped the seat at the card table. Two other dark-bearded men eyed her with humor before lifting their stare to Hank.

Behind her, Hank cleared his throat and muttered something while shuffling to the door. She pressed her lids closed at his embarrassment. It had to be done. There'd be no separation from Hank ever again. Not *ever*.

Hank found the livery at the end of the street. With emotions aboil, he let himself in and found an empty stall. One thing good about what had just happened. He didn't feel the cold anymore. His cheeks puffed out as he let go of a long breath, and then he backed the horse into the enclosure. His frozen hands fumbled with his saddlebags before reaching to unbuckle the girth strap. His hands stilled.

Maggie was his wife.

He tugged the saddle from the animal and plunked it on the side stall wall. With his hands resting across the leather seat, he leaned forward and hung his head. This wasn't the way his wedding to Maggie was supposed to be. It wasn't the proper time nor the proper place. No church, flowers, or loved ones were involved. Not even a preacher made the ceremony official—just some old small-town sheriff who they didn't know. How had this happened?

Never in his born days would he have ever thought he'd marry Maggie reluctantly. Yet he had. He'd let that little hundred pound dynamo join them in matrimony in ten minutes flat.

He rubbed down the horse, covered him with a wool blanket, and then poured a generous amount of cracked corn into the corner feed rack. Shivers overtook him, and he groaned. At least he could wrap himself around Maggie's small body tonight and let her golden

wheat hair fall against his cheek. He groaned. What was in the woman's head? This was no passionate honeymoon night.

He could just imagine her resenting him for how it had all fallen together. Maybe not tonight, but later. The horse nickered when he latched the half door on the stall, and Hank patted his velvet nose, yet his mind stayed fixed on Maggie. God, he loved her. His heart pounded just thinking about her being Mrs. Hank Sutter. But it wasn't right. He couldn't—

What in the world was he complaining about? The woman was his, bound by marriage, pitiful as it was. He'd waited so long, he could wait longer. Maggie had been so persistent. She nearly set a gun barrel to his head.

He swung through the front door and latched it. The wind stole his breath, and he buttoned the leather duster with cold-stiffened fingers. The street was dark, shrouded in falling snow. Flakes drifted down from the black sky. Danger lurked, Corbin waited, yet he and Maggie perched on the cusp of physical oneness. Maybe it wouldn't happen tonight, but soon.

And in that loft, he had the right to wrap his arms around her and hold her close. The mere thought sped his pounding heart. He quickened his jaunt and shook his head as the thick white powder swirled around him. It would work out. He and Maggie were meant to be together.

Trust.

He stared at the uneven slanted rafters above him. The mattress below him sufficed and the wool blankets warded off the cold that

turned his breath to a fog. They'd left both the trapdoor and the hallway door open. A meager amount of heat drifted up the leaning stairway.

The moon through the small arched window cast an eerie glow across the room. Encapsulated within his embrace, Maggie, fully dressed with her back to him, matched the contours of his body. Spooning her was one step from heaven's landing.

Maggie had been unusually quiet which was quite uncharacteristic. They'd turned in, covered up, and drifted off. He eased his ear under the corner of the blanket, and Maggie stirred in his arms.

"Hank?"

"Yeah?"

"I'm sorry."

Her sleepy voice dented a corner of his mouth. "For what?"

After a lethargic sigh, she replied. "For embarrassing you."

He gave a soft laugh. "Which time?"

She elbowed him. "You know."

"Downstairs? Shoot, that didn't embarrass me."

She pressed back against him like a lazy kitten. Her voice came like an intimate kiss, soft and whispery. "Still, I was a tad heavy-handed, don't you think? And you seemed pretty reluctant."

Another laugh escaped his throat. "I wasn't reluctant, Maggie, I was hesitant. Hesitant for your benefit. You deserve more than an emergency blizzard hitching at dusk. In a saloon."

She flipped over, letting in cold air as she did. "Woman, you can't be still, can you?"

A giggle answered him. Then her face popped up from the wool blanket and settled next to his. He let his eyes travel over her sleep-soft face.

"It's freezing in here."

She shuddered, and he drew her closer, which wasn't a hardship at all. Nope, not one bit. He ran his hands up and down her slender back. "I hadn't noticed."

Concern lit her eyes. "Are you still cold?"

A smile teased his lips. Was she kidding? "I'm warmer than you know."

She widened her eyes, and her mouth popped open. "Are you being fresh, Hank Sutter?"

He inhaled and studied her. "No, I'm flirting with my wife."

She chuckled softly and laid her hand on his bearded cheek. Her stroking hand against his chin nearly undid him.

Then her eyes grew serious. "How soon will we get to the reservation?"

His eyes slid closed. He'd hoped they could avoid this subject until morning.

"Hank?"

With a groan he pressed his lips to her throat. "A while."

She pulled from him, eyes lit with fire. "What? No. We've got to go as soon as morning breaks."

His molars compressed. "Maggie, there's no sense in you going. I'll take you to Bellevue then head north."

"No." She fought against his embrace.

"It's the best thing," he ground out, keeping her within his grasp until she lay still, ashamed he enjoyed her curves as she'd writhed. Her whimpers loosened his grip and dissolved his resolve. He stroked her back and snugged her closer against his chest. She gripped his collar and muffled her sobs at his throat.

"It'll only be a few days," he soothed.

Her head brushed back and forth on his chest. "No, they'll find me there."

He swallowed the knot in his throat while visions of Olin Leonard striding from Maggie's cabin filled his thoughts.

Small fists pummeled his chest. "You left me once, Hank Sutter. Don't you leave me again. You promised."

He blinked in the semi-darkness as she cried. *God, you know I can't endanger her. Please, make her understand.*

Chapter Twenty-Three

The next morning's ride stretched taut between them. She would watch his every move. He would not abandon her to the cabin. If she had to, she would tromp through the snow behind him. She would not be left alone.

They'd headed north before dawn had even properly broken through the sky. A few men lingered in the barroom but slept with their heads on the littered tables. The sheriff was nowhere to be seen.

The ride was cold and long, but at least the snow had ceased. Daylight had inched up the temperature, though it still remained well below freezing. They trailed up the Missouri River to link up with the ferry. Hank amazed her with his sense of direction. But she was still mad at him.

Hank soon had them loaded on the ferry, gliding across the Missouri, framed solid with frozen jagged edges. She huddled closer

to Hank. Even if she was mad at him, she had about turned into an icicle. Besides, there was something thrilling about nuzzling against her new husband. His thick arm came around, and she felt the press of a kiss on her head. She closed her eyes and soaked in the little bit of normalcy that she could. For presently, they would be in a throw down for sure. Yet, mad or not, an inexplicable joy raced through her. He was hers.

The flatboat crunched against the frozen ice at the bank, and the ferry captain worked to secure the vessel. Wooden planks clunked down on the stove-up ice floes bubbled up at the river's edge, to ease the travelers over the slippery expanse. From the temperature, they would need longer planks in the coming days.

Maggie's heart rose as Hank led the way off of the Missouri River ferry. But by the time they navigated the icy river bank and mounted their horses, her stomach told her it was after lunch. Maggie rode a second mount they'd secured in Glenwood, letting old Comfort take a rest for the time being. Even with the fresh horse, it had taken the entire morning to attain the Big Muddy. Hank leaned back to capture her reins and pulled them from her hands.

"What are you doing?"

Silence met her question.

"Hank, answer me."

A sigh came from him while he wrapped the reins around his gloved hand. He kicked his mount, and the two animals jostled together at the quickened speed. "We're not going to your cabin."

She snorted and shivered at the increased wind chill. "That's right we're not. We're going to get Corbin."

Her husband fell silent as the sound of the horses' feet plodded on. She huddled inside her hood. At the sudden change of direction, her head shot out of the black wool. "Why are we turning?"

The slope nearly unseated her, and she gritted her teeth. Her frozen hands grasped the saddle horn tighter, and she squeezed the horse's barrel with her legs. The animals heaved, zigzagging through the trees. When they reached the top, Hank urged their mounts down the hill, and once the land leveled, they set off in an easy gallop.

The freezing air flung her hat onto her shoulders and stole her breath. The speed and cold prevented her from any more questions, which she suspected was part of the plan. She yanked the hood back on her head while grappling the leather seat.

"Wh...where are w...we...going?" Her words came in a frozen chatter.

But Hank's back didn't reply. Snow flung from the horses' hooves as they bounded across the flats. Maggie leaned into her mount's neck to block the relentless glacial air current. As the miles rumbled past, she did her best to avoid the continual sting of frozen white chunks flying up from the ground. When she chanced a peek, a snow-covered soddy with a metal pipe emitting smoke appeared in the gloom of dusk.

Hank brought them to a quick stop, swung down and whisked her from her horse. She stuttered a demand which was snatched to the plains as he pulled her through the front wooden door.

The warmth inside comforted. The smell made Maggie want to retch. She pressed her wrist to her nose in a hopeless attempt to block the stench and glanced around the rough interior. The room

couldn't have been much larger than the back of a wagon. Lumpy sod bricks made up the walls, coated with hardened gray clay.

A table sat on the right, a small cot on the left. Atop the dark wool blankets, a black goat blinked ghostly gold eyes. It opened its bearded mouth and let out a bleat as loud and warped as ten screeching ghouls. A shiver raced up Maggie's spine.

"Shut it." A rough man-like voice growled.

Maggie's gaze swung back to the far wall where an ancient woman squatted before the glowing stone fireplace. The goat did a slight twist and then leaped in the air, landing with the grace of a prima ballerina. The demon-possessed creature let out another shriek, tossed its head, and tottered over toward the old woman at the hearth.

The figure rose, and the woman nearly looked eye to eye with Hank. Despite her age and weathering, the breadth of her shoulders indicated strength. A filthy flour-sack dress hung on her like old deerskins flapping from an Indian burial scaffold set high in a weather-whitened tree.

Hank held out his arm. "This is Old Polly. This is my wife, Maggie."

The woman grunted, the wrinkles in her face so deep they surely hadn't been scoured proper in years. The goat trip-trapped closer to lean against her skirt. "Done married her, did ya?"

Hank nodded.

One of her eyes opened large. "'Bout time. Yer mama will rest easy."

Maggie whipped the hat from her head. "Nice to meet you, ma'am. Hank, I—"

"Bunk up by the fireplace." Old Polly reached down and slid the stubborn goat to the far corner covered in straw. With quick hands, she hobbled the animal with twine.

"Much obliged, Old Polly." Hank turned and exited into the cold.

Maggie's mouth fell open. Was he serious? She whirled and strode through the door. In the near dark, she made out Hank's form leading the two horses to the barn soddy. She hurried through the deep snow after him, treading in the trough he made. A growl escaped when he disappeared into another low-slung mound in the lumpy moon-shadowed landscape.

Why was he being difficult? If he thought he was going to shake her, he thought wrong. She slipped through the leather door. More concentrated vile animal smells greeted her, and she grimaced. This, another tight space contained one horse, a cow, and several chickens fluttering about.

"Hank, stop this right now."

The hens fluttered, the horse's eyes flared.

"Lower your voice."

She clenched her teeth, but dropped her fury a notch. "We can't stay here. We've got to get to the reservation."

Hank tied their two horses to the center support and took up a brush. "Maggie, it's late. We'll start in the morning."

The horse in front of her shifted his hind leg, and she pressed against the door, eyeing the nervous animal. "We can't waste any time."

Hank paused and looked up. "Don't take a person long to die in weather like this."

She turned away, hoping to catch a gulp of fresh cold air near the door. "And the plan is to leave first thing in the morning?"

"Yes."

Maggie swung her head back to latch onto his gaze. "Promise?"

He nodded and went back to grooming his mount.

"How long will it take?"

The brush stroke sounds filled the small enclosure. The smell of manure wasn't as sharp as the other soddy. Perhaps the imperfect fit of the leather flap at the doorway had something to do with it. Even so, it remained biting cold. But, at least, the animals had a wind block.

"Maybe a week by horse."

Air whooshed from her and tears bit her eyes. A week? Exposed in this icebox weather? Well, maybe Hank didn't realize, but she would freeze to death to reach Corbin. That and much more.

She slipped through the thick flap at the doorway and stood in the moonless night, the wind freeze-burning her skin. Her gaze slipped to the stars. *God, why do You always make life so difficult? Why can't I for once do things like I want?* A piercing silence answered her as she ducked her head and stomped to the soddy's front door and swung it open.

Perhaps she had no quarrel with the Lord. He'd saved her from that horrid dandy and had spared Hank's life. Yet, she needed a miracle to rescue Corbin before Rupert Stilts laid his slimy hands on him.

Actually—she needed two miracles. Safely fetch Corbin, but first of all, not get left behind.

Maggie blinked awake from her pallet near the banked fireplace. Somehow she'd managed to fall asleep on the hard frozen floor butted up against the side of the chinked stone hearth. At least the jagged rocks maintained the heat of the fire. She took a deep breath and noticed the smell of the goat seemed less obvious. Doubting the smells had lessened, she could only surmise her nose had adjusted. That both disgusted and appalled her. Old Polly's sense of smell must be long dead.

This reminded her of the old woman. She fastened her gaze upon her formidable figure, attired in the same sagging dress, kneeling near the other side of the hearth. It had to be morning, it had to be, although without windows, the soddy was in perpetual gloom. Maggie pushed to a sitting position. "Good morning."

"To some, I s'pose."

Maggie rubbed her eyes. "Where's Hank?"

The woman stirred a pot of bubbling goo. "Best et whilst ya can."

Old Polly rose and plunked a bowl full of steaming food onto the small table. The black goat in the corner bleated. Nothing like eating in a place that more resembled a barn than a home. Maggie

eyed the wooden bowl as she stretched her sore muscles. Corn grits. At least it was hot. It was also probably seasoned liberally with black goat hair and grime, but Maggie wouldn't complain. Eat and get to Corbin. That's what counted.

Maggie swept up the blankets and folded them, careful not to shake the dust inside the house. Then she bellied up to the table and devoured the hot meal, thankful for the warm full feeling it gave her stomach. It made her sleepy once more.

With an iron hook, Old Polly tugged the black pot hanging from the swing crane and scooped out more gruel.

"Has Hank eaten?

"Yep."

Unease trickled down Maggie's spine. "Guess I better get packed up. Thank you much for the hospitality. Kindly direct me to the necessary."

The woman swiped the bowl from the rough boards and gestured to the right. Maggie wadded her wool blanket into a bundle and then tossed her cape across her shoulders. She found the outhouse in the general direction the old woman had gestured. It was nothing more than a third small swell in the thick layer of snow.

Another overnight dumping had wiped the landscape clean. Even the trough path to the barn soddy had drifted closed. And in the dim morning light, the gray, heavy clouds made it clear another snowstorm threatened.

Once she finished her business in the icy outhouse, she labored through the piled snow to the barn. No sooner had the leather flap

settled behind her than her breath stuck in her throat. Both horses—gone.

Hank had left. Just like that. He'd abandoned her without a word or a nod. And not only had he left her, he'd taken her horse. Anger, fury, and betrayal mixed a nasty batch in her chest. The lone sleepy swayback horse winked at her while the cow seemed to have some sympathy in her big brown eyes.

Maggie charged from the enclosure and stumbled through the irksome freezing globs, surely planted by Hank himself to slow her down. She fell through the door. Old Polly sat at the table, spoon in hand, while the goat nibbled corn at her feet.

She stood and dusted off. No sense wasting niceties on a woman who didn't even know the meaning of such. Besides, she'd partnered up with Hank on his clandestine exit. Her demand came out a tad too gruff. "Where is he?"

The woman squinted at her, chewing the bland, hot cereal mostly with her gums, given she'd nary a tooth left in her head. "Ye ain't as smart as I figgered."

Heaviness filled her. "He's gone, isn't he?"

The goat nickered as if answering her, reared up, and planted its front two hooves on the old woman's leg. The malevolent creature let out a belting bellow. Old Polly pitched some bits of bread to the floor and the goat pounced on them. Only then did Old Polly wink and nod, spooning a heaping portion into her mouth.

"Why didn't you wake me?" She snatched up the saddle bag and shoved her blanket inside. "I'll have to borrow your horse to catch up."

Without waiting for a reply, Maggie spun and hurried to the door to slog her way back out to the barn. At least her previous trek had broken away some resistance. Trouble was, her dress hem collected a new layer over the already formed icy clumps.

Maggie grabbed a saddle from a rack and only managed to deposit it on the floor. Dingus, it was heavy. With a grunt, she wrestled it up, wrapping both arms around it. But before she could take a step, a metallic click sounded behind her.

Old Polly stood at the door. Wearing only her soiled dress, her body appeared impervious to the harsh temperature. She swiped a dirt-encrusted hand to clear away the corn grits at the corner of her mouth and lifted the shotgun with the other.

"Cain't let ya do that."

Maggie caught her breath and let the saddle slide to the floor.

Chapter Twenty-Four

Hank shifted his weight, and the two horses beside him stamped their feet in the dirty snow. He cast his eyes to the Big Muddy, edged with rough, overlapping ice slab while sizable floes littered the current. The river had really iced over. Last night from his spot beneath Old Polly's plank table, he'd known the temperature had taken a dive. It had been one cold night which had made it easier to rise early. Thus, he'd avoided Maggie.

Meanwhile, now he waited and burned time. He had to get onboard and drift away from Maggie's clutches. She would not give up easily. He hoped Old Polly could keep things quiet and allow Maggie to sleep through the morning. He'd feel much better once he boarded the steamer and was underway. Yet, the ice floes drifting downstream didn't bode well for a smooth journey any time soon.

Nonetheless, Maggie would be hard pressed to track him once the steamer left port.

They'd be boarding some twenty feet from shore over the uneven chunks of ice, that is, if they boarded at all. The horses dropped their heads against a brutal blast of cold air, and Hank pulled up his collar, shooting a glance behind him. As light as it was, Maggie would surely be stirring by now.

Hank let a smile tickle his face as he thought about Old Polly's place. That place hadn't changed one bit since he'd filled out knickers. And the old woman had always seemed aged, from the first time she'd run off a violent customer of Ma's. Old Polly had a knack for turning up when things went south.

The smile drained from his face. Not such good memories. Might be best to change the flow of his thoughts. Maggie had settled well into the less-than-ideal overnight accommodations. Though the floor space hadn't allowed him to snuggle her into his arms, it had worked to his benefit in the long run for his early escape.

But that set his mind back to the night before. Sharing a bed with Maggie, even platonically—to feel her body against his, to have the right to wrap her closer, to watch the spark of shy playfulness in her eyes—had been pure heaven. When this mess was done, and she'd forgiven him once more, he'd do a whole lot more than hold her.

Maybe Corbin wouldn't mind spending a few nights at Old Polly's. A low groan buzzed in his throat. He'd better think on something else. Although, his unleashed imagination did warm his chilled body. He stomped his feet, both to encourage circulation and

to let out a bit of his impatience to be away before Maggie came up with some harebrained idea to follow him.

The *Miss Kitty Lee* moored before him crawled with deck hands. The vessel had been overloaded due to another steamer being ice-bound near St. Joseph, and the new passengers thronged the thick ice to load. Again Hank mulled the wisdom of going by steamer. But even with the Muddy's narrowed passage, he could be there by tomorrow morning. On horseback, in the snow, it'd be a torturous expedition to arrive in treble that time. He gave a sigh. At least Maggie was safe and sound at Old Polly's.

Maggie eyed Old Polly. The woman was one tough-cooked bird. Maggie could plead her case and waste time. Or…she could call her bluff.

"Shoot me then." Maggie lifted her chin. "Hank left me once. I won't be left again."

She lugged the saddle from the dirt at her feet. Then she pivoted and approached the old horse. Gathering every last bit of strength, she hurled the saddle onto the mount's bowed back. Maggie chanced a glance back at the old woman still at the door. The barrel of the gun now pointed at the hard soil, a vacant look in Old Polly's eye.

Sympathy climbed Maggie's spine. Had the old hag felt the sting of abandonment as well? She'd certainly had her share of rough living. "Please, Polly. Go back inside. I'll fetch the horse back once we find my son."

The woman propped the shotgun against the stacked-sod wall and strode over. Maggie released a sigh. So, she wasn't going to

shoot her. It had come down to a wrestling match, and even at Old Polly's advanced age, the woman towered over her. How motivated was Maggie to grapple an old lady to the floor of the frozen barn soddy? Yet, did the woman have any idea how important Corbin's precious life was to her?

But Polly stepped up and brushed her aside. "Ya fergot the blanket."

The old woman swept the saddle from the horse's back with little effort and yanked on the black wool blanket, smoothing the rumples down. Then she returned the saddle and strapped it underneath the swayed horse's potbelly.

"Ya take care of ole' Comfort. He ain't what he used ta be. But he's saved my sorry hide more 'n once. She adjusted the stirrups before continuing. "And if Hank asks ya, I was napping."

Polly grabbed Maggie's hand and plunked some coins into her palm. Then she twirled, stomped to the door, and snatched up the gun. Without another word, the old lady strode through the leather flap.

Maggie wished she'd have paid more attention on the journey through the blizzard yesterday. Thankfully the wind always helped orientate her. She set off with the biting cold at her back. Despite the horse's obvious age, he set a good pace. Maybe he was just as glad to get out as Maggie was.

Soon the line of trees came into view. And they—would be guarding the Big Muddy. She reached out and caressed the old horse's neck. Just where she needed to be.

She followed the river near the bank to avoid the hills as much as possible. Riding all the way to the reservation was out of the question. Going home to wait for White Moon made no sense. The only plan of action was to try and catch up with Hank.

Only…where had he gone? The land leveled out as she approached the edge of Omaha. She came around a copse of trees which afforded her a view of the icy river flowing from the north, and she pulled her mount to a stop.

Dotted on the distant landscape, skewed along the frosted ice lay numerous paddleboats. Some docked, some arriving, some exiting. Exiting? Hmmm. Soot poured from their stacks like some kind of Indian smoke signal, but it was still too far away to see much human activity,

Maggie crinkled up her face and pored over the scene. Wouldn't that be the most likely avenue to reach the reservation? Excitement tingled her from her frozen hands to her numb feet. Hank may not be there, but it was her best option to travel far—fast.

Time stretched like a cavernous valley before she reached the shabby hut. A hand-painted, weathered sign proclaiming the ticket office, hung at a slant above the doorway.. She glanced around to the industry around her. Wool-swollen people swarmed toward the frozen edge to board one of many paddleboats docked there. Others slogged up the snowy incline.

Maggie settled Comfort at the busy hitching post, drawing many male eyes. Curse Hank for leaving her unescorted. Maggie gritted her teeth. Unaccompanied or not, she would find Corbin.

Once inside the ticket office, Maggie sighed. The heat pouring from the pot-bellied stove made her chapped cheeks burn. She had to be insane taking such a trip in this type of weather. But she had no choice. The crowd thinned, and she leaned against the counter to inhale the warm air.

A slender, white-headed gentleman lifted his head and took a double take. "Where to?"

"Uh…" she lowered her voice, "the Omaha Reservation?"

The ticket man's wiry brows elevated in his wind-burnt thin face. "No steamer stops there, Ma'am. And not right proper for a young lady to travel to such a place, if you don't mind me saying."

Maggie was about to get her fill of folks directing her decisions. First Hank, now this nosy Joe. However, it wouldn't benefit her announcing to the room she was on a wild goose chase to the Omaha Nation Reservation—alone. No indeed. Her voice dropped another level. "Nevertheless, how close can I come?"

"Sioux City."

"How far is that from the reservation?"

The old man thumped a roll of tickets on the counter. "'Bout thirty miles of backtracking, I reckon."

Hope squashed in Maggie's chest. Would poor Comfort be able to backtrack such a distance? She chewed a sore spot on her bottom lip and glanced out the window. How could she—

Her eyes snagged on a familiar silhouette some ways out on the lumpy ice gorge. She drifted from the counter. Hank. *with her horse.* Her eyes narrowed and her mouth stiffened. Well, two could play the

disappearing act. She spun back and slapped Old Polly's money on the counter.

"I need a ticket to Sioux City."

The man nodded without hesitation, but censure shrouded his eyes. "Best hurry. They're loading up. Temperatures aren't cooperating."

She swallowed, pocketed her ticket and set off toward the door. Comfort seemed reluctant to leave the hitching post, poor thing. Being wedged in amongst the other horses had probably provided a respite from the wind. And the boat wouldn't be much of a picnic for the aged animal. Yet it couldn't be helped. Maggie dragged the horse behind her over the slippery frozen globs of ice, making sure to stay good and hidden in the crowd. No use Hank seeing her before the steamer was well on its way.

At last the group ahead of Hank shifted forward. He boarded and huddled up bow side behind a herd of cows on the main deck. He set his feet and remained with the horses until the boat's paddle reversed and set the huge vessel in motion. With a mighty rush of water striking the huge double-paddle wheels, the boat slowly worked up to a slow cruising speed.

To avoid the cutting wind, he tied off the two horses, churned up the stairway, and stepped into the main salon, a dim, dirty room in need of a good paint job. The space was filled with disgruntled people, huddled and rubbing freezing hands together. He found a spot near the window next to a couple of well-dressed men.

"By George, I intend to ship up several pallets of tartan wool in the next week. Given the temperature, I'm sure they will fly off the shelves. Nothing more stylish than appearing at a late winter ball wrapped in plaid."

The other man, black bowler tugged down with wool flaps at his ears gave a chuckle. "Doubtful these western ruffians will desire a fashionable ensemble. But they would appreciate warmth, I dare say. I'd move quickly if I were you. The river is liable to gorge and halt traffic."

"Ack." The first man took a long draw of his pipe. "'Tis the modern age of transportation. I'll have that wool moved by week's end. Plenty of winter left to sell cold weather attire."

Plenty of winter left. Hank blocked out the two trendy gentlemen's business conversation. Maggie's face entered his thoughts. Could he retrieve Corbin and return by the time this gentleman moved his wool? If the second man's predictions held true, and the steamers ended up buckled in ice, he wanted to have Corbin and Maggie safely back at the cabin as soon as possible.

While Hank had no desire to look stylish in a new tartan coat, nothing sounded better than gathering with Maggie and Corbin in the snug little cabin. He pictured them seated around the table with contented smiles. Then Maggie would clasp his hand and look at him, her love glowing from her beautiful violet-blue eyes. Yes, that would warm the coldest winter day.

His heartwarming family scene melted away and reality nosed in. When Maggie woke, she would be furious. She wouldn't cotton well to his desertion. Not at all.

The sternwheeler shuddered and Hank maneuvered through the crowd to the front of the salon. A large ice chunk blocked their way. There always seemed to be a wrench in the works, and he didn't need any more delays.

He couldn't dwell on the what-ifs. If only the river would cooperate, he could accomplish this undertaking and return—sans Maggie.

Hank only hoped she could find it in her heart to forgive him.

Finding a spot along the deck's edge of the paddleboat's portside Maggie leaned into the perfect place to block the wind and hide. She pressed herself against the horse's warm neck as the boat's horn scared the living daylights out of her. But Comfort lived up to his name and didn't move a muscle. The wooden planks beneath their feet shifted, and the din of the huge wheel sloshing behind them made Maggie search the perimeter. They were moving.

Several sheep in front of her nudged at her legs, and the grimy men near the animals leaned against the railing set her nerves on edge. She tied off Comfort to the deck's support pole tucked behind a pallet of baled cotton. Surely he'd be safe here while she found a more appropriate place to warm up.

Maggie slipped into the large salon, her eyes searching the crowded interior. Hank had to be here somewhere. Ah, he lounged on the far side. Fate had smiled down on her. She hunkered into the opposite corner from Hank, wedging a small seat at the end of a long bench. She had to stay low and out of sight. The man missed nothing. Her small stature was a definite advantage to keep him from

spotting her. And he would be on high alert with Moats's men possibly trailing them.

A smelly, dark-haired man covered in a cocoon of beaver fur settled next to her. He turned his wide, red face to her and flashed a huge smile. His pale brows jumped in appreciation. "Afternoon."

Ugh. She ignored him and turned her face.

"Beautiful woman like you probably isn't alone. Who's in your party?"

She stood and maneuvered away from the prying stranger, keeping her eye out for pickpockets. The last thing she needed was to lose what little money she had left. She thought of the gold she'd retrieved from the sheaves of wheat, not that she would have used it anyway.

She caught her breath. Glory, she'd left the pegs in the wall leading to the attic. That was like a giant sign pointing the way to the gold. Not only that, but it wouldn't take a genius to focus on the mound of straw covering the tidy pile of cotton bags filled with gold coins. Surely by now, Stilts's men must have cleaned it out. If they had, Corbin's safety could no longer be bought, as if it ever could.

A group of talking men loomed ahead, and she stepped behind them. Now somehow, before they landed, she'd separate her horse from Hank, and move him beside Comfort. The thought of the task amongst the roughnecks on the bottom deck repelled her. As much as she detested it, being unescorted caused her some concern. Nevertheless, it had to be done.

How she'd avoid Hank all the way to the reservation was another uncertain aspect. Plus, she had no clue how to backtrack to

the Omaha village. Perhaps she'd shadow him? Speak of the devil, Hank moved to the front of the cabin and the boat lurched below her.

She let out a low groan. What was happening? The men which shielded her dissolved toward the windows, and Hank turned. She glanced about and scuffled toward a group of ladies in expensive wool capes. If she could somehow meld into the gaggle of domed skirts, he might not catch sight of her. She moved her gaze between the talking heads and caught sight of him. His face hardened as he strode toward her. *Oh, dear.* She should have never left the seclusion of the outer main deck no matter how cold it was. She turned to force her way through the throng, only to feel strong hands upon her shoulders.

"Let me—" The rest of the words were snatched from her as the boat engines reversed, and the deck pitched below her.

Hank caught her and dragged her to the wall. She clung to him.

He pressed his lips to her ear. "You should be at Old Polly's"

She grabbed at his lapels when the vessel lurched again. "Yeah, well I'm not."

"Obviously."

Red-faced, beaver-fur man wedged closer. "This bloke bothering you, miss?"

Maggie opened her mouth, but Hank plowed ahead. "This is my wife, sir. Mind what you say."

The man bumbled a stuttered apology and melted into the crowd. Hank snorted. "You got a way of charming the bees from the hive, woman."

"I've no such thing. And don't change the subject. You abandoned me."

"I did not. I left you in good hands."

She tugged from his embrace, but his arm about her waist was like the oak plank she used to bar the cabin door. "You promised you wouldn't leave me."

"I merely promised to leave at first light."

"Well…" Blame him, he was right. "But, it was understood that we were staying together. Given our history, why would you leave me…again?"

She hated that tears thickened her throat.

He shook his head and then lifted his chin. "Maggie, you know why."

The sternwheeler thumped against something hard, and twitched sideways. Maggie discarded the idea of shoving away from him, though she was sorely tempted. She tamped down her anger and turned round eyes on him, rubbing his chest with her gloved hand. Resorting to artificial fair-lady wiles wasn't usually her style, but she'd run out of options. She fluttered her lashes at him and pulled a pouty face. "I thought you loved me, Hank."

His stern expression told her he hadn't been fooled by her coyness. He captured her hand and tugged her closer. "No games, Maggie. I could've returned Corbin within a week while you stayed warm and dry."

All pretense fell from her face, and she rolled her eyes and snorted. "With that old goat? And Old Polly? Sorry, that's two old

goats. Did you know she aimed a rifle at my head this morning when I tried to borrow her horse?"

Hank's lips twitched. "She values her animals."

A loud scraping sound caused Maggie to catch her breath. "What's happening?"

Hank's jaw clenched. "We're bypassing a huge ice chunk."

The chatters of the surrounding crowd hushed when the steamer convulsed and the engines cut.

Maggie cooed a startled cry and stared at Hank. "Why did the engines stop?"

He shifted until he could see out of one of the salon's windows. "Looks like we're drifting with the ice."

After several minutes of drifting downstream, the sternwheeler's engines vibrated to life. Large pieces of ice bumped against the hull as the vessel edged forward. Hank's body relaxed next to hers.

"I think it broke away. We're in the clear."

She glared at him. "Are we?"

He rubbed her shoulders and drew her under his arm. His cold fingers stroked her cheek. "Yes, Maggie."

The warmth of his body and the gentleness in his eyes banked her ire for the time being. Never would she admit she was grateful for his comforting presence. She'd loathed the idea of spending the day alone, ensconced inside the salon with opportunists dressed in beaver fur lurking about. However, questions swarmed her head. And he'd answer every single one. Oh, yes ma'am, he would.

Chapter Twenty-Five

Dismal dusk nosed in. Soon it would be dark. The ice floes had slowed the *Miss Kitty Lee* to a crawl. From the conversations around him, Hank had gleaned that the captain had put out double night watches on the hurricane deck. Maggie dozed on his shoulder. Exhaustion had finally caught up with the obstinate woman. A man sitting next to him on the bench rose and addressed the two women of his party.

"I've heard there are cabins available. I think I'll try to procure one for us. The weather seems to assure us that we won't arrive until late morning tomorrow."

Hank gripped the man's brown wool coat before he could stride away. The man turned, his bushy, gray-laced brows descended. "I do say, man, why have you seized me?"

"If you wouldn't mind," Hank dug into his pocket, trying not to disturb Maggie's slumber, "could you make arrangements for one more cabin for us?"

"Ah, very good. Please, if you would be so kind as to safeguard my wife and daughter while I take up the matter with the captain, I would be most grateful."

Hank nodded and the tall man strode away. The Lord continued to pave the way for them. The cabin would be much warmer, and after the cramped night in Old Polly's soddy, even the narrow cots would be a luxury.

The tree line out the window had vanished into complete darkness before the brown-wool-coated man had returned. But he brought news of the cabin, refused the extra coins Hank offered for the favor, and gathered up his brood to head to the upper boiler deck. Hank jostled Maggie.

"Are we there?"

Her breathy voice made him want to kiss her plump lips as she raised her sleep-softened face. He brushed back the stray hairs that framed her face and pushed away the thought of carrying her. That would bring on too much attention. "No. It's taking longer to reach Sioux City than it should. I've reserved a cabin for the night."

She blinked and then sat upright, suddenly completely roused. "A cabin? We don't have time for that, Hank—"

He set his fingers against her lips. "We don't have a choice."

Hank rose and clutched Maggie to his side, and they staggered to the stairs, both weary and stiff. They kept silent until Hank reached their cabin.

"Wait, Hank. Maybe the captain would let us off here. I mean, we are going beyond the reservation by some thirty miles. Couldn't we just ask? Then we wouldn't have to stay onboard. We could—"

Hank turned the door handle, scooped up Maggie and entered, tapping the door shut with his foot.

"Maggie. The captain won't stop. The banks are lined with razor-sharp ice. We have to stay the night. Please, for the love of God, just stop...battling."

He let her feet slip to the floor but she didn't step away.

"You're right."

Hank shook his head and fixed her with a skeptical gaze. "Did I hear that correctly?"

She nodded, a small smile lighting the corner of her cheek. "Yes. I've got to trust that God is protecting Corbin through White Moon's people. They are made of sterner stuff. Used to defending..." She shrugged. "And I'm so weary of this whole business. I need some sleep to be at my best tomorrow. We've got a long ride ahead of us."

Hank nodded, a little surprised at her wisdom. "I wish I could make it easier, Maggie. Believe me."

She lifted her chin, her eyes growing warmer by the second. Her fingers slid beneath his coat's lapels. "You are making it easier, Hank. Much easier."

Maggie rose on tiptoes and pressed her warm lips against the skin on his neck where his beard didn't cover. His pulse jumped in response. "Maggie, I don't think—"

"Hush. I'm tired. I'm sad..." Her lips warmed another spot on his neck, "and lonesome. I'm teetering on the brink of troubling worry and I just want it to disappear. If only for a few hours. What I need is..."

Her lips traveled to his ear. He shut his eyes, a growl of awakening in his throat while rivulets of pleasure trickled through him.

"...my husband to brush away reality and..."

Maggie's trailing kisses sent him into a state of euphoria. He let his hands navigate to the small of her back to snug her close and explore. His lips hungered to investigate the silky skin of her neck. He bowed his head and brushed his lips against her jaw, feeling the life pulse beneath her chin. Hank pressed a line of kisses down her neck, feeling her body arch backwards ever so slightly.

"Maggie," he groaned, trying to pull back. "You don't know what you're doing."

A satisfied coo exhaled from her lips. "Oh, I disagree. I know exactly what I am doing."

She reached back and flipped the lock on the door.

Light invaded her warm cocoon, and Maggie shied away from the glare and full consciousness. Snuggling her face and chilly shoulder beneath the cape, her mind grew more alert. Chilly shoulder? A sigh escaped, trying to assess why her shoulder lay bare to the biting air. Come to think of it, as she squirmed, she appeared thoroughly unclothed. That brought a lungful of rousing air, and she blinked her eyes open.

Beside her, warmth radiated like a pot-bellied stove, only much suppler. And then the pliant heater moved. *Hank.* They had spooned together after…hmmm. Her lips pressed together to stem a smile and a different kind of heat radiated up her neck. If only she could bask in their newfound union. But his body shifted next to her as his arms stretched above his head. Then he stilled.

"Maggie?"

"Uh-huh?"

His arms returned the warmth and tightened around her. "We better get up. The boat is slowing."

She pressed her eyes closed for just a second before swinging her feet to the floor. The clothing that had doubled as blankets slid off of them and the cold air's caress made her shiver.

"Good morning, Mrs. Sutter." One of Hank's brows bounced up and a possessive light entered his eyes.

She giggled and stood, grabbing her chemise. As much as she was tempted to flirt with her husband, for truly he was now her husband in every respect, they had a long, foreboding journey ahead.

Hank, too, commenced in readying himself and soon, they were whisking through the door to take the stairs all the way down to the bottom deck. Indeed, the busy port of Sioux City lay just ahead, as Maggie glanced about the frozen river.

They made short work of fetching Comfort and steering him to the bow of the ship to join Hank's two mounts. Maggie had nearly forgotten how cutting the wind could be on a Nebraska January day, especially cruising down the Missouri at approximately five knots an hour.

Docking seemed to take forever and equally as long to disembark, for the boat seemed chock-full of both people and goods. The temporary landing, the frozen Missouri, seemed an even longer expanse than at Omaha. But Maggie kept her hand buried in Hank's. His strong body guided their way across the planks and up to the land, keeping the horses in a line as they went.

Maggie glanced behind them at the long crowd balancing across the makeshift dock. Men carried crates while couples and families dodged the flocks of animals. Despite the dismal weather, one lady sporting a pink parasol departed the boat. As she watched, the delicate umbrella blew inside out and then whipped from the woman's hands. Gallant men chased the stray bit of fabric over the misshapen chunks of ice, stumbling as they went. Wait—

"Hank!" She yanked him to a stop, and he halted the horses.

"What?" his eyes searched the frozen floes, the people, the ship.

"The river. It's on the wrong side." She pointed to the timberline across the thick channel. "We should be over there."

Hank chuckled and he squeezed her hand. "Nothing gets by you."

He started to walk on, and she tugged at him. "I'm serious, Hank."

People and crates surged about them, bringing not just a few annoyed stares.

"I know. Sioux City is in Iowa. We'll have to take a ferry." He dropped a kiss on her forehead. "But first, we need to find a stable and feed our crew. Come on. We're blocking traffic."

"Oh."

The man apparently had everything planned. She wasn't sure if that aggravated or impressed her. And how had she not known that Sioux City was on the Iowa side of the river? Corbin would have known, with his little book of maps. How he'd pored over his small collection. She could just imagine him bowed over his new Christmas novel, perhaps huddled in a shadowy Indian lodge. Just thinking of him made her heart ache. She blinked away moisture and hurried her feet to keep up with Hank's long strides. Perhaps it was better that Hank led the way.

It didn't take long to set up the three horses in the closest livery for a quick rub down and a bucket of corn while they mosied to the diner down the street. Maggie shoveled in the ham and grits, anxious to be on their way.

By ten a.m., they were back in the stable, the horses saddled and waiting, looking sleepy and satisfied to be out of the weather. Hank searched the place for the livery owner and found him dozing off in the last stall heaped with clean straw. With a tap to the man's toe, he blinked awake.

"'Pologize. I was roused in the middle of the night by three men on a mission. Right busy evening." The graying man eased from the straw and Hank held out a hand to heft him up.

"Right obliged."

"Unexpected visitors, huh? Bad weather to be in a hurry."

"Yep. All fired hurry to get to the reservation."

Alarm shot through Maggie and must have cued Hank as well, judging by his question. "That's our destination. Wonder if they're friends of ours?"

"Uh…" The man meandered to a corner near the door where he pulled out a record book and money box. He ran his finger down the column. "Moats. He had a couple—"

Hank slapped money down on the wooden partition. "Keep the change."

Maggie rushed behind him to the tethered horses. She grabbed his sleeve. "Hank?"

His jaw hardened as he hefted her to the saddle. He scurried about connecting Comfort to the back of his horse. Then he handed the reins to Maggie.

"We gotta go. And we gotta go fast."

She would not let tears interfere. With a nod, he mounted up.

Hank had no business setting such a grueling pace with Maggie along. But lollygagging was out of the question. They needed to be at the reservation hours ago, and the delay of the sluggish ferry ride had him contemplating swimming his horse across the Big Muddy despite the insanity of such an attempt.

He'd ceased asking Maggie if she was holding up to the pace. Every time she told him to go faster. It was hard to ignore the exhaustion pulling at the planes of her face. But she was a mother needing her cub. He was sure her imagination was thundering like a herd of spooked buffalo.

Thinking of spooked buffalo, he couldn't deny feeling a little disturbed himself, entering and treading over Indian land. He hoped the two feet of snow would make the scouting parties more reluctant to investigate two lone palefaces on their lands.

Dark came way too soon. Slogging through the snow had slowed them down. Even on the best day, tracking back over thirty miles would take most the day. Somehow, he was going to have to break the bad news. But first, he'd had to find shelter. His eyes snagged a thickening to the right. Perhaps...

He turned to warn Maggie of the slight veer in direction, but she had hunched down over the horse's neck, covered fully with her cape and wool blanket. Poor woman. This ride was taking a toll on her. Hank glanced down to the icicles clinging to his horse's mane. It was taking a toll on all of them. But holing up for the night might not be too restful for anyone. As he neared what appeared to be an abandoned structure, he prayed it was sound enough to hold out some of the cold.

But the dilapidated three-sided lean-to did not give him much confidence as he led the way by moonlight. Hank put his hand on his Colt and pulled it from its holster. Most likely he'd only be scaring off the four-legged type of intruder, but he had to keep in mind that they were deep on reservation lands.

He pulled his horse to a halt and dismounted. Maggie didn't even move. She was most likely asleep. He searched the area, dipping his head into the open side. Other than drifted snow in the first half, it seemed still sturdy, and no one seemed about. Hank quickly made work of digging through the snow to gather what little wood he could, wondering if the kindling he had in his pack would light the damp stuff.

The horses were more than glad to enter the shack. At least the builder had situated the backside to take the brunt of the cutting

wind. Maggie's head rose beneath the wool and, with one hand, swiped away the coverings from her face.

"Corbin?"

Hank took a deep breath. "We gotta stop for the night."

"Stop? Aren't we there?" Her voice took on a sleepy wail.

The flame, only by God's miracle, took hold and blazed. Hank carefully held the kindling bundle in his hand to blow the spark to life. Then, he settled it beneath some crisp sticks and the driest bits of wood. Then he went to Maggie who'd finally sat up fully.

"Hank?"

He reached for her and cradled her against him. She felt as cold as he did. This was going to be some night. "We had to stop. It's too late to go on."

Tears sparkled in her eyes as he carried her near the fire and the buffalo robe splayed on the bare earth. "Moats will get to Corbin before we will."

A sob wedged forth from her lips as he laid her near the fire. "He's protected, Maggie. Remember that."

She sniffed and nodded while he fed the reluctant fire. Hank unloaded the horses and stacked up the snow as high as he could across the eight foot opening. It wasn't a toasty lodge by any means, but at least they had some warmth. He huddled up close to Maggie and held out his freezing hands to the fire. She tugged a wool blanket over his shoulders. They were in for a long night.

Once he'd thawed his hands, he pulled his saddle up close and cushioned his head against the worn leather. Maggie snuggled in close, and he pulled up the blankets. No matter how satisfying it was

to have Maggie in his arms, they were in for a miserable, bitterly cold night.

Maggie fought off the cold as long as she could. Even being swaddled by the wool blanket, pressed against Hank and a pitiful fire burning nearby, she was freezing. She tugged the wool blanket down as streaks of orange and pink ribboned the eastern sky. Daybreak. She pressed her eyes closed, her eyeballs warming beneath her lids.

But she had to get up, for Corbin's sake. Riding several hours in the weather to reach their destination did not appeal at all. But Moats's gang would have already arrived. Perhaps she would have been wise to let Hank go alone after all. He could have traveled faster without her. No, she refused to be a liability.

Finding the Omaha village would be hard enough, though they knew the general direction. Wandering around in the snow would only delay their arrival. Moats could have nabbed Corbin by that time and headed for parts unknown. No, somehow they would have to find the settlement. If only White Moon were here. What a great comfort and guide she would have in the small child.

Braving the cold, she flipped back the blanket and sat up. Hank groaned beside her. A movement caught her eye and she turned her head. Three tall braves, layered with buckskin and buffalo robes, their legs encased with fur boots stood at the doorway. All three carried rifles. Fear skyrocketed up her throat. Their stern faces beneath the hooded fur had her nudging Hank.

Hank pushed to a sitting position, and two of the Indians brought up the muzzles of their guns.

Maggie raised her arms. "Wait. We come...for my son, Corbin."

This statement didn't faze the three forms at the door who appeared carved from weathered wood.

"Please, we're looking for my son." Maggie struggled to rise.

Guttural commands from the center brave froze her movements. Hank stepped in front of her.

"Maggie...hush."

She stomped and slipped from behind him, thankful she remembered White Moon's native name. "Mi'wa thon."

Hank's hand gripped her, but the Indian in charge gave a jerk of his head. She only had one other word she knew. White Moon's name for Corbin. "Zo^{n}de."

This started a string of native words muttered between the three of them. But more importantly, the guns lowered. Hank draped the wool blanket over her trembling shoulders as the discussion continued. The middle brave stepped forward and barked a command.

"Horses."

Maggie kept her eye on the natives as they quickly broke camp. The braves mounted and arranged their three horses between the leader in front and the two shotgun-wielding Indians in the back.

"Do you think they are taking us to Corbin?" Maggie turned her head to whisper into Hank's neck, thankful they were riding double on the stronger mount. It felt good to have him at her back.

"They're talking too fast for me to understand anything." He grunted. "But, they're taking us somewhere."

Chapter Twenty-Six

Several hours of slogging through the deep snow put them at the bank of what must be a small creek. Down the slope nearly unseated her, but Hank's strong arms kept her firmly aboard. Going up the other side was just as alarming, looking at only sky until the horse took an awkward leap to level ground.

There—a spotty circle of both teepees and mounds of earth lodges lay quilted under the snow. As they grew closer, Maggie could detect an organization of some sort. In the center of the homes stood a tall pole, covered in ice and snow. They were directed to an earth lodge and grunted at until they dismounted. One of the Indians that had followed them, pointed to the door of the lodge with his shotgun.

"Wait—"

Hank gripped her and swept her inside. She tugged from him. "Really, Hank they owe us some answers."

He held up his gloved hands. "Let's just give them a few minutes. We're not exactly welcome."

Maggie stared at Hank inside the small earth lodge. The long ride on the *Miss Kitty Lee*, dodging ice floes, plus two days on horseback shuffling through the snow had brought them here, into the circle of the Omaha village. Yet, they were no closer to any answers.

Hank knelt to stack wood into the fire pit in the center of the dirt room. He brushed the snow away and made a nest of kindling beneath thicker logs.

Maggie's eyes drifted upwards to the small hole in the ceiling of turf. "This makes no sense. Where's Corbin? Why haven't they taken us to him? And what about Moats's men?"

He glanced up as he flicked the flint into the kindling. "We need to sit tight."

Her peripheral vision caught a dark shape behind her and she spun. But it was only a dark shadow the weak light from the smoke hole had not illuminated. She let out a long breath. This whole waiting business made her jumpy. She paced and then headed for the buffalo skin draped across the wooden entrance. Suddenly a hand gripped hers and Hank's voice boomed next to her ear.

"Stay inside. Mr. Gore won't appreciate our presence here."

"You scared the living daylights out of me." She gave a huff. "White Moon's family is always sneaking away from this place to hunt. I doubt the Indian agent would know one way or another."

"He may not, but I don't want to start any problems. The Omaha don't always receive their federal money, even though it's part of the treaty. And from the looks of it, White Moon's people could use it."

Maggie fell silent and turned from the door to find herself in Hank's arms. His eyes bore into hers, and her heart sped up.

"Trust, Maggie." He whispered. "He's fine."

Her heart thudded and the niggling question slid out. "Where did you go?"

A puzzled expression flickered across his features. "When?"

"When you left Bellevue. You know…before."

A silence stretched between them as they assessed one another. Finally, he sighed. "I hunted meat for the Union Pacific."

"Why did you leave me all those years ago, Hank?"

He took a deep breath and threaded a strand of hair behind her ear. "To raise a large amount of cash in a short amount of time."

A chilling breeze wafted in under the buffalo skin, causing her to shiver, and Hank eased her from the doorway. Impatience grew like a bubble within her. "Why? Why was that money so important?"

His face grew serious. "I told you. I had to have something to offer…you."

She pushed from him and wrapped her arms around herself. Why she dredged up ancient history in this charged atmosphere, she had no clue. "You didn't have to earn me, Hank. We were inseparable. I always thought we'd marry. I didn't care about your family background or whether you had money."

His jaw stiffened. "It mattered to me."

"Why?"

He stared long and hard at her before he murmured. "My mother prostituted herself, and I was the result of one of those unions. I had no worth, Maggie. I went to find it."

She crept toward him, her face crumbling in sympathy. "I just needed *you*. If you hadn't left, I wouldn't have married Ax."

His brow puckered. "And we wouldn't be here, waiting for Corbin."

She filled her lungs with cold air. "I could never wish away my son. He's the only good thing that came from my disastrous marriage."

He reached out a hand and stroked her cheek. "We've both made mistakes because we chose our own destiny instead of leaning on God's wisdom. My time hunting buffalo was the worst time of my life. We lost a lot of men and boys to the Indian raids. After I learned of your marriage, I began to figure dying wasn't the worst thing."

Maggie groaned and buried her face against him. "I'm so sorry."

He caressed her back and kissed the top of her head. "No. I'm sorry. The only thing we can lean on is something good always comes of trying times. Wisdom. Faith. I learned to lean on God and ask for His direction. And here I am."

"My husband." A warmth filled her being in the cold room. "But why are we…"

Hank pressed his finger against her lips and studied her eyes. "Trust."

She nodded and laid her head against his chest as his arms tightened around her. A rustle behind them drew them apart. A solemn, dark-skinned Omaha dressed in thick buckskin stood there with White Moon at his side. Maggie stepped closer, eyeing first the erect proud Indian man then turning to Corbin's friend.

"White Moon?"

The child nodded and her lips quirked into a tiny smile. "Corbin not here. Evil-Heart men come. We hide Corbin."

Maggie caught her breath and her hand moved to her throat. "What?"

Hank stepped up beside her. "Where?"

White Moon motioned toward him. "You know, Man-Who-Cheats-Death. Your healing place."

Hank glanced to the tall, silent man, but the child continued.

"Two Bears no speak white man talk. But he want to see Man-Who-Cheats-Death."

Maggie knelt, eye level with White Moon. "Who are you speaking of? Who is this Man-Who-Cheats-Death?"

The girl nodded to Hank, and understanding washed over Maggie. Surviving the death dunk in the Missouri had earned Hank an Indian name of high praise. "But who is Evil-Heart?"

The child's sincere dark eyes locked on her and she laid her cold hands on Maggie's cheek. "You know, Man-with-Three-Legs."

Maggie shook her head in bewilderment.

"Black Crow." White Moon tried again, her eyes flaring wide.

Hank pulled Maggie up, and she turned her puckered face to his. His stiff features sent shivers of fear down her backbone. "Rupert Stilts."

Rupert Stilts. Maggie pressed her eyes closed. Yes, she had to accept he was the very same man her mother had swooned over in her journal. Maggie spun to White Moon. "But you said, Evil-heart."

The tall Indian rattled in guttural syllables to White Moon before she turned to answer. "He has many names. Black Crow, Evil-Heart, Man-with-Three-Legs. He is my mother's father. He no claim her. Only violate her same as grandmother. She die in grief."

So, what Moats's gang had alluded to was true. The horrid man had not only raped White Moon's grandmother, but his own daughter, White Moons' mother. Oh, dear heavens. How low could this despicable man go? She knew he was cruel, but to abuse a child?

He was capable of terrible, unspeakable things, had done terrible unspeakable acts. And now he wished to possess her son. White fringed Maggie's vision. Her name echoed from a distance, and then arms supported her.

"Corbin." She whispered hoarsely.

A large hand tapped her cheek, and she heard her name again. She blinked. Hank's concerned face came into focus. His deep voice reverberated through her as he continued to address the child. She clutched his lapels as Hank's voice continued, laced with a thread of desperation.

"The healing place. Is it the earth lodge in the bluff?"

"Yes. Hurry. Two Bears say Father leave soon." Here, the child's voice quivered. "Burial ceremony for Pacoosa, White Swan, is done. Father burn fire for mother to find land of happiness."

Maggie pulled from Hank and knelt in front of the girl. "Your mother? She's dead?"

The eyes of the small Indian girl glittered with unshed tears. "Yes. No more hunting for Father."

"I'm so sorry, White Moon."

Her eyes closed momentarily while the lean, dark man beside her turned and slipped through the hide at the doorway. White Moon opened her eyes and then stepped to follow him. "Go. No waste time. Find Corbin."

Hank nudged his horse and the animal blew out a belly full of air. He tightened the cinch. Maggie stood beside him stamping her feet and clutching the wool cloak about her. Why the woman couldn't wait inside the lodge was beyond him. The frigid Nebraska air stiffened his finger joints as he double-checked his rigging.

He'd been wrestling with the notion of tying Maggie up and going it alone. Dragging her directly into the melee didn't make one iota worth of sense. Short of driving the grip of his revolver into the back of her head, he didn't foresee a way of stopping her from charging right in. Who knew what awaited at the bluff? Stilts and a whole mess of miscreants could be housed there.

And what of Corbin? Remorse shuddered through him. If he were his son, he wouldn't be able to stay away either. Yet...it was

Maggie. After more than a decade apart, he was ashamed to admit at this point, being parted from her scared him solid.

"What's taking so long? We need to leave." She jumped and clapped her hands together to rustle some warmth.

He straightened and turned to her, her face pink in the early darkness. Even if he never saw her again, he had to attempt to separate. "It's best if you stay here, Maggie."

Anger swept across her features. "Stop it, Hank Sutter. We're not going through this again. I'm your wife now. We'll do this together."

Hank inhaled a deep breath and drew himself up. It was just as well. He wasn't totally comfortable leaving her here in the Omaha circle. Weariness pulled at him. Last night had yielded little sleep in the three-walled shack, as had the previous night and many more before. Her arms encircled his waist, lighting a flame of strength that coursed through him.

"I'm sorry, Hank. This is just one big horrible mess. I don't know what I'd do without you, and I've never once thanked you for all you've done. I've given you nothing but grief with my impatience and snippiness. Please forgive me."

The huskiness in her voice made the words ring true, and Hank wrapped his arms around her. "This might be dangerous."

"I know."

"Someone could get hurt, or—"

She wrenched from him. "*Trust*, Hank. Remember?"

He nodded. "Let's pray, Maggie. I don't want us to do this by ourselves."

She nodded and sagged against him. Maggie's eyes flooded with tears as Hank's deep voice implored the Lord Almighty. Something morphed within her. A realization of man's dependence on God's wisdom and guidance swept over her. But more importantly, she acknowledged her need of Him. That no matter what happened, God reigned sovereign, and all of creation belonged to Him. Therefore, all their destinies were orchestrated by Him. This all-knowing Being loved them beyond comprehension…including Corbin. Her son was not hers, but God's.

She'd known this since she was a child, but she'd pushed it away when adversity had heaped its cares and sorrows on her. Now, it was time to embrace the God who'd never given up on her and had never left her. She breathed a silent plea for forgiveness, a prayer that begged the Lord's pardon for her unfaithfulness. With a shaky breath, she pulled from Hank who'd long grown silent. The cold air remained, but a new fervor blossomed through her body.

She scrubbed a tear from her chapped face and shot him a small smile. "All right. Whenever you're ready."

The journey through the snow, picking up Comfort, the trip aboard the return steamer back toward Bellevue and the earth lodge proved a test of patience, one Maggie determined she would master. She prayed off and on throughout the journey for safety and success, but also conceded God's will.

Strange how she suddenly realized Hank's weariness hanging on him like a cloak. The air in the steamboat proved warm enough for him to grow drowsy. Yet he straightened and kept himself alert, and love for him bloomed in her chest. "Lay your head back and rest."

He gave a crooked smile. "I'm fine."

She straightened his collar and touched his coarse beard. "You'll be sharper if you rest."

His dark eyes sparkled as he chuckled. "Mother Hen."

The wooden bench felt like granite after so much sitting, and she squirmed, but grinned. "Someone has to nag you."

His brows danced. "Looking at her."

Her mouth flew open, and her eyes blinked wide. "Hank Sutter. I'm offended."

A lazy smile appeared between beard and mustache. His arm tightened around her. "Best get used to it. I may offend quite often."

A shiver brought goose bumps. *He was her husband.* Throughout the scuttle of retrieving Corbin, grasping the full implication of that concept proved difficult. They were joined, futures fused.

"When everything becomes normal, what will we do?"

His dark brow elevated. "What do you want to do?"

Excitement dented the corner of her mouth. "I want us to live in the cabin, harvest successful crops, and have lots of children."

A soft laugh echoed from him. "Picture me a farmer, do ya?"

She nodded as her face grew warm. "And a good father."

A mischievous glint lit his eyes. "Probably ought to put some practice into being a good husband."

"You already are." Concern matted her brow. "What about Corbin?"

He caressed her arm. "Already feels like mine, and I don't even know him."

She drew in a long breath. "What about you, Hank? What's your dreams?"

He looked across the long, crowded salon. "I've always known that if you were my wife, the rest would fall into place."

Tears ached to be released. "Oh, Hank. I love you so much."

He pressed his forehead against hers. "Always love me, Maggie."

"I will."

The dark shore at Omaha stretched even farther away from the steamer as they disembarked. Floating down river had been faster than going up, though it had to be after midnight. Hank parked Maggie on one of the horses, and they picked their way through the jagged ice. They gained solid ground and Hank swung aboard his mount and glanced back.

"All right. Start praying. We'll catch the ferry and then we've got a long journey."

She shook her head. "No, Hank. We need to overnight at the cabin."

He halted and waited for her mount to draw closer. "Come again?"

She took a deep breath, glanced off ahead, before turning to him with resolve on her face. "We need a good night's rest. White Moon said he was safe. And I know God has him within his grasp."

Hank studied her. "Are you sure?"

"Look, it's been dark for hours. It's late. By the time we get to the ferry, it'll be the middle of the night. Really, Hank. I think it's best. Don't you?"

He hesitated. Maggie asking his advice? *Interesting.* Hank took a deep breath. A good night's rest would sharpen his senses. He glanced at her, soft pleading in her eyes.

"I agree. Some rest would aid success."

He tamped down the image of Maggie, soft and compliant before the fireplace, with strategies of tomorrow's recovery of Corbin. His prayers shot up as he planned ways to stymie any unexpected turn of events to protect the people he loved.

The trail to the cabin stretched long and harsh, yet no new snow hid their tracks. With relief, he swung from the horse in front of the barn and lifted Maggie down. The cow was conspicuously absent, probably thanks to Moats's men, but that allowed plenty of room for the three horses.

Hank made a quick trip to the cabin and returned to the porch. "The cabin's empty, a bit mussed, but empty. I checked the attic too since the hatch was hanging open."

She hesitated a moment. "The gold? It was under a pile of straw."

"I got news for you. It ain't up there no more."

Her shoulders deflated. "I figured. Guess we've lost our bargaining power."

"We ain't lost nothing. *The Lord is the light of my salvation; who shall I fear?*"

Maggie chewed her lip and her eyes sparkled with unshed tears. "Yes."

"You head on in." Hank took the horses' reins. "Start a fire if you can, and I'll bed down the horses for the night."

She nodded and whisked her wide skirt toward the cabin.

He escorted the horses inside, brushed out their damp coats, and covered them with blankets. All three animals stepped up eagerly to the trough when he poured in the cracked corn and oats. With one last pat, he turned and secured the door. The moon and stars glowed above him in the clear black night. Again he sent a prayer heavenward for tomorrow's mission.

He swung the cabin door open. Maggie stood in front of a roaring fireplace, clad in a thin white shift. Her hair, the color of ripe wheat, flowed about her shoulders. His body shuddered to a stop.

She sent a shy smile his way. "Shut the door, silly."

If only everything were right in the world. The uncertainty in her eyes turned over his heart. For all her confidence and swag about waiting till morning, she was broken inside without her son. He lurched forward and wrapped his arms around her.

"Oh, Hank."

Her sobs muffled against his chest.

"Shhh. We're close now. By tomorrow this nightmare will be over."

She nodded against him.

At least, he certainly prayed it so.

Chapter Twenty-Seven

Maggie pulled the cabin door shut and breathed in the frosty air. Today she would hold Corbin in her arms. She gritted her teeth. God willing.

And she was Hank's wife. Yes, today marked the start of her new life. She snugged the wool cape about her shoulders as Hank came around the corner, leading the two horses minus Comfort, packed and saddled.

He stopped at the porch and grasped her waist. A fierce determination flared in his eyes. "Are you ready?"

She threw her arms about his neck. "Most ready."

With gentle hands, he lifted her aboard the horse then mounted his. He surveyed the cabin a moment. "Your pa built a good solid cabin. It will be right comfy to pass the winter in."

A small smile of remembrance lit her cheek. "Yes. Back then, Pa always made sure it was a happy place. And maybe today…that will be true again."

He nodded, his jaw set tight. A sound below them caught their attention. A young boy on a small pony navigated the slippery hill. Maggie's brows furrowed. Hank dismounted and scrambled down the slope to assist. When at last they gained the level ground, Maggie swung from her horse.

"Mrs. Robbins?" The flushed boy held out a yellow paper.

She cringed, but nodded. "I'm Mrs. Sutter, now."

"Telegram, ma'am."

Fear jolted through her like a spank of an angry horse's hoof. "Telegram? From whom?"

The boy shrugged and swept his hand through his tousled hair. He wasn't much older than Corbin, and there he stood in a ragged jacket with no hat. She swallowed and reached for the note. Flicking her glance to Hank, she flipped it over and read it aloud.

"Mrs. Robbins—stop—Thank you for your service—stop—The gold is recovered—also the boy—stop—My new amalgam assistant—stop—is quite intriguing—stop—Desist from searching for us—stop—for you know not my name—stop—Rupert Stilts."

Maggie was dimly aware of Hank shaking the boy and demanding who'd left the missive. She set a hand to her heart and gripped the saddle with her other, fearful she'd collapse.

300

"I don't know, sir. I only do what they tell me at the telegraph office."

Hank let go of him, handed him a coin, and strode to Maggie. The child clambered on the red pony and dashed down the dangerous hill. A sob rose in her throat, and she pressed her head against the stiff leather. Then hands lifted her to the saddle.

"We gotta go—now, Maggie. And hard."

The horses leaped to a canter before Hank settled into his seat and the animals, sensing urgency, pranced down the icy slope.

"Hold on."

Maggie closed her eyes, pressed herself against the coarse dark mane, and prayed. They arrived in double time at the ferry but had to wait for its return from across the Missouri. No words were spoken while they shuffled to hold their balance aboard the weathered skiff. No sooner had they landed than Hank had them mounted and galloping across the plain toward a huge bluff some distance away.

The hurling speed threatened to unseat her. She dug her nails into the resistant leather. Hank slowed the horses when they left the flood plain and entered the tree line. Maggie ducked to avoid the clawing branches scraping at her. Hank's head shot from left to right as if searching.

"Are we lost?"

"Shhh…"

Maggie pressed her lips together to still the questions raging in her brain. He brought them to a stop and studied the surrounding trees and snow-covered briar patches. Did he know where he was going? His legs again urged his mount forward before stopping again

to scan. Finally, he slipped from the saddle and worked his Colt Peacemaker from the saddle bag. He came back to help her dismount. She blinked at him as he laid a thick finger against her lips.

He turned, still clutching her hand and crept through the bare underbrush. At the thickening of several trunks leaning against the base of the bluff, he looked at her and jerked his head toward the bank. She nodded.

Hank stood tall and led through an opening in the branches with his gun drawn. He whipped aside the buffalo skin that blocked the doorway. Maggie gave a cry when they gained inside access, but the interior was empty. He let go of her hand and stepped to the fireplace, still glowing.

"They've not been gone long."

Maggie swallowed the tightness in her chest. "But was Corbin ever here?"

Hank pulled something from the bundle of skins in the corner. She gasped at the blue scarf she'd knitted for him. "That's Corbin's."

Hank nodded, his face stern, eyes sharp as he handed the item to her. With a whimper she brought it to her cheek.

He spun from his task of searching the remaining items. "We'll find him."

Back outside, they quickly mounted, and Hank steered them free of the restricting woods. They bounded over the frozen ground.

"God, please let them be at Stilts's cabin," Hank whispered the words to the rushing wind while the horses hurtled across the

landscape, dodging copses of trees. Could Maggie withstand the long ride? He hoped and prayed she could. This could all be nothing but a waste of time. But it was the most obvious choice.

Hours came and went. It neared noon but the thick, overcast sky made it seem like dusk. Hank slowed the exhausted mounts and perused the area. If Corbin was inside, Stilts's men had been busy trailing and capturing him. Was the boy safe? Had Stilts used his conjured emulsions to injure the boy? With big money involved—seventy-five thousand according to Maggie—it wouldn't have been hard to recruit Moats's gang of men to do the bidding of Stilts's perverted ideas.

He tallied the possible opponents. Worthy had met his maker and Eakins also, who'd draped the horse the day he'd rescued Maggie. That left Fingers Stanley, the murderer, plus Leonard and Gibbons. Then there was Jeether Moats. Would that man, so full of his own pride, continue to be at Stilts' beck and call? As much as he despised the man, he doubted it. Yet, Moats was all about the gold. The other three weak brains would most likely still be in the deal.

He closed in as near as he could, the outline of the barn barely visible with hazy fog slipping through the trees. There was no sign of any movement, but fresh prints of two horses led to the clearing. A strange, quiet rustle echoed through the trees, and Hank froze.

Maggie grabbed him from behind and whispered, "What was that?"

He cast his gaze around the area and shrugged. Again the shuffling sound, so very still it seemed non-existent—like a distant group of horses shuffling through the snow. Maggie's fingers

tightened on his jacket. Yet after several moments of silence, he relaxed. Then he fixed his sight on the cabin.

Creeping closer, no light shone from the window. Hank flanked a wide arc to the right and stared at the cabin from the backside. Here's where he'd spring. That way, if anyone was holed up in the barn, he'd have the jump before they could gain access from the front door.

Wishing for darkness for cover, he hunkered down and sped to the cabin, Maggie hot on his heels. He flattened himself against the log exterior and edged to the window. All was shadowed. Gripping the pistol, he spun and eased the back door open, shoving Maggie behind him for safety.

Again, nothing. He took a deep breath and clamped his teeth. Maggie appeared at the door, shooting him with anxious eyes. But her gaze then scanned the room. Her wrath turned to fear as her eyes returned to his. He grasped her hand and led her to the front door.

"Stay here."

Her eyes grew huge, and she shook her head.

He lowered his voice to a murmur. "If they're in the barn, or positioned in the woods, I'll be stepping into the crossfire. Stay here."

Indecision danced across her face before she nodded.

Hank reached for the leather strap and popped the door loose. With a prayer on his lips, he maneuvered through the opening. The door eased shut behind him, and he at least had the peace that Maggie would bar the doors. He looked left and then right. No time like now.

He strode to the small building with his gun drawn. Still, quiet surrounded him. He scurried to the cover of the barn and slid through the unlocked door. He halted. There, in a stiff wooden chair, Corbin sat, roped and gagged, eyes wild. Hank hurried forward and pulled the cotton from his mouth, noting the tears on his face.

"You okay?

He nodded, his eyes still wide with fear.

"Don't be afraid, your mother's here."

The boy's face crumpled into soft whimpers.

"Shhh. Hurry. Tell me who's here."

Corbin blinked back the tears. "Ju...just that one guy. With the cane."

"That's it?

The boy nodded, and Hank rubbed his shoulder. "I'll be back."

Hank snuck from the barn then hurried back to the cabin. Maggie opened the door, and he slinked inside.

"Corbin's in the barn."

"What?" She lunged for the door.

He grabbed her and whispered in her ear. "Be careful. Stilts is about."

She nodded, biting her lip. He reached up, pulled out a spare revolver that hung in a holster beside the door, and checked to be sure it was loaded.

Hank clasped her hand when they exited the cabin. Then he pulled her to him to protect her as much as possible. Then, he nearly carried her across the lumps of hardened snow to gain entrance to the barn. Maggie broke away from him in muffled sobs and rushed to

Corbin. Her fumbling fingers tore at the rope binding him while whispering words of comfort to the boy.

Hank turned his attention outside. Stilts was somewhere. His eyes scanned the area over and over. A large, dark indention of snow lay east of the back of the cabin near the outhouse. He didn't' remember anything being there, and his neck hairs prickled. Behind him, Corbin rested in his mother's embrace, both clinging to one another, sniffing and whispering.

"Maggie. You need to watch this door. I gotta check out something."

She shook her head, her face stiffening in dread.

"Yes. We're not safe yet."

Wrapping Corbin in one last hug, she rose and stood next to him. He took in her tearful face, pressed his handkerchief into her hand, and then gestured to the dark object.

"See that?" At her nod he continued. "That's where I'm going. Take this, and shoot anything that moves but me."

Her eyes widened when he pressed the extra pistol into her hands.

"What if I shoot you?"

The beginning of a stiff grin lit his face. "You won't."

Maggie's hands shook around the cold revolver. Hank stepped from the shelter and scrambled toward the cabin. He eased along the cabin's wall until he gained the corner. Whatever he saw loosened his caution, for he strode from the building to the object and knelt. His hand reached down for a moment then returned to his lap.

"Stay here, Corbin."

"Mama." The fear in his voice tore at her.

"I'll come back, I promise."

She hastened to Hank over the stiff ice. A body, with pink snow blooming around his form, lay face up, sightless eyes fixed on the gray sky.

"Maggie, no. Get back."

But the macabre scene drew her closer. The dandy, Rumble Stills, aka Rupert Stilts, lay dead, decked in his cape, his cane upright in the snow some five feet away, and he hadn't even paled yet.

"Oh, my." She dropped the revolver and flung her hand to her mouth. There, embedded dead center in his heart, rested her kitchen knife, buried to the hilt. The dent in the handle was clearly visible.

Then Hank was there, blocking her view, cradling her and hustling her back to the barn.

The next several hours passed in a blur. Hank loaded them up and headed to Glenwood. They spent a couple of hours in the sheriff's office before making their way to the saloon. Hank secured a better room than their last visit with two beds and a window.

Then, despite Maggie's protests, he left them to house the horses and wait for the sheriff's return from the murder scene. She and Corbin dined on a tray full of hot food shortly before a hot bath arrived. Corbin sank shoulder-deep in the small tub, while Maggie scrubbed his head.

"Who is that man?" He squeezed at the bubbles floating across the surface of the water.

"Hank Sutter." She cleared her throat. "My husband."

Corbin started and turned wide eyes on her. "But he was with them."

Maggie nodded. "I know. He was undercover. Or he thought so."

"So, he's good?"

She worked the suds up in his hair. "Yes. Very. I knew him before…you know."

Her son sat very still. "Before Axel Robbins?"

A sigh escaped her. "Yes."

She poured the cooling water over his head then fetched the towel. He shivered as he stepped from the tub and welcomed his mother's rough rubbing. She paused to kneel in front of her son, placing her warm hands on his cheeks. Her gaze searched his uncertain dark eyes.

"Listen to me. There's no need to be afraid. Hank will be a better father than your real one ever was, I promise you that."

Corbin nodded solemnly. "He'll teach me to carve."

A sob shuttered up Maggie's throat. Already, Corbin had better memories with Hank than he ever did with his biological father. "Yes, if you are very careful. And he'll teach you so much more. He's a good man. He'll be a good father."

Corbin slid into one of Hank's clean shirts. "My true Father is God, not Axel Robbins."

Maggie caught his chin in her hand. "I've come to realize that is true, Corbin Alan. But even Jesus had an earthly father. And you've

now been given the very best one. Perhaps we can check into changing your name to Sutter."

A small grin tugged at his mouth. "I'd like that, Momma."

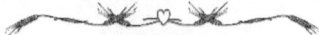

Corbin drifted to sleep while Maggie hummed a hymn, stroking her son's dark silky hair behind his ear, his sweet innocent face content and at peace in the muted light of a full moon. Then she washed up and snuggled beneath the heavy wool blanket, thanking God for deliverance and hoping Hank would return soon.

A soft knock sent her scurrying across the floor. She opened the door at Hank's quiet voice. And then she was in his arms. Tears gushed to her eyes, and she bawled unashamedly against his shoulder. Her family was together and safe. A new start beckoned and God's protection and love surrounded them. God's plans to give them hope and a promising future had finally come true. Even through the most frightening times, God had been there. And now, she was home…in Hank's arms.

Chapter Twenty-Eight

Hank hammered the last board into place on the cabin's new addition. Two bedrooms, one for Corbin and one for him and Maggie, made the original house look almost stately. Though the boy would most likely spend only a small amount of time in his new bedroom. Corbin continually eyed the attic, and Hank figured that would be his next project. But he had no worries. The new bedroom would house the next arrival.

He rounded the corner to the front of the house and stepped back a good twenty feet. New roof and fresh whitewash made the cabin gleam in the broad daylight. Maggie's pa would be right proud of the structure he'd started with his own hands. At least, Hank thought so. His gaze touched on the newly painted red barn he'd

enlarged a few months back. Now the animals had their own section and the crops another. Then Hank scanned the surrounding fields.

Late August had colored the tall corn so green it hurt his eyes the more he stared. Or maybe that was just sentimentality pushing its way through. Golden tassels topped the stalks and multiple ears of corn nestled below, ready to be harvested. The wind set the heads of golden wheat bundles piled high in the barn nodding, awaiting their turn to be threshed into bags. Maggie had been right. He was fast coming into being a decent farmer.

Laughter filtered up the slope behind him, and he turned to see his wife and Corbin returning from town aboard the horses. He filled his lungs with air and thanked God yet again for his new family. His gaze dropped to Maggie's swollen abdomen, and his mind contemplated the children yet unborn.

He shook his head. Why that woman had to run to town today was anyone's guess. But he couldn't deny her. Even when she insisted on riding. Even now, he wrestled with allowing her out of his sight, being as the gang was still at large and Stilts's killer had not yet been apprehended. 'Twas a relief they were home. Yet seeing her joy, he knew letting her go this morning had been the right decision. Besides, what human could possibly hem in his feisty woman? Well, perhaps he could. But he'd have a good fight on his hands.

He approached and he soaked in her form. She was his. Forever. Her beautiful face wreathed in a contented smile as they gained level ground, and Hank met her and lifted her from the horse.

"Gonna have to lay off the corn, woman."

She laughed, slapped his arm, and then patted her belly. "You know full well I'm loaded with more than corn."

He leaned forward and pecked her lips despite Corbin's interested stare. He'd think the boy would be used to it by now. "Safe trip?"

"Uh-huh." Her eyes glittered with secrets.

He studied her. "Why do I get the impression something's going on?"

She giggled and grasped Corbin to her side. "We might have something up our sleeve.'"

He shook his head and threaded his hand through his hair. "You know I don't like fuss, Maggie."

She smiled a grin with the light of a thousand angels. "Everyone ought to have a party for their birthday, shouldn't they, Corbin?"

The traitor grinned and nodded.

They reached the porch before Hank stopped them. "Now, I need that boy for chores, you know."

The dark-haired boy broke away with delight on his face. "Yeah, Momma. I ain't no girl."

Maggie stuck her fist on her hip. "Hank Sutter. I believe you've ruined my baby. And don't use 'ain't,' Corbin."

The child merely beamed from Hank's side. "I'm not ruining him. I'm making him into a man. You want him cooking cakes and prancing about the insides of the cabin looking for socks to darn?"

Maggie put on a stiff face, but her eyes danced in glee. "I expect not."

Hank put an arm around the boy. "This is my right-hand man. You'll get your girl eventually."

They turned at her chuckles and strode toward the barn.

Maggie felt a shiver of complete peace steal over her. Hank meandered to the barn, arm about Corbin's young shoulders. The corn ripened in the late summer sun, and the Missouri River shimmered in the east. The wheat rustled from the barn loft, a reminder of a chore yet undone.

A burst of joy filled her, sending tingles to her nerve ends, and she rubbed her swollen tummy. *God, how did you do this?* She giggled to herself, letting out a whispered, "Hallelujah."

Long after chores, dinner, and birthday cake with icing, they reclined on the porch. Corbin presented Hank with some new work gloves. Maggie also laid three handkerchiefs in his lap with hand-tatted S's in the corner along with a couple of new shirts. He chuckled then pulled her close for a good, long kiss.

They settled back in the swing. Down on the wooden planks, Corbin trotted his little horse Hank had carved for him between the marbles that served as bushes in his little make-believe adventure.

At the sound of a whinny, they glanced up and saw the sheriff of Glenwood ride up. He dismounted, and Hank stood to meet him on the steps. Corbin grew quiet.

"Howdy, folks. Good to see y'all in this fine weather."

"Welcome, Sheriff. What brings you by?"

He shrugged and reached a hand up to twirl the long dirty-blond mustache. "Not much. Checking in with my Bellevue contact."

Hank nodded.

"Crops look good."

Maggie rose and stood beside her husband. "Would you like a drink, Sheriff?"

"Naw. Just had one." He peered at Hank and leaned on the porch post. "That gang's still on the loose. Be nice to get a tip on recovering that seventy-five thousand. Pretty clever hiding that stash in wheat straw. Reminds me of a childhood tale."

"Rumpelstiltskin."

Corbin's voice broke into the conversation. The boy was now perched on the porch edge, very attentive, his hands cradling the carved pony.

The sheriff nodded. "Yep, that's right, little fellow. And that dandy's name was right akin to that."

"Dr. Rupert Stilts," Corbin volunteered again in a whisper soft voice.

"Right again, son." The sheriff winked at the boy. Then he set his gaze on Hank and Maggie. "Boy's right intelligent."

It bothered Maggie not a little that Corbin knew so much about the whole horrific experience. Talking about the murderous incident in front of her son made her nervous, and from that glint in the sheriff's eye, Maggie knew there was more information to come. "Corbin, why don't you go and read your new book?"

He tilted his head with a shadow of a grin. "In my bed?"

Maggie gave a soft laugh. "Yes, of course. You don't have to be outside all the time."

Corbin spun, collected his marbles into a leather bag, and disappeared into the cabin.

Maggie's hand fluttered to her neck. She grabbed Hank's hand and led him down the steps. Both men followed her a slight distance from the cabin. She sighed. "Yes. All we know is that he went by Rupert Stilts or Dr. Rumble Stills."

"'Twert no doctor, ma'am." The sheriff harrumphed. "Fact is, the man is known as the Fairytale Slayer, wanted in several states back east. His real name is Rufus Stilitz, wanted for poisoning his entire family. We've also pinned the death of Willet Eakins on him with Mrs. Sutter's testimony. But that dandy is also linked to several other bizarre and gruesome killings."

Chills brought out bumps across Maggie's arms. Her gaze flicked to the cabin, glad Corbin was safely inside, protected from the horrifying news. "So, not a doctor and not a fairy tale."

"No, ma'am." The sheriff squinted at her for a long moment. Then he stepped back and took a deep breath, scanning the slope toward the Missouri River. "You know, there's not been hide nor hair of who might have killed that dandy. If you folks remember anything else, you'll let us know, right?"

"Of course." Hank's firm voice comforted her.

"'Bout forgot. I do have something for you." He strode to his horse and pulled a brown paper package from his saddle bag. "I believe these belong to you."

He returned and handed the bundle to Maggie. She pulled the string and caught her breath at the contents. Her mother's

daguerreotype, her ring, and her watch fob rested in the crinkled paper.

"Oh, my. I thought I'd never see these again." Tears flooded her eyes. She sniffed and fixed a grateful gaze on the sheriff. "Thank you so much."

He nodded with a grin. "Well, I'll let you fine folks get on with your evening. I got a long ride and wanna be back by bedtime. The wife will worry."

Hank waved and the officer tipped his hat, whistling as he turned his mount to take the slope

The two of them climbed the porch steps once more and settled back into the swing. Maggie caressed the prized objects resting in her lap, so thankful to have this little bit of her mother back. "Hank? You know the strange whispers we heard in the woods before we entered Stilts's cabin?"

He stiffened beside her. "I reckon."

"You know who moves like that?"

A long silence stretched between them, and she turned her gaze on him. He stared at her, crossed his arms, and tucked his hands beneath his armpits. "Yep. I listened for them while hunting buffalo."

"Indians."

He cleared his throat. "*People*, Maggie. People make that noise. But we don't know who it was."

They rocked a bit in the cool breeze, and Maggie squinted when she perused the yard. "But I gave my kitchen knife to White Moon…"

Hank reached to encase her hand in his. His eyes bore into hers. "We don't know who got ahold of that knife, Maggie. And we don't know if it were Indians making that rustling sound in the woods before we found Stilts. I sure wouldn't want to put the sheriff on a wrong trail, would you?"

"It could have been Moats." At his nod, she continued, "Or Leonard, or Stanley, or Gibbons."

He smiled. "Or anyone else. I'm sure Stilts, or rather Rufus Stilitz, had a lot of enemies."

A shudder ran through her. "What if those men come back? What if they—"

"What if the grasshoppers return? Or the sun disappears? Or the sky falls?" Hank chuckled. "Trust, Maggie. God wants us to prosper, not fail."

She released a pent-up breath. "It's hard to let go of those fears."

He nodded and set the swing in motion. "Reckon so."

"Harder than spinning straw into gold."

Hank slapped his leg and gave a crooked grin. "Now, woman, God even did that for you."

Her laughter joined the sweet robin's song. "I suppose you're right, Hank."

The swing lulled her body into total relaxation. She laid her head upon her husband's strong shoulder.

"No more fairytales, wife. Let's enjoy real life and bask in the happiness God has blessed us with." He reached over and laid his

hand on her abdomen. A kick brought a smile to his lips. "Someone else agrees."

Somberness stole over her as she stilled the swing and laid her hand upon Hank's smooth cheek. "You bring me great joy, Hank Sutter. I love you."

His eyes glittered while he leaned forward to draw her into his arms. "And I love you, Maggie Annette Sutter."

Maggie's lips pressed to Hank's to seal the bliss God bequeathed upon them. And with the Almighty's blessing, they lived happily ever after..

PEGGY TROTTER

Ransomed-Ever-After Fiction

Dear Reader~

Isn't fiction great??? Especially Christian Fiction that allows a reader to escape the pressures and responsibilities of life for a few precious hours to travel in destinations and different time periods. And isn't it great that when you read Christian Fiction, you're in a safe space? Sure, there are book scenes that make you cry or rage, but in the end, it's wrapped around a world that recognizes God as the creator and orchestrator of life. Then, and the end, the novel is tied with a bow of happily-ever-after.

But are you in real-life eternity's safe space? Reading is fabulous and enjoyable, but in reality we have but a scant few years of life on this planet before we all face eternity. Eternity is never ending and there are only two destinations—Heaven or Hell. Everyone will spend forever in one of these two places. Heaven is a place of paradise and Hell is a place of torment. In the latter, there are no books that allow a few hours of escape from the horrible agony of eternity in Hell.

As a default, we are all bound for Hell, **BUT God sent his one and only Son, Jesus Christ, into the world to take our sins, become our Savior, and thus provide a way for you to spend forever in His presence.** All you need to do is pray to accept Jesus—pray with a heart full of conviction, humbleness, and true repentance. Perhaps your prayer might go something like this:

Lord Jesus, I know you died on the cross for me and rose from the dead. Please forgive and cleanse me from all my sins. Come into my life as my Savior. Mold my life to always follow and trust you.

Jesus is the only real happily-ever-after.

Please find and join me all around the web and sign up for my newsletter:

peggytrotter.com

peggytrotter.blogspot.com

diamondsinfiction.blogspot.com

Twitter: https://twitter.com/Peggy_Trotter

Facebook: https://www.facebook.com/PeggyTrotterAuthor

Goodreads:

https://www.goodreads.com/author/show/13778873.Peggy_Trotter

Amazon Author's Profile Page:

amazon.com/author/peggytrotter.com

Instagram: https://www.instagram.com/peggy_trotter_author/

Pinterest: https://www.pinterest.com/PeggyTrotterAuthor/

LinkedIn: https://www.linkedin.com/in/peggy-trotter-44a29b95/

BookBub: https://www.bookbub.com/authors/peggy-trotter

Find all my books @https://www.amazon.com/Peggy-Trotter/e/B00V15P2LU

Ready for you next reading adventure? Take a sneak peek into:

Year of Jubilee

Orphaned and widowed, eighteen-year-old Jubilee Stallings clings to her southern Indiana farm as her only refuge. The wilds of Gibson County are just being tamed in the year of 1850, and Jubilee ekes a meager existence. But when Rafe Tanner, a cousin of her abusive dead husband, shows up with the deed to her property, Jubilee's dream of her own home dissolves.

Rafe, stinging from his ex-fiancée's rejection, offers a business marriage, throwing him and Jubilee together in an effort to make the farm successful. But scars from the past keep her in constant fear of her new husband. The pair masquerades as a love-struck couple at Rafe's family farm, enduring the romantic notions of his family, and the jealousy of his ex-fiancée. Once home, Rafe realizes his newfound love for Jubilee and sets out to court her.

Meanwhile, Jubilee fights demons from her past as her husband reveals his interest. Can Jubilee let go of her distrust and pain to embrace God's plan of true love and finally find a place to belong?

__Chapter One__

Gibson County, Indiana, December 31st, 1849

Jubilee Stallings' forehead collided with the wall. Stars flashed behind her closed lids. She lay completely still. Her face heated and her body ached, yet she dared not move.

"You're worthless," her husband's slurred voice continued.

She heard his footsteps stagger across the floorboards.

"You're nuttin' but a dog, and…and…a piece…of dung."

The floorboards thundered as his body hit the floor. Scraping sounds emitted from the other side of the room.

"I…oughta…"

He continued mumbling unintelligibly. Jubilee pressed her bruised brow against the icy wood of the wall and prayed. Fresh tears wet her face. Please fall asleep. Almost on command, Colvin gave a snore. Jubilee continued to lie immobile, although, now that the initial rush of adrenaline had worn off, the frigid air made her naked body want to shake. She clenched her teeth and fought against her body's urge. Snores filled the air.

She pushed to a sitting position and eyed the straw mattress where Colvin had sprawled. Moving as cautiously as a newborn colt, she crawled to her dress by the door. She pulled it on as a set of shivers ripped through her body. With her sweater in hand, she crept to the fireplace. Only dying embers remained, but Jubilee couldn't risk adding another log. Her teeth chattered as she tucked her feet

beneath her skirt and pulled up the ragged cardigan to ward off the chill.

She grimaced as she rubbed the swelling on her neck where he'd choked her. The moonlight broke through the clouds, highlighting the marks scratched into the wall near the stone mantel. She'd carved the last one this morning—December 31, 1849. More than a full year had come and gone since she'd begun marking. Tomorrow would be her second birthday in this house. Once again, tears threatened. She'd be eighteen.

The day had dawned in a gray haze, but the day of her birth marked a new year, which always buoyed her with hope. The hours had passed pleasantly. She'd filled the wood box, baked fresh bread, and gone to bed looking forward to tomorrow. Until Colvin had exploded through the door, startling her from a deep sleep. She closed her eyes and her mind. It was always the same. More tears spilled from her swollen eyelids.

She tensed as Colvin sputtered a few times before going back to his ear-splitting snores. Noting where his pants had dropped, she decided to wait a little longer before she pilfered a couple coins. Any more and he'd notice and beat her senseless. Now, time to rest and recover her strength. She'd make sure she wasn't near the cabin when he woke. Hopefully he'd follow his usual pattern and be off and gone for the next several weeks. Let it be months, she prayed. I don't care if he ever shows up again. For now, she needed rest.

She woke a short time later, collected a few coins from Colvin's pockets, and opened the door, thankful for the quiet leather hinges. Because of the cold, she wouldn't head to the woods, her favorite

hiding place. She'd settle for the barn, a huge hulking structure. Her breath formed a ghostly fog about her in the chill, crisp air. Fear licked at her, and she ran from the evil sleeping in the cabin.

Inside the barn, she moved quietly so as to not stir the cow, who loved to greet her in the early morn. She scrambled into the loft and buried herself in a cave of hay. The exertion left her body panting, but warm. With the protection of the sweet hay around her, she fell asleep.

***

Jubilee started. She blinked a few times before she realized where she was. Dust tickled her nose. Noises caught her attention. Colvin saddled his horse in the stall below. He spoke in gentle tones. The man had always been kinder to his beast than he had been to her. A door opened with a creak and a low thudding indicated man and horse made their way to the exit. Good riddance, she thought as the barn door closed.

With Colvin gone, Jubilee took up residence once more in the cabin. Her hands were like ice blocks as she started a fire from the few remaining embers. Once her fingers warmed, she brought the coins out of her pocket. They needed to be hidden. Jubilee climbed on the rough table and located the canvas bag she kept behind a loose board in the eaves. Not much left. The stash might last two months if she were careful. After climbing down, she pulled the bench as close to the hearth as possible. Some birthday. She sighed. At least a warm fire burned in the fireplace. Perhaps now she'd have a time of peace.

Spring arrived and by mid-April, Jubilee's desire for peace fought with her need for food. She'd dropped a good amount of

weight since Colvin's visit. All the meager supplies she'd managed to purchase in January had long since been used. She'd run out of flour six weeks ago, and out of salt in early February.

She'd killed five of the chickens, one by one, save the last hen and one rooster. Now she only took an occasional egg for breakfast, hoping there'd soon be a new brood of babies. Otherwise, the chickens would be gone too.

Elsie, the old cow, had been nothing but a sack of bones wrapped in leather in early March, although now she found tender grass to revive herself. She'd gone dry, and without a bull, she wouldn't freshen soon.

Jubilee turned her attention to the task at hand and drove the cutting edge of the shovel into the packed sod once more with her bruised heel. She paused a moment to wipe the sweat from her brow and survey her accomplishment. The small eight-by-ten patch of newly-turned soil made it hard for Jubilee not to let discouragement grip her.

Her stomach clenched in hunger. A drink of water would help, but the bucket and dipper stood a good twenty feet away, which was too much work. She thought of the thin wild onions and dandelion greens she'd laid on the table for lunch. The meager meal duplicated what she'd eaten every day for weeks, but she could hardly wait to devour them. Yet she had to wait. This garden was vital and had to be big enough to allow her to store sufficient food until next year. She sighed. It needed to be four times this size.

Jubilee pushed herself away from the handle of the shovel and rambled to the water bucket. She settled in the new grass and

grabbed the dipper. Her life depended on getting the ground dug, raked, and ready for planting by mid-May.

Her ears picked up another sound. Her brow wrinkled and her eyes flew open. A horrible dread washed over her. Hoof beats. Distant, but very real. Her head snapped up.

Colvin.

Of course him. Who else? Seldom did anyone come out this far. Her weary body, so tired before, tensed with fear. She glanced from the woods behind her to the barn. Where could she hide?

The creak of saddle leather was audible now. He'd soon be coming through the tree-lined pathway. The cabin blocked his line of sight if she headed for the trees now. But it had to be now. She turned and trotted past the outhouse, praying she'd reach the woods before he saw her.

Another sound stopped her dead in her tracks. Whistling. Colvin never whistled. She changed direction and crept to the side of the cabin.

***

Rafe sat easily in the saddle. He tilted his head toward the sky and shielded his eyes with his right hand. Had to be near past lunch. He looked ahead and saw a break in the thick branches. That had to be it. He urged his Appaloosa to a faster pace, anticipating laying eyes on his new property.

Sure enough, the trees broke and Rafe took the path. He located a clearing up ahead. As he emerged through the tangle of limbs, he pulled the animal up in surprise. The barn, the biggest he'd seen in the area, greeted him like a castle on a hilltop. He grinned. Colvin

had said it was worth twice the land and he had, for once, told the truth.

He swung his gaze to the cabin. The front porch sagged, nearly detached from the main house since the foundation had given way at the steps. He'd have to walk uphill to reach the door. Stumps, waist high, littered the yard. The place would require some industry, but he hadn't come to sit on his thumbs.

His eyes caught a movement at the edge of the shack. What was it? A face?

"Hello?" he called.

Silence greeted him. His hands yanked the shotgun from the scabbard at his leg, and he urged Horse closer to the house. He dismounted quietly and motioned the animal to stay. Horse, well trained, stood steadfastly, watching him.

Rafe sidled up to the left corner of the cabin with his gun held across his chest. In one swift movement he stepped out, weapon raised, prepared for anything. But the yard stood empty. With quick movements, he pressed himself to the wall. He reached the back corner again and popped out in ready stance, shotgun cocked.

It was a girl. She stood with hands out next to the outhouse, about fifty feet away. Hunched over, she poised for flight. He took a deep breath and brought the gun down. As thin as she was, she presented no threat. Must be a neighbor girl.

"Hello?" he called again, and she back-pedaled a half a dozen steps. "Wait. This the Stallings' Place?"

She stepped behind the outhouse and peeked at him.

"Hey there. Can you tell me if this is Colvin Stallings' place?"

She never moved. Was she addled? He strode toward the outhouse. Time for some answers.

No sooner had he taken a step, when she took off running. He jogged to get a good glance at her, but by the time he reached the outhouse, she neared the edge of the trees beyond what had once been a cleared field. Now, scattered with young trees and weeds, it'd soon turn the open meadow into a woods. He gave a sigh. What did it matter? She was probably trespassing and wouldn't return.

He turned and took a step toward the shack. The hand pump caught his attention. Ah, that would come in handy after a long day of tending crops. His eyes fell on another sight. A shovel was stuck in the soil, the handle straight up in the air, mid-row in a small patch of freshly turned dirt. He stopped short, wheeled around, and studied the edge of the woods. Why would a woman be digging in Colvin's yard? This had to be the place. The barn matched the description.

He moved to the back door of the shack and pushed it open. What he saw made him want to choke his dead cousin. The floor appeared swept. In front of an ashless fireplace, a table stood, topped with a bowl of dandelion greens and wild onions. Herbs and strips of cloth hung from the ceiling. But, worst of all, was the worn quilt on a straw mattress on the floor, directly to the right of the door. The bed was carefully made.

He stuffed his hands into his pockets. Colvin had sworn no one lived on the place and now this. Rafe turned and looked toward the trees. Did that girl live here? Was she a squatter? Well, he could hardly set up house until he found out. With an aggravated grunt, he left the shack and mounted Horse. He'd have to find her.

***

Jubilee climbed higher. This had always been her lucky pine. Never once had Colvin located her when she'd shimmied up this tree. The problem was, the farther she scrambled, the thinner the trunk. And, although she'd slimmed down quite a bit, the five-inch trunk tilted dangerously and creaked louder at each sway.

She closed her eyes and hugged the bark to her face. The pine smell always soothed her, the sap did not. The rough bark made a plumb uncomfortable seat. In her weakened condition, she knew she couldn't clutch this tree for the rest of the day and into the night. Already she shook from the effort of climbing and holding her position in the rocking tree.

Snap. She caught her breath and her eyes flew open. The stranger had found her. Twigs continued to crunch under the horse's hooves as they neared.

"Hello? Can you hear me? I must talk to you."

Jubilee shivered and her muscles trembled. Sensing him below the tree, she squeezed her eyes shut.

"I need to know who you are." His voice grew fainter. "Colvin Stallings is dead, and I own the property now."

Jubilee nearly lost her hold on the trunk. Had she heard right? Colvin was gone? Her breathing sped up. How? Surely she couldn't be free of him. Her face puckered in distaste, disgusted she'd be thrilled at the possibility of a man's death. She prayed the Lord understood.

But, if the first part were true, the last part must be true as well. A sob rose in her throat. She was free of Colvin, but now had no

home. Nowhere to go. Stickiness clung to her hand and face as she wiped the moisture from her eyes and contemplated her situation.

She needed to think. Her throat constricted with tears. Her numb mind grappled for something practical to do. First, she'd stay hidden until he left the woods. She'd check her fishing lines. Then make her way back to the house. Maybe, by some miracle, this invader would've disappeared.

With a mind full of worries, she carried out her plan, begrudging the time she should have spent digging the garden, and landed a middling catfish at the creek. A blue cat was more appetizing than the yellow belly she held by the string, but she wouldn't complain. She'd carefully cut out the mud vein, fry it up, and feast. Now, if only her visitor had vanished.

Near dark she crept toward the outhouse and paused long and hard, searching for signs of the man she'd seen earlier. Please let this all be a horrible dream. Cautiously, she stepped past the garden and approached the house. Her hunger drove her to be careless. She grabbed a couple of pieces of wood from the meager pile against the cabin to start a fire and reached for the door. Suddenly, he loomed before her. She gasped and dropped her load to flee for the woods.

But his hand, like a steel trap, clamped down on her arm and she screamed. He had her. Jubilee kicked and flailed for all she was worth until he released her. She collapsed in a writhing fit and clawed her way through the tall grass until she reached the hand pump. Her arms hugged the metal as if it were a lifeline.

Find all my books

@https://www.amazon.com/PeggyTrotter/e/B00V15P2LU